I0692424

MISSING MEN

THE STORY OF
THE MISSING PERSONS BUREAU
OF THE
NEW YORK POLICE DEPARTMENT

BY
CAPTAIN JOHN H. AYERS
AND
CAROL BIRD

Foreword by ALFRED E. SMITH

GARDEN CITY PUBLISHING COMPANY, INC.
GARDEN CITY, NEW YORK

COPYRIGHT, 1932, BY JOHN H. AYERS

MANUFACTURED IN THE UNITED STATES OF AMERICA

TO
LYNN CARRICK

FOREWORD

I HAVE known Captain John H. Ayers for more than thirty years and I have seen his work as a member of the New York Police Department and as an officer of the Reserve Corps of the United States Army.

When I first met Captain Ayers he was a patrolman in the precinct which I considered my home for the greater part of my life. Nobody has ever called him a "parlor cop."

When I first became acquainted with him he was walking a beat on Cherry Hill, considered one of the most difficult and dangerous neighborhoods from a police standpoint in the city of New York. I have watched Captain Ayers' career as he advanced through the grades of the Police Department to his present position as Commander of the Missing Persons Bureau, one of the most important and constructive units of the Department. He has had in his police career every phase of police duty from patrolman through detective and executive work. I know full well that he is now in a position to tell some detective stories that are real tales which will settle for any one the assertion that "truth is stranger than fiction."

Captain Ayers has "broken" many of the most baffling mysteries which have confronted the police of the world's largest city and his position in command of the Missing Persons Bureau is unique in police history. His work has brought him widespread commendation from all parts of the world and his methods of dealing with missing persons cases have been widely copied by police departments throughout the United States.

In a difficult position, Captain Ayers has made himself not only beyond criticism in the conduct of his office but he is a psychologist, analyst, humanitarian and policeman, all in one. No one with less than unusual tact and diplomacy could deal with the problems that reach the Bureau.

His stories are true, they draw a colorful picture of the humanity that is crowded into the city of New York.

I know that every lover of real life "men who do things" will enjoy these authentic detective mysteries.

ALFRED E. SMITH

CONTENTS

PREFATORY NOTE

EVERY one of the cases described in this book are in the files of the Missing Persons Bureau of the New York Police Department. They are among the actual cases which have been handled by this Police unit during the fifteen years I have been its commanding officer. Most of the names and addresses, however, have been disguised, for the reason that those involved in these dramas are now, in most instances, readjusted to society. It would, obviously, be unfair to direct attention to them now, and thus revive details of happenings which occurred in those chapters of their lives when they were on the "Missing Persons" list. Real names are used, at times, where crimes are involved, as, for example, in the chapters on Murders, Kidnapings and the Unknown Dead.

J. H. A.

MISSING MEN

I. THE MISSING PERSONS BUREAU

NEW YORK BANKER MISSING

FRANK E. BENNETT MAY BE VICTIM OF FOUL PLAY

Frank E. Bennett, of 680 Parkview Avenue, mysteriously disappeared from his home yesterday. Mr. Bennett, who was forty-six years of age, was an investment banker. Mrs. Bennett, distraught with worry, and near collapse, can supply no motive for her husband's disappearance. . . .

Mr. Bennett, always punctilious about appointments, failed to keep a dinner engagement with his wife at the home of Mr. and Mrs. Joel Franton, 221 Merryvale Place, and when he had not returned by midnight, and no word had been received from him, the matter was reported to the police. The Missing Persons Bureau is now conducting a search for the missing man. . . .

—New York Globe Dispatch.

When the average citizen, munching toast and drinking coffee, reads a news item like this, he begins to speculate. A mystery! He instinctively forms his own solution of it, according to his individual bias.

MISSING MEN

Has Bennett been murdered? Has he dropped dead of heart disease? Has the banker joined the Other Woman? Is he a victim of amnesia? Has he been kidnaped and held for ransom? Or has he committed suicide? The man with a humorous turn of mind might even visualize Bennett nursing a star-studded headache, off in some Turkish bath, after an all-night "bender." *Anything* might have happened to the man who has entered that mysterious realm which the romantic writers like to call the Port of Missing Men.

But when the average citizen finishes his mental game of trying to solve the mystery, he tosses aside the newspaper, puts on his hat and coat, goes to his office and—promptly forgets all about Bennett and his fate until perhaps some one else brings up the subject, or until Bennett has been found. It is up to the Missing Persons Bureau to conduct the real hunt. How is the machinery of this police unit set in motion? What actually happens when a Mr. Frank Bennett or a Mrs. John Morris drops suddenly out of sight and the search is on?

After dealing with over a quarter of a million cases of disappearance (ninety-eight per cent of which have been solved) during the fifteen years that I have been in command of the Missing Persons Bureau, I have, naturally, enough, come to know something of the human animal and his network of emotions. These emotional elements enter very largely into the picture when an attempt is made to describe the work of the Bureau.

Each individual case calls for a separate analysis, a different kind of investigation. Since human beings are not robots, but complex men and women, there can be no standardized plan of action for us when a person is reported as missing. What steps we will take depend largely on the make-up of the absent individual, and we can no more adopt a general plan for the hunt, than a physician can prescribe the same medicine for all his patients. Everything depends on the diagnosis.

It is not enough to tell of the teletype and radio broadcasting, of descriptive circulars distributed, of letters written, of telephone calls made, of foreign-language communications translated, of the interviews obtained, and let it go at that. People's emotions and their reactions to certain situations and happenings often guide us in our work, for the friends and relatives the missing man or woman leaves behind frequently offer valuable clews and supply motives for the disappearance. Plain common sense does the rest.

First of all, we must recreate a lifelike picture of the missing person for, after all, we do not know him, probably have never even seen him. Second, we must try to identify ourselves with him, so we will be in a position to know how that particular person would act under certain given circumstances. We fashion a likeness of the one who has disappeared by "digging into his life" and, from the material secured, reconstructing him. We must know all about his past, his present, and his possible future, and we must not depend entirely upon the often biased opinions and unconsciously colored information we are able to secure from relatives and friends.

When the wife of a missing man tells us: "Joe and I were ideally happy; we never had a single quarrel," we must take her declaration with a grain of salt and a spice of suspicion. Experience has taught us that Joe, who is so "happily married" to Maud, frequently has a red-headed enchantress just

5

around the corner. So we poke about into his life until we find, perchance, an unprejudiced acquaintance who gives us a real line on our man.

Once one of my detectives ate luncheon for days at the same table where a missing man he sought used to sit, until eventually the restaurant proprietor saw and pointed out a certain man who had entered the place and was heading for this table. He was a chance acquaintance whom the missing man used to talk with at luncheon time, but from him the detective got an important lead. Men, you know, will often open up to almost total strangers though they behave like clams with friends. The man who had disappeared had made a confidant of his restaurant companion.

Very often the home or business environment of the missing man or woman yields a clew to the disappearance. Most people leave home voluntarily; very few vanish through suicidal intent or the act of another. It is most often business difficulties, the stale marriage, the love that has proved a mirage, the nagging, boring, hypercritical, or spendthrift mate, or general domestic difficulties which cause men and women to drop suddenly out of sight. As a result, our Bureau much of the time resembles a Psychological Clinic or a Domestic Relations Court rather than a Police Department unit.

We thresh out all sorts of family difficulties, secure tell-tale admissions, observe people under emotional stress brought on by the disappearance of a loved one, study the reactions of those we interrogate, seek the confidence of others who may help us in the search. And since our Unit happens, necessarily, to be a constructive one, because it is our duty primarily to *find* people—and not to arrest them—

and restore them to their families and their place in society, helping to stabilize them in the process, assisting them to adjust to their environment, our work does not always end when we have found our man. We learn that there is often an anticlimax and that we must continue on as counselors, aiding in overcoming the difficulties which originally drove him from his home.

But as these various phases of our work will figure in the following chapters, I will here attempt merely to give a brief picture of the bare mechanics of our job at the Missing Persons Bureau of the New York Police Department. Let us take the case of Bennett, who figured in the hypothetical newspaper dispatch, which might have been clipped seventy times each day of the three hundred and sixty-five days of the year 1931 from any of the New York daily papers.

In other words, twenty-five thousand three hundred and twelve cases involving a mysterious disappearance were reported to the Missing Persons Bureau during that year. Our imaginary clipping is similar to many thousands that from time to time find their way into the public press. It contains the potential elements that might call for the employment of all the machinery in the possession of the police for the work of solving the mystery of a disappearance.

Here are some of the questions to be asked and answered before an intelligent and effective search for the missing man can be prosecuted:

What is the domestic background?
What is the business background?
What are his personal habits?
Who are his social and business associates?
Has he had a serious illness, or has he been the victim of

a serious injury? If so, who were his physicians? What sort of temperament does he possess? What is his cast of mind?

Does his family tree show any decayed fruit, such as insanity, suicide and the like, depending from its branches?

Questions like these and many others must be answered before a successful search can be undertaken. If all these questions asked could be satisfactorily answered, the prospect of an early solution of the mystery might be expected. In that case a motive would have been established and, once having a motive, a detective can get off to a good start. But the difficulty with which the police are constantly confronted is that informative and truthful replies to questions often cannot be secured, either because of lack of information, or because of the desire of those questioned to evade the truth either through fear of consequences, or to shield themselves or the missing man from unfavorable revelations. There is little to be gained by conjecture, either. What we need are facts.

Bennett will serve to reveal the *modus operandi*. He will be a composite picture evolved out of the substance which makes up the material of many a missing person's case. And if we are forced to murder Bennett in the end, do not censure us; we shall do it only in the interest of public enlightenment. As likely as not, Bennett's marriage has been a failure; he may be "fed up to the chin" with the monotony of his particular surroundings; his business relations may not be what they appear on the surface; or he may have underworld contacts of which his everyday acquaintances and friends know nothing. In short, Bennett may be, during regular business hours, a man of integrity and honor, scrupulously honest and upright in all his dealings; in the remaining time he may be an entirely different man, one whose associates and dealings, if discovered, would shock every one who knew him as an apparently respectable member of society.

But the dark secrets and family unheavals will all have their place when actual case histories are told. Meanwhile, what happens when Bennett disappears? His attorney may have reported his disappearance to the missing man's resident precinct, or the lawyer and Mrs. Bennett may have called at the Missing Persons Bureau to report it. If they take the first course, they are asked for a physical description of Bennett, along with accurate and detailed information regarding what he wore at the time he was last seen, whether he had on brown cheviot or blue serge, a soft felt or a derby hat. The desk officer or a detective of the precinct immediately transmits the facts, through the Telegraph Bureau of the Department, to the Missing Persons Bureau.

If Mrs. Bennett calls at the Bureau instead, the man at the desk in the outer office, realizing the importance of the case and the many possibilities figuring in the disappearance, brings the matter to my attention at once. I talk with the lawyer and the wife in an effort to secure all the information there is to be had regarding the missing man, his life, his work, his habits, his health, his possessions, his friends, his recreations, his troubles, in order to discover the possible motive for his disappearance.

Sometimes I learn much during an initial interview of this kind; but often those interviewed are reserved and reticent, because they fear publicity. Still others are by nature inarticulate, or else they do not talk freely because of some obscure reason which I hope to learn later on. What people do *not* tell is often as enlightening as what they do. Occasionally there is a skeleton in the family closet, one whose bones cannot be rattled too carelessly. But generally one soon penetrates this veil of concealment, which obscures so many of the facts of vital importance to us if we are to do our job intelligently. Subsequent interviews often bring out all the necessary facts. We sometimes have to discount much that we learn, for people lose their perspective when a case comes up which involves some one near and dear to them. They are too close to the picture to get the proper color values.

As for the Bennett case, I find that Frank E. Bennett is a man who has widespread financial transactions. His wife tells me also that her husband was in an automobile accident a year ago in which he received a fractured skull and pelvis. She tells me that he has had frequent and violent headaches since, and at times semi-paralysis of the right leg. She confides that sometimes he has appeared discouraged about his health and his ultimate recovery. They had often discussed the possible merits of a sea voyage. I get the details of the accident, the names of the surgeon and the brain and nerve specialists who treated him at that time.

After Mr. Bennett disappeared his wife searched his room and found that he had taken a Gladstone bag, a suit of underwear, a change of linen and some toilet articles. She had not seen him as he left the house, as she was a late riser, and he had come to her room to kiss her good-by as was his custom. Mrs. Bennett does not know how much money her husband had on his person at the time he departed. He may have carried a considerable amount, for he was known to be in the habit of having in his possession at all times sums ranging from several hundred to as many thousands of dollars. So far the facts might indicate that Bennett had committed suicide because of ill health; he might have registered at a hotel for the final act; or the Gladstone bag might point to a planned journey.

I ask Mrs. Bennett for a photograph of her husband, and she supplies it. Faces and photographs interest me enormously. I discover much about men from these two sources: scanning faces, perusing photos. When, let us say, I studied Bennett's likeness I felt that he was shrewd, acquisitive, and possibly unscrupulous in his dealings with others, although his wife had described him as approaching perfection.

Since Bennett carried a large amount of money he might have been robbed and killed. It is always necessary to do some theorizing at the start of a man search. I at once assign one of my detectives to make the preliminary investigation. He "digs in," as we term it. He interviews members of the family, business associates, social acquaintances, the specialists who treated Bennett following the automobile accident. He talks with the brain and nerve men for the purpose of ascertaining the condition of Bennett's mind, or uncovering a possible tendency to commit suicide, or to discover whether he was likely to be the victim of amnesia.

All these inquiries are directed toward the discovery of a motive for Bennett's dropping out of sight. Was it premeditated? Compulsory? There follows the inevitable routine of elimination. The possibility of kidnaping for ransom is considered and finally discarded. One motive after another is taken into account and ultimately rejected as untenable.

But, during the time that the man I assigned to this job is at work tracking down leads, checking up on the missing man's contacts, his life, his actions, I direct the immediate sending out of a teletype alarm. This goes to all precincts and detective squads of the New York Police Department, to the police of other cities, and to State Troopers of adjoining states within the zone covered by our teletype system. Later Bennett's name and description are placed on the General Alarm, which is a list of all disappearances for each twenty-four hours, and which is compiled once each day.

This list is transmitted to hospitals, morgues, public lodging houses, branches of private, semiprivate and public institutions of shelter, in brief to all the places to which a person might be brought in an emergency, if he met with an injury, was killed accidently or otherwise, or where he might seek refuge under stress of necessity. This General Alarm is mimeographed and distributed through departmental channels. We have, say, five hospitals within a certain precinct. Copies of the alarm are sent to that precinct, and the officer on post drops in at the hospital leaving a copy at each stop.

Within the past year the method of sending out alarms has been revolutionized. A year ago we were sending alarms on missing persons to precincts and different detective groups throughout the city by means of the telephone. Today we send them by the speedier and more accurate teletype. The teletype has recently come into general use by police departments. It is a very great improvement over all methods previously employed in disseminating police information.

Briefly, the method is this. Assume that New York City is the point from which a "general alarm" is to be sent. The "alarm" is typed on a master machine, which resembles an ordinary typewriter with this difference: it is electrically connected with receiving machines, not only in the police precincts of the city, but in police headquarters of many other cities as well. These receiving machines are similar in type, roll and shifts to the master machine, except that there is no keyboard, and they are operated automatically by the electric energy released and controlled by the master machine. Each letter or symbol struck on the master machine, each shift of the carriage, is duplicated on the receiving machine. The paper employed is of standard width and is fed in from large rolls. A message transmitted in this manner is simultaneously and accurately received at as many points as are provided with properly connected reception apparatus.

Circulars play a rôle in the hunt also. I arrange for one on the Bennett disappearance. A cut is made from his photograph, and this is inserted in the specially prepared circular which gives a complete description of Bennett, and any other details that may be important in identifying him. These circulars are sent to out-of-town police departments for their information, for posting, or for such other use as may be considered advisable. Sometimes we direct the commanding officers of our own Police Department to post the circulars in public places, such as railroad stations, ferryhouses, hotels.

A good photograph is important. Often the family of the missing person does not even possess one. "He hated to pose for a picture," they tell me. Sometimes we are forced to pick our man fourth from the end in the sixth row of a group picture, which shows little more of him than a blurred profile or half a pompadour. Once, tracing a missing man who later was found to be a murderer, we resorted to the use of a small glossy print which had been submitted by the man when he applied for his driver's license.

This description of Judge Joseph Force Crater, Justice of the Supreme Court, of the State of New York, missing since Aug. 6, 1930, will give an idea of the kind of material we use to construct a word picture of a man, augmenting his actual photograph:

POLICE DEPARTMENT
CITY OF NEW YORK

MISSING SINCE AUGUST 6, 1930

HONORABLE JOSEPH FORCE CRATER
Justice of the Supreme Court, State of New York

DESCRIPTION—Born in the United States—Age 41 years; height, 6 feet; weight, 185 pounds; mixed gray hair originally dark brown, thin at top, parted in middle, "slicked down"; complexion, medium dark, considerably tanned; brown eyes; false teeth, upper and lower jaw; good physical and mental condition at time of disappearance. Tip of right index finger somewhat mutilated, due to having been crushed. Wore brown sack coat and trousers, narrow green stripe, no vest; either a Panama or soft brown hat worn at rakish angle, size 6⅝, unusual size for his height and weight. Clothes made by Vroom. Affected colored shirts, size 14 collar, probably bow tie. Wore tortoise-shell glasses for reading. Yellow gold Masonic ring, somewhat worn; may be wearing a yellow gold, square-shaped wrist watch with leather strap.

I also direct that steamship offices be queried on the possibility that Bennett might have taken passage for Europe, or· some other foreign shore. Arrest, hospital and morgue records are checked, as he might have been arrested or been the victim of an accident. These are the preliminary and immediate steps taken in the search. After that I give instructions that the Passport Bureau be communicated with for the purpose of learning whether Bennett had applied for or was the holder of a passport.

In the midst of this the detective assigned to the case telephones me that he has just talked with the head of the bank where the missing man carried a large balance. This banker tells him that he knows of no reason in connection with the missing man's business which might account for his disappearance. The banker thinks that Bennett was assisting a foreign government in negotiations for a large loan, but he states there were no upsets so far as he knew in Bennett's own business affairs which might occasion him to drop out of sight. The detective also informs me that he has interviewed the brain specialist who attended Bennett subsequent to the automobile accident, and has learned that no condition existed which might lead to a mental breakdown or to amnesia. The doctor stated that nothing of that sort was liable to occur.

When the detective rings off, I direct that a radio broadcast regarding Bennett's disappearance be made through Municipal Broadcasting Station WNYC. We give a complete description of the missing man; his age, height, weight, color of his hair, eyes, the clothing he wore, his teeth, scars, birthmarks.

Identification is often made through an article of apparel,

15

jewelry, cuff links, tie, and most important of all, the laundry mark on shirt or collar. We have at the Bureau what is known as "The Laundry File"—probably the only file of its kind in any Police Department in the country—which consists of a carefully compiled, classified list of laundry marks or "indicators," as we term them, with the addresses of the laundries using them. These are collected by the police from the approximately six thousand laundries in the City of New York, and they are kept up to date by frequent checkings with the laundries. Each laundry has its distinctive indicator with which all shirts and collars of its customers are marked in India ink.

This mark may consist of a letter, figure or symbol, depending on the whim or choice of the laundry employing it. The laundry ordinarily never changes its "indicator." Following the "indicator" is what is known as the "customer mark," a second letter, figure or symbol, a different one for each customer. This mark identifies the customer and is also never changed by the laundry using it. These customer marks, followed by the name and address of the person to whom they are assigned, are recorded in a book maintained by all laundries.

These laundry marks, when all other identifying media have failed, have proved most useful in establishing the identity of many victims of accident, illness, or amnesia, or of unknown dead from any cause. Not infrequently a first time criminal has been identified through the laundry mark on collar or shirt.

When the detective is engaged in the work of compiling a complete description of a man, he gets the name of the maker of his suit, coat, hat, gloves, shoes. He finds out the kind of underwear he had on, the size, color and design of his hose. An old scar, an appendicitis operation, a mole, a tattoo mark, all help in tracing a man's whereabouts or in identifying him when found.

On one occasion a nude man, found drowned, was identified through his shoe, the only piece of apparel found on the body. The manufacturer of the shoe knew to which jobber it had been sold, the jobber had a record of his retailers, and the retailer in turn had a list of all his customers. There was one man who had been in the habit of buying this kind and size of shoe at regular intervals. A study of the books revealed that he had not bought any shoes for a period very much longer than the usual interval. So trivial a thing as a collar-button has been instrumental in helping to identify a man.

Teeth are extremely important means of identification; in fact, they are of more significance than any other. Teeth do not change after death as do other parts of the body, and we find them our most reliable means of identification. Sometimes hair, particularly if it is of an odd shade or special texture, is an excellent means of identification. Not long ago the few remaining wisps of hair on the body of a man who had been in the water a long time helped to identify him. The hair was gone from the head, as a result of the water-soaking process, but a few strands of it on other portions of the body remained to tell the story. It was red and the hair of our missing man was red. The name of the man was found on our list of those reported missing.

Now to return to Bennett. His social life is thoroughly probed. Who were his companions during his hours of leisure? Were they friends of his wife or gay night-club girls he met outside his home without her knowledge? Was there the "inevitable woman" and, if so, who is she and what part might she have played in his disappearance? Was she, perchance, even indirectly responsible for it? Is there a jealousy motive somewhere? But we find, in this case, that the missing man's life was singularly regular in this respect; it was free of any of this kind of entanglement. He is not involved in any clandestine relations with other women.

On the third day after Bennett's disappearance, the detective reports that he has met, in the course of his investigation, a man who was said to have had certain business relations with the missing man. From him he has learned that Bennett was frequently seen in the company of questionable characters, men believed to have contact with the underworld. Bennett, leading a dual life in so far as his business was concerned, is found to have advanced money to supply the means of carrying on certain illicit transactions. This opens up a new field, affords a possible motive for the disappearance. We dismiss the previous picture built up of Bennett as a respected and influential investment banker. The question is: did Bennett arouse the enmity of any of these underworld characters with whom he was said to be dealing, and if so, why?

We concentrate on this angle. A few days later we learn that the missing man had a serious quarrel with the representative of a large bootleg ring. Threats were made that if he did not comply with certain demands which had been made and supply a large sum of money for the purpose of extending the operations of the ring, he would be "taken for a ride." A hurried check-up is made upon amounts he had withdrawn from his banks of deposit during the few weeks prior to his disappearance, and it is found that no unusual sums were withdrawn. Apparently, he did not "come through." Nothing remains but for us to conclude that, since Bennett did not comply with the demands of the ring, they had carried out their threats against his life.

On the morning of the tenth day after Bennett's disappearance it is brought to our attention that the Marine Division has reported the finding of a body floating in the Upper Bay, off the shore of Staten Island. The body is sent to the City Mortuary, at the foot of East Twenty-ninth Street, and a careful description of it is prepared by the detective assigned to that morgue. As soon as our man telephones us a description of the dead man, we find that it tallies with the one we have of Bennett. A more careful check-up is made, and the mystery of the disappearance of Bennett has been solved. The body is swollen and distorted as a result of submersion, but the Bennett family dentist examines the dead man's teeth and recognizes his own bridgework, fillings, inlays.

Bennett has been murdered. The Medical Examiner, whose duty it is to perform the autopsy, has found that there was a gunshot wound in the left breast. The bullet has penetrated the heart, and this has been the cause of death. The body was dumped in the water after Bennett had been killed. These facts are immediately reported by us to the Homicide Squad, and the work of the Missing Persons Bureau in connection with the case is ended.

But before we leave this hypothetical case and go on to actual disappearances, it is necessary for me to digress a bit in order to describe the organization of the Missing Persons Bureau. From fifty to fifty-five detectives are assigned to this Unit. For the convenience of the men, and in order to save time, we zone the city, and each man has a certain zone. When a person is reported missing from a particular area, the detective responsible for that section handles the case. We know from past experience that certain districts will yield an average number of cases a month. I assign men to the various zones, and the assignments are so arranged that all detectives will have about the same number of cases throughout the year. I hold certain men in reserve, however, for unusual or emergency cases. They may be termed specialists.

All of the men are instructed in regard to making contacts with the Consuls General of foreign governments, and if Bennett's name had been Zaretzki the detective working on the case would have sought out the Polish Consul General for information. If a missing man or woman is a foreigner, the detective immediately gets in touch with the Consul of his country. And if Pedro Ramos, a Spaniard, who is not a citizen of the United States, is reported missing and is later found dead in a lodging house with the name of relatives or friends, who are abroad, in his effects, notification of the man's death is sent to these people through consular channels. We do not attempt to notify them direct, but supply the Consul with all the facts in the case.

People out of town frequently report people missing in New York, through their local police departments, which in turn communicate with us. Approximately eight per cent of the cases handled in New York are of this kind. The missing people are visiting, seeking employment, or have come here for any one of the dozens of reasons which bring people to a large city. These out-of-town cases, and even local ones, make it necessary to call on Uncle Sam in the search. Letters of inquiry are sent to people at various places, people who might furnish a clew to the missing one's movements, or who might be able to give helpful information. Thus the teletype, radio, printed circular, telephone and cable are supplemented in our work by the typewriter.

II. MURDERS

MURDERS always make exciting reading. Newspapers play them up on the front page, often with flash headlines and exciting details. The public's appetite for murder stories is insatiable even in fiction form. They afford, for one thing, an opportunity for vicarious detective work. There are so many elements of drama involved, so many mysterious motives at work, so much of the kind of stuff that congeals the blood and sends cold shivers up and down the spinal column. People like to be shocked and thrilled in this way. It is a form of entertainment they avidly crave, and the more grewsome the details of the crimes, the more eerie the settings, the better they like it. This love for the macabre is an odd strain in human nature, and I will not attempt to analyze it.

Since I want to set forth samples of the various types of cases handled by the Missing Persons Bureau, I am going to tell some real murder stories. These cases are in the New York Police Department records. It must be borne in mind, however, that the solving of murder mysteries is seldom a task that falls to the lot of our Bureau. When it is known, or even suspected, that the crime of murder is involved, the services of a group of specially trained detectives, known as the Homicide Squad, are called upon. It is only when an investigation, originally taken up for the purpose of discovering the whereabouts of a person reported missing, discloses the fact that the man sought has been murdered that our Bureau carries on to the point where arrests are made and prosecution had.

"Murder will out" is a trite, if not always a true saying. But many times a murder is discovered although the murderer may have been confident that no clews had been left that could possibly lead to the discovery of his crime. There are other times when a disappearance can be accounted for in no other way than by the murder theory; when every circumstance surrounding it points to no other conclusion; when the killer or killers are known, to a moral certainty, but yet where no indictment can be secured for the reason that the body of the victim of the crime cannot be located. The *corpus delicti* is lacking, without which no prosecution may be conducted. I am confident that some disappearances reported to the Bureau can be explained in no other way, and specific instances will be touched on later.

The disappearance of approximately one quarter of a million persons has been reported to the Missing Persons Bureau during my fifteen years as commander of the Bureau. Among them are a few examples where the mystery has been solved by discovery that the missing one was murdered. In the following actual cases I will describe how the machinery of crime detection functioned in bringing to light the cleverly hidden handiwork of the criminal, first explaining the motives involved in the commission of the crime, and the steps taken to cover up the act. The entire process of the work up to the point where arrests were made and

23

the criminals brought to justice for their crimes will be revealed.

A love intrigue figured in the Bauer case. Late one fall Frederick Bauer reported to us the disappearance of his wife Frieda, the day before. He told us he had no knowledge of her whereabouts and knew of no reason why she should have left her home. He added, however, that he suspected she had run off with another man, and went on to say that he had noticed recently her frequent absences from home in the evening, and that when he questioned her, she had explained by saying that she had been attending motion picture shows.

"Now that she's flown the coop, I'm beginning to see through her little game," said Bauer. "She was giving me that moving picture line to cover up her doings with the other fellow."

"You suspect your wife of having had improper relations with some other man?"

Bauer nodded.

"Sure! What else can a fellow think now?"

Bauer was a combination of Nordic races, blonde, stockily built. He was about forty-five years of age. I studied him closely as he sat in my office talking. There was, I observed, something bestial about the man. His mouth was sensual, his eyes held a cruel gleam. He was, too, a man of low-grade intelligence. As he discussed his wife he showed no concern over her absence or over the fact that harm might have befallen her. His manner was offhand, indifferent.

The detective assigned to the case was unable to secure any clew which would guide him in a search for the missing woman. The husband was interviewed again and again, as were the neighbors; and Tekla, a girl of sixteen, daughter of Mrs. Bauer by a former husband, was also closely questioned. The detective asked the girl whether or not her mother had taken her into her confidence as to her plans, but she professed to have no knowledge whatsoever of her mother's possible whereabouts. She said she could give no reason why her parent might have left home. The detective prosecuted the search diligently, but without digging up a single clew.

Then, a week later, Tekla voluntarily came to see me. She was a clear-skinned, full-bosomed girl, physically developed beyond her age. She and her mother were Polish. The moment the girl walked into my office I sensed that she knew more about the case than she had revealed. At first she rambled on about her mother in a pointless, disconnected way. Finally she blurted out: "I think my stepfather killed Mother."

Questioned as to why she made this assertion, she told me a sordid story and one which she apparently had not intended to divulge when first she called to see me. This is what she related:

Her stepfather was infatuated with her. He had at frequent intervals made improper advances to her and on several occasions she had had intimate relations with him in the absence from home of her mother. She told me all about the affair.

"He said that if anything ever happened to Mother he would marry me," the girl declared. "I've thought, from the first, that he put her out of the way."

Tekla was precisely the type which would appeal strongly

to a man of Bauer's nature, and although she had carried on a liaison with her mother's husband, nevertheless it was plain to be seen that there was a certain bond between daughter and mother. The girl appeared to love her absent mother and to be appalled by the thought that she might have met death at the hands of her stepfather, as a result of their illicit intimacy.

After hearing the girl's story and cautioning her to withhold her suspicions from her stepfather, who, in the absence of the mother, had been making more ardent approaches than ever to the daughter, I instructed the detective working on the case to undertake a close examination of the cellar of the house owned by Bauer and occupied by the family, on the theory that the husband might have made away with his wife. A cellar makes a convenient burying ground, for a killer might find it embarrassing, to say the least, to carry the body of his victim any distance.

Searching the cellar, detectives found that a portion of the floor had been freshly cemented. It developed that the work had been commenced by Bauer on the day following the disappearance of his wife. Tools were at once procured, and this recently laid piece of concrete floor torn up. Beneath it, in one corner of the cellar, was found the body of the missing woman. Her head was nearly severed from her body, apparently by the blow of an ax. Later the ax with which the crime had been committed was found hidden in another part of the cellar, still bearing marks of the murderous use to which it had been put.

Bauer was arrested and admitted murdering his wife so that he would have a clear field to court and marry the daughter. At this point the case was turned over to the

Homicide Bureau. It is, as I have said before, primarily the task of the Missing Persons Bureau to *find* a missing person. When he or she is found, either dead or alive, our job is done.

Coincidence played a part in the Graff case, which came to our attention August 8, 1924. On that day Aaron A. Graff, seventy-one years of age, of West 107th Street, New York City, was reported by his attorney missing since August 1. The investigation by the detective I assigned to the case revealed that Graff's wife had been absent from home at the time of her husband's disappearance. She had told neighbors several days before August 1 that she expected to be away from home for a few days on a visit to friends. She did not mention any name or address.

When the disappearance of Graff was first reported it was thought that he had joined her. Ten days later she returned, and it was only then learned that she had no knowledge of her husband's whereabouts. In fact, she did not hear of his disappearance until she came home and the neighbors told her about it. On the theory that she might know something of her husband's probable destination, or the reason for his leaving home, the detective questioned her closely. After a rather extended quiz, he was, in a measure, convinced that the reason back of her husband's disappearance was as much of a mystery to her as it was to others.

However, the detective did learn that the missing man conducted a loan business. It was Graff's custom to make loans at a usurious interest rate to finance houses of prostitution and other dubious enterprises, accepting the notes of borrowers. Among these notes was found one due August 1,

1924, and it had been given Graff by one John Lugosy, of West Twelfth Street, near Sixth Avenue. Do not overlook the August 1 date, which was also the date of Graff's disappearance, for it is of much significance in this particular case.

Lugosy had a radio cabinet shop on Sixth Avenue, just around the corner from his residence on Twelfth Street. When the detective working on the case sought to interview him, he found that he, too, had disappeared! Lugosy had vanished on August 9, his wife having reported his disappearance to the Police Department on August 12.

Since still another missing man was now involved, a second detective was assigned to that case. The two detectives working on the Graff and Lugosy cases compared notes, and came to the conclusion that the disappearance of Lugosy so shortly after that of Graff was a suspicious circumstance. They decided that Lugosy might even have been responsible for the disappearance of Graff, because of that significant August 1 date.

The detectives searched Lugosy's shop on Sixth Avenue. They found nothing suspicious in the shop itself, and then turned their attention to the cellar, the place which in many houses has held dark secrets, as was seen in the Bauer case. Descending to the basement they found that it extended a considerable way back, and connected with the cellar under Lugosy's residence on Twelfth Street, forming an L-shaped catacomb filled with rubbish and waste material from both his cabinet shop and home.

Poking around among the rubbish, in the damp atmosphere of the cellar, which was like a dark subterranean vault, the detectives, using flashlights to discern objects in the dimly lighted place, came across a covered box. It was

28

in the portion of the cellar under the Twelfth Street house, and measured about 4 x 2½ x 1½ feet. The detectives summoned Mrs. Lugosy, who explained that her husband used the box for the purpose of melting varnish used in making cabinets. From its size it did not appear to offer concealment for a body, but the two detectives had a feeling of suspicion about that box. They opened it.

Prying off the lid, they peered inside, and at first the flickering light revealed that it was filled apparently only with varnish. But, on closer inspection, the detectives saw, imbedded in the varnish, the dismembered portions of a body which later was proved to be that of Graff. The body had been sawed across with a dull saw, and this implement was later found secreted under some trash in another corner of the cellar. Portions of Graff's flesh still adhered to the teeth and blade of the saw. But the startling feature of the find was that Graff's face was lifelike in appearance, fresh and showing scarcely any sign of decomposition. The box, his temporary coffin, was zinc-lined, and some of the chemical properties of the varnish had served as a semi-preservative for the body.

After the finding of Graff's body, the matter was turned over to the Homicide Bureau, which is still conducting a search for Lugosy.

Two persons were implicated in the disappearance and tragic fate of Jennie Becker, whose murderers eventually went their way to the electric chair. One was merely a cat's-paw, under the domination of a will stronger than his own.

Mrs. Becker was first reported missing on April 8, 1922, by her husband, Abraham Becker, of East 150th Street, in

the Bronx. The detective working on the case got the following story from Becker. On April 7 he had gone to work at
his place of employment, and when he left home, his wife
was still in bed; but when he returned at noon for his dinner,
he found his four children alone in the apartment. His wife
and all her wearing apparel were missing.

Becker offered no genuinely helpful information, but after
several conferences he told the detective he thought his wife
might have returned to England, where she was born. When
asked to which part of England she might go, he became
vague, saying his wife had never spoken much of her old
home. The detective persisted in his queries about England,
but Becker became more and more uncommunicative, stub-
bornly refusing to say anything more about that country,
or even to divulge where his wife's relatives lived over there.
He said: "I'm not going to the trouble of looking her up.
I won't attempt to get in touch with her people. Why try
to hold a woman who wants to run away?"

No progress was made until the early part of July, when
the detective again visited Becker's home, only to find that
he had moved, leaving no address with the janitor or tenants.
He then called at the place where Becker was employed at
the time his wife had disappeared, and was told that he
had been discharged from their employ, and that his present whereabouts were unknown to them. But on August 24
the detective located Becker at a factory where he had
secured employment.

Because of Becker's persistent refusal to give information
regarding his wife's habits and associates and her English
relatives, our suspicions had been aroused. We decided that
the man knew more about his wife's disappearance than he

wanted to tell, and that the District Attorney's office might
be able to get some information from him. Becker was therefore brought to the office of the District Attorney of Bronx
County, and was questioned by an Assistant. Becker told
him that his wife had left of her own accord, and that her
mother resided in London, England. After this interview the
Assistant District Attorney concurred with us that something
was amiss. He was of the further opinion that Becker should
be kept under surveillance, and that a communication should
be sent to London, to ascertain if Jennie Becker's mother
had any knowledge of the whereabouts of her daughter. A
query was immediately sent abroad through the British Con-
sulate of New York.

Following this conference, neighbors and friends of the
Beckers were questioned, but they could throw no light on
the woman's disappearance. In November Becker was again
taken to the District Attorney's office, and again examined.
Because so many discrepancies appeared in his story, he
was now ordered arrested as a material witness. Four days
later, after several more witnesses were questioned, the detective was directed to search the dumps in the Hunt's Point
section, where Becker was in the habit of disposing of saw-
dust. Several detectives engaged in this work, but without
result.

A short time later the detectives, still out for leads, located
Harry Monstein, of East 114th Street, a friend of Becker's,
who told them that Becker had confided in him the fact that
he had had his wife killed. It was further learned that
Becker, through a friend, had had a telegram sent from
Philadelphia, purporting to come from Becker's wife, and
addressed to Becker, which read as follows: "Having a good

time. Do not worry about me." This red herring message was intended to divert suspicion from Becker, and make it appear that the woman had left voluntarily. It was also to bolster up Becker's original suggestion that his wife had deserted him.

Later Monstein was sent by the District Attorney to visit Becker in his cell. During the conversation between Becker and Monstein, Becker told his friend that Rubin Norkin had assisted him in the murder of Jennie Becker. Following this overheard confidence, the District Attorney, the detectives and a patrolman went to Norkin's home on Southern Boulevard, in the Bronx, and planted outside the house all night. He did not return, however. But two days later he was picked up in the vicinity of his home, taken to the local precinct station house, and later brought before the District Attorney's office for questioning.

At first Norkin said that the only knowledge he had of the Becker case was what he had read in the newspapers about Mrs. Becker's disappearance. But a little later he broke down and admitted that the woman had been murdered, and agreed to take his questioners to the lot where the body was buried. Accordingly, the body of a woman was uncovered that same day in a boiler pit in a lot at 140th Street and Southern Boulevard. She had been strangled to death, and her body sprinkled with chloride of lime. Norkin was promptly arrested as a material witness.

After the finding of the body Becker was taken to the Fordham Morgue where it awaited identification, but he refused to say the remains were those of his wife. When he was taken to the boiler pit he was stoical, shrugged his shoulders and stoutly denied all knowledge of the crime.

Then, as so frequently happens when accomplices in a crime are cornered like rats, Becker and Norkin behaved like rodents. They tried to run to cover. Each blamed the other, and Becker openly accused Norkin of doing the actual killing of his wife. Norkin, in retaliation, said he would tell all.

"Becker came to me about Christmas time last year, and asked me if I wanted to make a little easy money," declared Norkin. "He told me he wanted some one buried. I replied that I had never made any easy money in my life. That ended the talk then. But Becker came to me again on New Year's Day, and this time made advances to me on the matter of getting rid of his wife. He said he was fed up with her, and wanted her out of the way. After that he bought a car from me, and also asked me if I had a shovel. I told him I guessed there was one around somewhere.

"A little while after that, Becker found a shovel, and he placed it at the side of the building. The next morning Becker came to my shop very early, before I arrived, and when I came in told me he had buried his wife in the pit. When I bawled him out for what he had done, he said to me:

" 'You can't bring the dead back to life.'

"Then he grabbed my hand, and asked me to promise not to tell any one. He offered me a drink and said:

" 'Let bygones be bygones. Don't be yellow!' "

This statement was later accepted as evidence at Norkin's trial, proving him to be an accessory after the act.

My detective who carried this woman search to a successful conclusion was instrumental in obtaining the indictment of Becker by the Bronx Grand Jury for first degree murder of his wife, and on December 4 Rubin Norkin, his accomplice, was also indicted for first degree murder. Both men were found guilty, were sentenced to death, and later executed.

A more recent disappearance mystery which brought to light a crime concerned Henry Levy, whose wife reported him missing. Levy was a John Street jeweler. There is a distinction between a Maiden Lane jeweler and a John Street jeweler. The former has a place of business; the latter maintains desk space with several other jewelers in the same office, and carries his stock under his hat or, to be more exact, in a case in his pocket.

Mrs. Levy reported that her husband had had an appointment to meet her at 3:30 one Saturday afternoon to accompany her on a shopping trip. When he failed to appear at the appointed time, she decided that he had merely been delayed, and waited a couple of hours for him. Finally she telephoned her husband's brother, a lawyer, and told him of the occurrence. Her brother-in-law suggested that she wait a little longer, since her husband might have had a last minute customer who had caused the delay. He mentioned a number of business contingencies which might have cropped up to detain him. After waiting several hours, the wife telephoned her husband's office, but received no reply.

She returned home, hoping to receive some word. During this interval she and her brother-in-law had several telephone conferences, and shortly before midnight they decided to report the matter to the Missing Persons Bureau. There appeared to us, at first, nothing unusual in connection with the case. Many men fail to keep appointments with their wives.

MURDERS

The detective assigned to the case took the matter up the following day, but since it was Sunday little progress could be made due to the fact that the business associates of the missing man were not available at their places of business; and their home addresses were not easily obtained. The detective did, however, succeed in interviewing a few of Mr. Levy's business friends, but without securing any information which'would supply a lead or clew.

Monday morning the brother of the missing man came to my office and, with the detective present, we went over the entire situation. Mr. Levy said that his brother represented his father-in-law, a well-known Amsterdam jeweler, in the handling, in New York, of precious stones, mostly uncut diamonds; that he usually carried a stock valued from twenty-five thousand dollars to fifty thousand dollars on his person; that inquiry had been made at the safe deposit vaults where this type of dealer in precious stones leaves his stock overnight or on Sundays and holidays, and it had been learned that his brother had not left his gems there as usual.

This information opened the door to two possibilities. One was that the missing man had absconded with his stock of jewelry for some purpose best known to himself. The second was that he had been "taken for a ride" for the purpose of robbing him of his stock. The brother was an exceptionally frank man. He was able to take the objective viewpoint, something I have found few relatives able to do under stress of emotion.

The brother said: "I understand human nature. Because the man happens to be my brother does not alter the situation in the least. But because he is my brother I happen to

35

know him better, perhaps, than any one else does. So I
will try to give you what you ask for—the intimate slant
on him."

I asked him about the possibility of there being another
woman in the missing man's life. Experience has taught us
at the Missing Persons Bureau that a woman frequently
enters into the situation of a husband's delayed homecoming.
I term this siren the Inevitable Woman. The brother, with-
holding nothing that would throw light on the character of
Levy, assured me, however, that there was no other woman
in Levy's life.

Referring to the kind of business his brother was carrying
on, and the people with whom he dealt, the lawyer said he
was convinced that his brother was fundamentally honest.
When questioned as to the state of the jeweler's business,
the lawyer was forthright. He gave me detailed information
regarding his brother's creditors, and the amount of his indebtedness to them. He knew all about his obligations in this
respect, because he was frequently consulted regarding them.

I accepted the brother's story with certain mental reservations, despite his obvious sincerity, and began a systematic
inquiry for the purpose of sifting various theories we held.
With us it is a process of elimination. We work out one
theory after another; some collapse, others stand up, and
we carry on with the latter.

Detectives began a canvass of John Street, interviewing
the man's acquaintances and business associates, and finally
two men were found who recalled having seen Levy standing
across the street from his office at 1:30 on the afternoon of
the day he disappeared. He was in conversation with a man
they were unable to identify. From that moment all trace

of Levy was lost, and a most thorough inquiry failed to disclose a single trace of the missing man.

A number of men in the same line of business were interviewed. Some of them were international jewel dealers, with foreign connections, and with cosmopolitan experience. One of them had been employed by a foreign government as an appraiser of jewels. These men gave us valuable information as to the methods employed by foreign jewelers in sending their goods to this market on memorandum. Incidentally, they also gave us some interesting tips as to ways in which ingenious smugglers had been accustomed to get valuable gems into this country free of duty. (A recent lowering of the tariff has put a stop to the smuggling of jewelry. There is no longer money in the racket.)

Circulars describing Levy were prepared and distributed to Police Departments throughout the country, and also among the jewelry trade.

As our investigation progressed we confirmed the lawyer's opinion that no member of the opposite sex was involved in a way that would lead us to believe Levy had been remiss in his social and marital duties. During the two or three weeks following the disappearance, searching investigations were conducted. The probability of his having absconded with his stock of gems was checked upon, and found not tenable. This left only one theory: that some outside agency was responsible for his disappearance. So by the process of discarding one theory after another, we had them narrowed down to the point where only one held water.

At about this time a new element entered the picture. Mrs. Levy received a telephone call from an unknown man, and one whose voice was strange to her, telling her that her husband had been kidnaped and was held in custody by him. He gave her this warning: "If you want to see your husband alive, have ten thousand dollars ready to turn over to me through a medium of which I'll advise you later. After I get the money Levy will be released. Now keep your trap shut about this! Let out a peep to the cops and your man will be bumped off. Don't forget!"

Mrs. Levy, shocked and terrified by this message, asked the man when she would be expected to pay the money.

"I haven't decided yet on the time or the means," replied the unknown voice. "But stand ready to turn the money over to me on a moment's notice. I'll instruct you later how to go about this...." Click. The man had hung up the receiver. One can readily imagine the agony of the distracted wife. With strained nerves she began a vigil, listening for the ring of the telephone, awaiting a visit from the postman. But for several days following this first call no further approach was made.

Then Mrs. Levy received another telephone call asking her if she had received a registered letter. She said she had not, and her telephone caller admitted that he had probably addressed the letter incorrectly, but told her that he would write her another. A day later she received it, and this time she was informed that five pigeons had been left at a place of which she would later be advised. The writer said that, upon receiving the address, she was to get the pigeons, take them home, attach a one thousand dollar bill to both legs of each pigeon, and then release the birds with their ten thousand dollars ransom.

One morning a few days later the telephone bell rang, and the now familiar voice instructed her to go to a certain cigar store in the Borough of Queens where she would find the five pigeons in a box.

"Don't lose any time," he warned her. "Come through with the money as directed, and your man will be back home with you almost at once."

All of these conversations between the unknown man and Mrs. Levy were at once repeated to me. After each telephone call I got a report on what had been said. While at first Mrs. Levy was inclined to believe that her husband was being held captive for ransom, I was able to convince her that there was absolutely nothing to it. I told her that the pigeon scheme was simply a new and ingenious kind of racket, which was being worked as a result of information secured through newspapers regarding the disappearance of her husband. At first she was reluctant to see the matter in this light, but she was finally brought to the realization that some clever, designing crook was attempting to shake her down and cash in on her anxiety over her missing husband, and was dissuaded from parting with any of her money. Her brother-in-law supplemented my arguments so that she was eventually convinced that her telephone caller had no power to help her, and was merely attempting to take advantage of her credulity.

This and other types of attempted extortion which have figured in missing persons cases will be described in a later chapter. Suffice it to say here that we checked up on the pigeon plot, and developments showed that the man who tried extortion by this original means knew nothing whatever of the whereabouts of Levy.

By this time the detectives, the Levy family and I all felt that there was but one way to account for the disappearance of the jeweler, and that was that he had been murdered for his stock of jewels. Up to this time I had delayed broadcasting the Levy disappearance by teletype to out-of-town police departments for this reason: had Levy been murdered it was to be assumed that his body would be thrown into some inaccessible swamp or woods, or into some of the waters surrounding New York. It was winter and the weather was still cold. A body disposed of on land would not be as readily detected as when the weather warmed up. A body cast into the water would remain submerged until such time as the water warmed sufficiently to cause the generation of gases in the tissues, when it would come to the surface. Therefore, I did not send out the teletype alarm until early in April, for I wanted to bring the matter freshly to the attention of police departments outside of New York at a time when there was a probability of the body's being found. The soundness of our views in this connection was borne out by the fact that on the evening of May 1, a message was received by us from the Nassau County Police to the effect that at about 10 o'clock that morning a fisherman, while fishing about one thousand feet off the shore at Glen Cove had discovered a body floating in the water. He towed it to shore and notified the police.

It was the opinion of the Nassau County officials that the body was that of Levy, since it tallied with the description the Missing Persons Bureau had recently sent out by teletype, and that it had probably been in the water from the day of his disappearance.

A cursory examination of the body disclosed that the legs had been bound tightly together at the ankles with several strands of picture wire. Strands of wire had also been drawn tightly about the throat, and there were marks on the wrists which indicated that they, too, had been bound together, although the wire had broken and fallen off. The supposition was that a weight had been attached to the wire binding the wrists, and that either the movement of the body in the water had worn the strands of wire through until they had broken and the weight dropped, or that they had come in contact with some other agency which had severed the strands.

Shortly after the discovery of the body a Coroner's physician made an examination of it, and ascertained that there were five gunshot wounds, two through the head and three through the heart. It was evident from this that whoever perpetrated the crime was taking no chances as to the death of the victim.

Immediately upon receipt of the message reporting the finding of the body I went to the headquarters of the Nassau County police, accompanied by the detective who had worked on the case, and Levy's brother. Inspector Harold R. King received me at his office. Right here I want to say that Inspector King is thoroughly up on his job. He had assembled everything that would serve to identify the body of the murdered man. Portions of clothing that still remained were all there. Both upper and lower jaws had been removed and brought to the Inspector's office to facilitate my inspection.

The hair from the man's head had entirely disappeared owing to the long submersion in the water, but some from the body had been saved. The hair, by the way, was a very important item helping toward identification in this case. Levy had red hair, and the hair placed before me was the same shade of red. Of course, the teeth were more important still in the matter of identification. We had consulted with the dentists who had done professional work for the missing man, and they had given us an accurate and detailed description of the fillings and bridges they had made. This description had been embodied in our teletype broadcast and circular descriptions of the missing man. Even to the unprofessional eye the condition of the teeth was seen to tally with that given by the dentists.

Then the brother identified articles of clothing worn by the missing man, particularly portions of the trousers, for they were of a peculiar weave, with gray predominating in the color scheme. Levy had purchased them in Amsterdam, Holland, and a button on the piece of trouser still remaining bore the name of an Amsterdam tailor. That practically settled the matter.

A few days later the Coroner's inquest was held, and identification of the body made positive through an examination of the teeth by the dentists who had worked on them during Levy's lifetime, and through the exhibition of a second pair of trousers belonging to the same suit. The identification was established, and the Coroner ruled that Levy had come to his death by being shot or strangled by some person or persons unknown at the time. A search for the perpetrators of the crime is still being conducted jointly by the Nassau County Police and the Police of New York City.

With the finding of the body of Levy came confirmation of our contention that the man who had been attempting extortion by means of pigeons, trying to persuade Mrs. Levy to part with a large sum of money, had known nothing whatsoever of the whereabouts of the man he claimed to have in his custody. Evidence showed that he had made all his attempts at extortion long after the missing man had been murdered.

As for our Bureau, our duty was ended the moment the body was discovered and identified.

Splendid detective work was done in the case I am about to narrate. When it first came to our attention no unusual circumstances surrounded it, but clever sleuthing uncovered a secret and illegal happening, one which involved several people, and which resulted in a death shrouded in mystery.

Since the crime occurred about fifteen years ago, I have been obliged to refresh my memory regarding it through the aid of the detective responsible for the adroit work. He has submitted to me a memorandum of his notes, and I think it will be well to quote from them direct, omitting only some of the more or less unpleasant medical data. The detective tells the story in his own unemotional way, setting down cold facts in a matter-of-fact fashion, without attempting to take any credit for the really fine job he did. His report simply shows results step by step as he worked them out.

I have, in the cases preceding this one, with the exception of the Bauer case, used real names, for crimes were involved and the facts matters of police record. But, for various reasons, I shall change the names and places in the following history. Several of the physicians figuring in the case are, due to insufficient evidence of criminal participation, unfortunately still practicing, and the family of the girl victim survives.

This mystery concerned a young Austrian girl, whom I

shall call Hilda Weymar. During August, of the year 1917, Mrs. Hannah Luringen, living in Washington Heights, reported that her sister Hilda Weymar was missing. She described the girl as eighteen years of age, weighing 128 pounds, with gray eyes, chestnut hair, dark complexion, fine teeth, and with good physical and mental make-up. The sister said that the young girl wore, on the day she disappeared, a white shirtwaist, a navy blue skirt and coat, black laced shoes and black stockings, and a navy blue hat, clothes reminiscent of another style period.

Now to quote the detective direct:

"At about 12 noon, August 17, I called on Mrs. Luringen and interviewed her and her mother. Mrs. Weymar being unable to speak English, Hannah Luringen acted as interpreter. She stated that her sister Hilda was living in a furnished rooming house on West 41st Street, somewhere between Seventh and Ninth Avenues. And she said that the last time she saw her was around June 1, 1917, but she could not fix the date positively. The sister said that, after they had attended a performance at a theater uptown, Hilda had left her saying she was going downtown. That was the last time she had laid eyes on her.

"The sister also stated that a Sidney Blaustein, musical director of a Broadway theater, must know where her sister was, as he had given her the privilege of getting things at several stores and having them put on his charge account. He also paid for her room and board. The sister said she had called at the theater on August 16 and had talked to Mr. Blaustein, who stated he had not seen Hilda for the past two or three months.

"On Friday, August 17, I called to see Mr. Blaustein. He

stated to me that he had not seen the girl in two months or more, and the only interest he had in her was that she came to him crying one day, and said she had no friends in New York, and her folks were living in Philadelphia. So he said he then took pity on her, and told her he would pay for her room and board until she got a job, providing she would be on the level and live straight. He then brought her to a family named Makin, on Lexington Avenue, but she stayed there only about one week, coming back to the Broadway section where Blaustein said he did not want her to be, as he stated he told her she would go wrong if she did not stay away from there.

"So then she came to him some time later crying again and told him she was ill, so he told her he would have nothing more to do with her. He then stated that about two months ago he received a telephone call from an uptown hospital, but paid no attention to it, and that was all he knew about the girl and he had not seen her since. I called up the hospital and was informed by the entry clerk that Hilda Weymar was not there any more. I then asked him what address she had given as her residence, and he replied giving a number on West 41st Street.

"I called there and inquired of Mrs. L. O. Graddis, the landlady, if she had a Hilda Weymar living there. She replied that Hilda Weymar had lived there but was now dead, having died at the hospital around June 16, 1917. I then asked her how long the girl had been living there. She stated, after looking up her book, that she had hired the room May 21, 1917, and left there on a Wednesday or Thursday, June 6 or 7.

"Hilda told Mrs. Graddis that her folks lived in Penn-

45

sylvania, and that she was a model, but was then on her vacation. I next asked the landlady if Hilda had any visitors and she stated she did not allow any men to go to any of the girls' rooms, but a man whose name she thought was Blaustein had brought Hilda home to the door one evening when she was on the stoop talking to her brother, and that was the only man she had ever seen with Hilda.

"I then called the hospital again, telling them what I had learned, and this time they told me that Hilda Weymar had died there of natural causes at 5 :30 P.M., June 16, and was buried by an undertaker named I. Sankermann. She gave her age as twenty-three, and said she lived at West 41st Street with her husband Max. I called at the undertaker's shop on August 18 and was informed by his stable man that the boss was not there and he did not know where he lived and could not tell when he would return. I then went to the hospital, and was informed that Hilda Weymar was brought to the hospital in an automobile about 10 P.M., Tuesday, June 12, by an elderly woman whose name they did not know. Hilda Weymar was entered as a private patient at twenty-five dollars per week, and that a Dr. Abe Sorker telephoned everything would be all right in regard to the money as she was his patient. She was operated on on June 13 or 14 by Dr. Sorker, and had died from natural causes.

"Accompanied by another detective from the Missing Persons Bureau I called at Dr. Sorker's, and he stated in our presence that Hilda Weymar was brought to his attention by a Dr. Jacob Ratter, who paid him one hundred and fifty dollars by check for his trouble. He also stated it was Ratter who performed the operation on Hilda Weymar at the hospital, with the assistance of Dr. Moisellwich. The other detective and I called on Dr. Jacob Ratter, who stated Hilda Weymar came to him on June 12 and said she was sick and wanted to be treated.

"So he asked her how she came to be sent to him, and she said she was recommended by a friend. So he examined her and found she had a very high temperature and was very sick. He then informed her he would have to call in another doctor, and believed she would have to be operated on, and that would cost her quite some money, and she replied that she would return with the money.

"She returned with three hundred dollars that evening, and said that would cover the expense for the operation, and she would be well enough by the time that was used up to get some more, providing it cost any more. He then stated he called his nurse Fannie Caxton, who brought Hilda to the hospital in a taxi. He also stated that it was Fannie Caxton, of Second Avenue, who, after Hilda had died at the hospital, attended to her funeral and so on, at his request, as he felt sympathy for the girl and wanted to see her get a decent burial.

"He did not know just what cemetery it was, as he had left everything to his nurse, Fannie Caxton, and that she was not at home now, as she had gone to visit some friends in Jersey, and he did not know just what time she would be back, but that as soon as she returned he would telephone to us giving us the name of the cemetery, and the plot she was buried in. He thought he would be able to let us know by 2 P.M. that day.

"After that the other detective and I called at Second Avenue and saw Fannie Caxton, who is a midwife, and who was not out of town as Dr. Ratter had informed us. She

47

stated in our presence that she was the one who brought Hilda Weymar to the hospital on June 12, at the request of Dr. Ratter. She then stated that she was visiting a friend at the hospital on June 13, and stopped in to see Hilda while she was there and asked Hilda where her folks lived, and Hilda replied she had a stepmother, father and sister living in either Philadelphia or Boston, and she did not want them to know of her condition, but that she would go back home to them when she got better.

"The midwife said: 'So I saw she would give me no further information so I left her and saw her no more until June 17, when Dr. Ratter came to my house and told me the girl had died and asked if I would do him one more favor and see that the girl got a decent burial, and he would stand the expense, which he did.

" 'I then got an undertaker, and we called up the cemetery to open a grave for us, and we buried her that same day, June 17. About two or three days later I sent my daughter Renie to Dr. Ratter's office with the receipts, and that is all I know about the case.'

"Leaving Mrs. Caxton's, the other detective and I called at Dr. Ratter's again, and he stated that he had been looking for the receipts for the grave and that he was going to let us know where Hilda Weymar was buried as soon as he found them. He then went into another room and came back in about five minutes with the receipt for the grave, which he said we could have. It called for one grave for Hilda Weymar at $29.00, Row No. 16, Grave 40, at a Long Island cemetery.

"I then called at Washington Heights and saw Hannah Luringen and Tillie Starecky, another sister of Hilda's.

Hannah said she went to a corset and underwear store on Columbus Avenue, in which Sidney Blaustein had a charge account and where Hilda could get what she wanted on his account. Mr. Blaustein lives across the street from this store. A blonde girl and an old man in this store told her Hilda had been operated on in a hospital and had died, but they refused to tell her who told them about it. On August 16 Mrs. Luringen saw Sidney Blaustein at the theater, and he told her Hilda was pregnant and that he had brought her to a doctor and the doctor had refused to touch her.

"He also stated that Hilda had been in several hospitals, and that she was in the fourth or fifth month of pregnancy. Tillie Starecky, the other sister, said that Hilda told her three months ago that Blaustein was going to send her to the Catskill Mountains, and that Hilda would write Mrs. Starecky when she went. And Hilda told her Blaustein was going to buy her all kinds of good clothes, and that he even promised to put her on the stage. He also sent her to a dentist and paid $50.00 to have her teeth fixed, and he would give her money any time she needed it. She also stated Blaustein was supposed to have charge accounts in several stores and restaurants along Broadway.

"I then told the sisters I would be able to give them definite information relative to what had become of Hilda on Monday, August 20. On that day I laid the facts of my investigation before the Missing Persons Bureau. I was ordered to place them before the District Attorney of New York County, which I did. I talked to the Assistant District Attorney in the Criminal Courts Building. He immediately gave me summonses for all the hospital records in the case of Hilda Weymar, also for the entry clerk, the private nurse for Hilda, and several others in the case. August 21 I brought Sidney Blaustein on a summons to the District Attorney's office, but we were unable to get a statement from him.

"On August 24 I had the undertaker come to the District Attorney's office, where he stated he had received ten dollars for supplying one hearse and one carriage on June 17 for the funeral of Hilda Weymar, being hired by the shamus, Moses Stoddels. I brought Stoddels to the District Attorney's office where he stated that Fannie Caxton came to him June 17, and told him to make arrangements to bury the girl, which he did, as he does for several lodges, and that Fannie Caxton paid him for his trouble and expense.

"Another officer and I called at Fannie Caxton's on August 22, where we obtained some clothes of Hilda Weymar's, which consisted of one blue serge skirt and coat, one waist, one silk chemise, one silk corset cover and one pair of silk bloomers, which were put in the property clerk's office at the District Attorney's. Fannie Caxton stated that Dr. Ratter had paid her for the funeral, and she did not get anything for her trouble. She said she left the shoes, stockings and hat belonging to Hilda in room number 9, which Hilda had at the hospital.

"On September 19 Dr. Sorker was served with a court summons. He was later arrested, and charged with issuing a false death certificate. An autopsy was held on the body of Hilda Weymar at the City Mortuary. Dr. Ratter was also arrested, charged with being implicated in the death of Hilda Weymar, who died from the effects of a criminal operation."

There was seemingly nothing unusual about the Weymar girl's disappearance when the case first came to the attention of the Missing Persons Bureau. But, due to the persistence of the detective working on it, a criminal operation which resulted in the girl's death was discovered. The shocking feature of the whole affair was the fact that a dozen or more people knew about the death and secret burial of the unfortunate victim of the criminal act, but that her own family was kept in total darkness regarding it through the connivance of those implicated in the crime. Long after the girl was buried, members of her family still sought her as though she were temporarily missing.

Only a short time elapsed between the day the case was first handed to the detective and the hour when he discovered that a crime had been committed, and that the girl he was seeking was dead and buried. He made a habit of dropping in at the doctor's office, apparently just visiting and chatting with him in friendly fashion, with no hint that he was trying to "get something on him." In this way he secured some good leads. Through him he found out where the midwife lived, and she proved the key to the whole situation. It was her testimony which secured the conviction of the guilty men.

Several years ago one of the most grewsome of mystery murder cases came to our attention under the following circumstances. Near Long Island City, in a depression in a vacant lot, the legless body of a girl was found through one of those chance occurrences, which are sometimes responsible for the discovery of a crime. The body was lying in a pond at Queens Boulevard and Rawson Street, wrapped in an oilcloth. The hollow place where the torso was discovered, by a worker in the sewer department, was filled with water due to recent rains. The City employee had waded into the pond in order to wash his boots as had been his custom when in this neighborhood, which he had not visited for about six weeks. As he waded into the water, he found the victim of the brutal crime. He found a raft about fifteen feet from the shore of the pond, placed the body on it, and immediately told his foreman of his discovery. The foreman, in turn, reported it to the police.

It was estimated that the murdered woman had been about five feet one inch in height, had weighed about one hundred pounds, and that she had been dead about four days. She was approximately twenty-two years of age, had hazel eyes, and hair described as "auburn." The ears had been pierced for earrings, making it probable that the victim was either foreign-born or the offspring of foreign-born parents. A small woven raffia ring was on the little finger of the murdered girl's left hand, and there was an imitation tortoise-shell comb in her hair. According to the detective's report the celluloid comb had "nine teeth missing," a detail which goes to show how minutely a crime of this kind is described. There was also one black metal hairpin and one small yellow bone pin in the victim's hair.

Further details of this grewsome murder are given in the detective's report: "The body was dismembered at the hips. There was a deep cut at the base of the right thumb of the left hand, and a wound on the left shoulder. A piece of olive green cotton made in the shape of a belt, with a large celluloid faced button attached, was found tightly tied around her neck, causing strangulation, from which her death had apparently resulted."

One of the outstanding features, by which identification might be made, was "red hair." The first description we received of the body came to us from the local precinct in which it was found, and I immediately caused a careful check-up on all still unsolved disappearances on our records, seeking a missing woman with red hair. But I found none who tallied in any other particular with the description of the murder victim.

I visited the Morgue personally, and viewed the body or, rather, the portion of it which had been found. It was not a pleasant sight. It was apparent that the legs had been chopped off, and it was easily seen that the one who had dismembered the body was not familiar with surgery or anatomy. No effort had been made to dismember at the joints, and the work had been executed crudely by one who was, doubtless, in a hurry to get the thing done. The face of the dead girl was badly swollen as a result of being immersed in the water. I noticed at once the pierced ears, but it was the hair of the murder victim that attracted my attention. I was puzzled by the shade, which did not seem natural or genuine to me. It appeared to be red, and yet the shade looked artificial and strange.

Oddly enough, it did not look dyed, either, or as though it had been hennaed or "touched up" with any chemical. This curious circumstance aroused my interest, and I decided to experiment. I secured a strand of the hair, brought it back to my office, and gave it a careful washing in clear water, without using soap or any chemical. It was immediately restored to its original color, a mousy shade of blonde, the kind of hue sometimes crudely called "dirty blonde." The bowl in which I washed the hair was now filled with water tinged with red.

After the strand of hair had dried I placed it on a piece of

53

paper on my desk, and called in one of the men at Head-quarters:

"What shade of hair would you call this?" I asked him.

He gazed at the lock of newly washed hair.

"Mud-gutter blonde," he promptly replied.

When I told him that it was the same lock of hair of the strange red shade he had seen a little while before, he was astonished. I explained that, because the torso had been lying so long in a pool of bloody water, the blood had soaked into the woman's long hair and dried on it, giving that queer shade of red which had at first caught my attention.

After this discovery I immediately changed the description of the victim, substituting "drab blonde" hair for red. A widespread search was made for the killer in this case, but he was never apprehended, and to this day the identity of the girl has not been established. The description of the murder victim did not tally with any on our list of missing women. The mutilated torso is still preserved in alcohol in one of the morgues of New York City.

Hard-headed police officers do not often engage in so futile a pastime as guesswork, but in this instance there is seemingly nothing one can do but conjecture about the details of the girl's sorry end. She was probably the victim of an assault; possibly she resisted, and in the struggle was killed, the murder taking place in a house or an apartment. After the crime the killer cut up the victim, so that her body could be more easily disposed of. Perhaps she was assaulted, and because she recognized her assailant, he decided it would be well to put her out of the way before she identified him and reported the matter to the police.

A strange coincidence in connection with this case was that

just about the time I was conducting the investigation, another grewsome murder find was made. While I was at the Morgue one day inspecting the legless body of this unfortunate woman, a brown suitcase containing the mummified remains of a man was brought in. The body was found in the suitcase in the store-room of a local hotel. It had been abandoned in a room in the hotel a long time before and sent down to the storage-room by the management, who did not know what it contained. One day, years later, when employees were clearing out old baggage from the store-room, the suitcase was opened and its sinister contents discovered.

Since the suitcase had been gathering dust in the store-room for a number of years, the hotel people could not check back and find out in which room it had been found or who had left it at the hotel. The manager notified the nearest precinct, and the grim relic found its way to the Morgue.

The body had been dismembered, but all of it was there in the case. The flesh was still on the bones, and the body had evidently been subjected to a drying process of some kind which gave it the appearance of a mummy. Unlike the torso of the woman found in the pool of bloody water, this body had been dismembered by one who was familiar with anatomy. It was an expert job. Anthropologists who were later called in to examine the remains said that the dead man had evidently been a Japanese or a Chinese, or at any rate, an Oriental.

In this instance, also, one can but hazard a guess. If murder was involved, the killer probably went to the hotel for the express purpose of ridding himself of the fatal suitcase by leaving it behind. From his standpoint his plan seems to have been both simple and sound. The drying or embalming

55

process left no odor, and it was evidently assumed by the management that the suitcase had been forgotten or abandoned, or that it might be called for later. Once it was sent to the storage-room it was forgotten, and the passing of years made it difficult to recall events or persons connected with it. It is barely possible, of course, that the suitcase might have belonged to a medical student, and the remains have been a cadaver used in his medical studies. This theory is not so plausible, however, because of the fact that flesh still adhered to the bones, and a medical college cadaver, once it has been used by the students, is usually well reduced to its skeleton frame.

Both the torso and the suitcase mysteries are still unsolved, and the bodies remain at the Morgue in the event of possible future identification.

III. SUICIDES

SURPRISINGLY few of the disappearances reported to the Bureau are accounted for through suicide. We have only about ten suicide cases a year; approximately one hundred and fifty have come to my attention during the fifteen years I have been in charge of the Bureau. Sometimes a disappearance is reported where no apparent motive for the act seems to exist. Upon investigation we may find that the absent person has a real or fancied reason for taking his own life, and then we turn to the possibility of suicide. The motive is all-important, and in every case, whenever possible, we attempt to learn what it is.

We have found business failures to be responsible for the largest number of suicides; domestic difficulties hold second place; incurable disease third. Disappointment in love has long been supposed by the sentimentally inclined to be the motivating force behind many suicides. But, strange as it may seem, this celebrated and traditional cause for self-destruction has apparently not accounted for any of the suicides which have come to my attention in more than a decade. Men and women put a period to their earthly existence but—not for Love! The love interest figures indirectly in several of the case histories I am going to relate, but disappointment in love was not the chief reason for the act of suicide. I am sorry that honesty compels me to shatter another romantic idol with the hard logic of fact.

Suicide is an interesting subject upon which to speculate. A wide field for controversy presents itself the moment one takes up its discussion. Opinions vary as to whether or not it is, under certain circumstances, more valorous to die than to live. What degree of courage, moral, physical, or both, is necessary for the act which destroys the complicated assemblage of cells that means a human life? Is suicide ever justifiable? I have listened to many debates on this subject, and have yet to hear a common conclusion reached. What my own opinions in the matter are is of no importance. Academic discussions ill become a policeman. My job is not to theorize, but to find missing people, dead or alive. I can often tell by looking at a man, or at his picture, whether or not he is likely to commit suicide. But whether his act would be noble or base, heroic or cowardly is a problem for philosophers rather than policemen, although, oddly enough, a policeman is sometimes a philosopher. But now for some suicides in cold fact and without the accompaniment of idle speculation.

About seven years ago, Mrs. Luella Thurmer, a socially prominent widow and a philanthropist, was reported to us as missing. She lived on lower Fifth Avenue, was forty-five years of age and a widow. She gave much time to social welfare work, and was well known not only in society, but also in charity circles. All of these facts we learned when constructing a picture of the missing woman's life. We found also that Mrs. Thurmer dwelt alone in a large and luxurious home, except for a staff of servants and a paid companion, Miss Myra Gwynne.

Mrs. Thurmer, who maintained an expensive car, disappeared one evening after her chauffeur had driven her to 59th Street, near First Avenue. That was the last any one saw of her; she had passed completely out of the lives of all who knew her. She was described to us by friends and servants as a woman of slight build, weighing about one hundred and twenty pounds, a decided brunette, who always dressed well and fashionably. The day on which she started out with her chauffeur in her imported car she was wearing a dark tailored suit, a small, close-fitting hat, long black gauntlets, and carried an expensive French beaded bag, believed to contain a considerable sum of money. It was her custom to be well supplied with money, so that she would be prepared, at a moment's notice, to meet calls from the needy. She was known as an extremely generous person.

Almost at the start of our investigation we secured a clew to the possible motive for Mrs. Thurmer's disappearance. The detective assigned to the case and I both talked to Miss Gwynne, the companion, who was also a trained nurse. She told us a story which revealed Mrs. Thurmer as leading a rather lonely and unhappy life, despite her social prominence and wealth. It seems that for years she had been suffering from a peculiar type of epilepsy. The attacks occurred with unusual frequency, and each year they increased in number until, at the time of her disappearance, she had been suffering from as many as a dozen or more a day. Sometimes the seizures would last but a few minutes, at other times for a more extended period, although they were never violent in form.

One odd feature of Mrs. Thurmer's ailment was that she might be seized with an attack when others were present, and no one but herself be aware of the fact. She might feel one coming on at the dinner table, in which case she would grow a little rigid, stare straight ahead, and remain motionless in suspended animation for a brief period. She would simply cease talking, appear not to be listening, and to all eyes but those of the trained nurse, nothing otherwise peculiar was occurring. She might easily have been merely lost in reflection over a remark made during the conversation.

But it is easily understandable how this strange malady would have a tendency to lessen Mrs. Thurmer's social contacts. The embarrassment which her epileptic attacks might occasion deterred her from visiting friends often, or doing much entertaining herself. As time passed, and these attacks made their appearance with greater frequency, the lonely woman grew depressed. Thus, regardless of the fact that she lived in material comfort, had plenty of money with which to procure the luxuries of life, and outside interests which her philanthropic nature created for her, she became more and more hopeless. After a day of twelve or fifteen attacks she would show the effects of the strain in both appearance and manner.

Questioning people who knew Mrs. Thurmer brought to light the fact that while she had a wide circle of friends, there was scarcely one to whom she could really unburden herself. Since Mrs. Thurmer felt she had certain obligations to discharge in order to maintain her social position, she kept in touch with people, but there were no real intimates. She had no release from the pent-up worries over her health and her ultimate tragic fate; everything was locked in her own mind. Miss Gwynne, the nurse-companion, told us that while Mrs. Thurmer seldom referred to her "illness," as she termed it, and was not given to complaining of her trouble, she felt confident that her patient fully realized the hopelessness of her physical state, and understood the condition toward which she was slowly drifting: complete irresponsibility and helplessness. When I discussed the matter of Mrs. Thurmer's health with her physician, he told me that before the passing of much time she would be a hopeless invalid, in other words, an imbecile.

After learning all these facts, and being confident that Mrs. Thurmer thoroughly understood the progressive nature of her ailment, I felt that the probable explanation of her disappearance was suicide. Life held no promise for the future; she did not have even a thin hope of eventual recovery. With nothing left to buoy her up, suffering in the present and despairing of ever being cured, one could easily imagine her making the obvious choice between a hopeless future and death. I believed that a woman of Mrs. Thurmer's type, judging her in the light of her friends' description, would decide to terminate an existence which was certain to become a burden to herself and others.

To guard, however, against the possibility that this theory would not stand up, we checked with officers assigned to duty on the 59th Street bridge, and found two or three who were there about the time that Mrs. Thurmer had been driven to 59th Street. These officers believed they had seen her around the entrance to the bridge, and a newsboy who had a stand near the entrance was positive he had observed her loitering near-by. He even believed he had seen her walking out on the bridge. This, of course, dove-tailed with our theory of suicide.

We checked up carefully on all bodies of drowned persons that came to our attention. I instructed our Morgue man to advise me immediately of recovery of the body of any woman answering Mrs. Thurmer's description. Inquiry was then made of the superintendent of the cemetery, in which the widow's husband was buried, as to whether he knew her, and if she had recently paid a visit there. He made a canvass of cemetery employees, and one of them said he knew the woman very well as a result of visits she made to the grave. He stated positively that he had seen her in the cemetery two days after her disappearance, but was unable to say in which direction she went after he had seen her standing near the grave of her husband. We cannot always depend upon the accuracy of casual observers, however, and memory, too, is a tricky and deceptive thing. But every bit of information concerning a missing man or woman is, nevertheless, always welcomed by us.

A confidential request was sent to units of the Police Department throughout the city, asking them to be on the watch for a case of this kind. All hospitals were carefully checked since, in Mrs. Thurmer's condition of health, anything might have happened to her. Not a clew was found, however, and no solution of the mystery came until about two months later. At that time I received a report that a Government dredge, belonging to the War Department and working in Ambrose Channel, had found the answer. This dredge was of the sandsucker type. The sucker of the dredge had suddenly become clogged, a condition which the dredger always finds extremely annoying, for in situations of this kind it is necessary for the sucker to be raised from the water, the suction stopped, and substance responsible for the clogging removed. The obstruction in this instance was the body of a woman. Her head, one arm and shoulder were wedged tightly into the mouth of the sucker. The other arm was hanging free, with a long black gauntlet on it.

As soon as the workmen found the body, it was turned over to what was then known as the Harbor Squad; they brought it to shore, and at once notified the Missing Persons Bureau. An immediate examination was made of the clothing still remaining on the body and of the dental work; and as a result we were almost immediately convinced that the body recovered was that of the missing Mrs. Thurmer. Later, when the autopsy was performed, it was found that the woman came to her death through submersion, which indicated that she had of her own accord put an end to her unhappy life.

This case again impressed upon me the importance of chance in our work. Consider this angle in the case of Mrs. Thurmer. It was assumed that she plunged into the water at or near 59th Street. Divide the total area of the East River and the Bay down to where the dredge was anchored in Ambrose Channel by the area which would come under the influence of that sandsucker, and you can picture to what extent luck was involved in the recovery of the woman's body. The ebb and flow of a few more tides, and the Atlantic Ocean might have held forever the mystery of Mrs. Thurmer's fate.

A case filled with pathos, and one which followed closely on the heels of the world-wide economic disturbance with which we are all too familiar, concerned Anton Mollick, a forty-six-year-old metal worker, who lived on Southern Boulevard with his wife and five children. It was a struggle for Mollick to keep things going, for he had only a part-time job, and his earnings did not stretch very far. Notwithstanding this, he managed to keep fairly happy, for he was devoted to his wife and children. On April 1 of this year, however, fate played him a grim April fool's joke. Mollick returned home on that day to find that he had been dispossessed. His wife, his five children and their few household belongings had been put out on the street by a city marshal while he was at his place of employment. But what filled him with terror was the fact that while the few sticks of furniture were there on the curb, his wife and children were nowhere to be seen; nor could his neighbors enlighten him as to what had become of them.

It never occurred to Mollick that the Police might be a source of information and help. He grew more and more desperate as the hours passed, and he was unable to learn the whereabouts of his loved ones. Frantic, miserable and homeless to boot, his family lost, he jumped in his hysterical condition to the conclusion that his wife had deserted him; to his simple way of reasoning she had grown disgusted with his failure to keep a roof over their heads. Eventually some one suggested that he report his wife as missing, and he did so. We tried to cheer up the poor fellow by assuring him that we would soon locate his family, and that we were confident that all was well with them.

Mollick was a splendid workman, and as soon as his employer heard of his plight, he promptly offered him the privilege of sleeping in the shop, and even supplied a cot and blanket. But this kind treatment proved of no avail. In the middle of the first night in his new quarters Mollick swallowed a quantity of muriatic acid, easily obtainable, for it was used in the shop for soldering. After swallowing the poison, he was soon in such agony that he staggered out to the street, where he was discovered by the officer on post and taken to a hospital. Later the same day he was removed to Bellevue where he died a few hours later.

In the meantime our search for Mrs. Mollick continued, and we learned from the Department of Public Welfare that the three oldest children had been sent to the Children's Society, and that the mother and the two youngest children, both little more than infants, had been taken to the New York Foundling Hospital. The wife, of course, had no intention whatever of deserting her husband; she had simply gone where she could find shelter for herself and her little ones.

When a young person dies by his own hand, the act seems particularly tragic. And when a young man who appears to be endowed with a multitude of blessings voluntarily walks out on life, one's curiosity is immediately aroused. Why did he do it? What cause could have been sufficient for an act which robbed him of many years of an apparently promising and happy life?

When, four years ago, young Merton Loring, a student in his senior year, suddenly and mysteriously vanished from a well-known Eastern college, every one who knew him was surprised. He was a brilliant, fine looking boy of twenty-two, and apparently had everything in the world any youth could desire. His parents were well-to-do, and had a charming home on Riverside Drive. Loring had recently become engaged to an attractive young girl of good family, and the wedding was to take place immediately after his graduation. Then one day he left his dormitory, apparently to go for a stroll, and did not return. His unaccountable disappearance was reported to his family by the Dean of the college, and the family reported it to us.

We learned that the boy was extremely happy in his choice of the young woman he was to marry, and that his home life was eminently satisfactory. His future looked particularly bright, and he showed every promise of a successful career. He seemed, in fact, a most fortunate young man, for he had wealth, social position, and friends to help him toward his desired goal, whatever it might be.

No motive seemed to exist for his disappearance, which occurred just before a mid-term examination. At first we thought that he might have fallen down in his studies and was afraid of flunking. But a talk with the Dean quickly removed this possibility from the motives for his disappearance; his standing in his studies was so high that he would have been exempted from taking examinations in several of them.

About a week after his disappearance, Mrs. Bruce Jayson, a married sister of Loring's, who resided in a small New Jersey town, came to see me at the Bureau. She appeared to be under a considerable strain, and was highly nervous and troubled in her manner. It was her first contact with the police, and obviously an ordeal for her. Realizing that she was upset, I decided that she was perturbed about my possible attitude toward her. My first task was to put her at ease, and relieve her mind of any anxiety about the part the police were to play in connection with her brother's disappearance. I reminded her that her brother was not a culprit, that we were not seeking him in order to punish him for a crime, but merely prosecuting a search for a person reported to us as missing. Mrs. Jayson soon unbent, and after we had talked for a while, she suddenly asked me to pledge myself to secrecy regarding something she was about to tell me.

"I have decided to take you into my confidence," she said. "What I am going to tell you is a family secret. It is rather— well, you see,—it is quite an unpleasant one," she stammered.

Then she proceeded to tell me that when her brother Merton had last visited her, which was about a month prior to his disappearance, he had alluded to his father's health. His father had been suffering for years from locomotor ataxia. Her brother told her that he had worried much about this, and had been informed that this father's condition was the result of early indiscretions. Loring had taken the matter to heart very seriously, and had even consulted medical authorities about the disease as it related to himself. They had advised him that there was a strong possibility that he had inherited the ailment, and that in any case it would be unwise and also unfair to marry under the circumstances. The boy said the doctors had told him that while he might not manifest any signs of the disease itself, he could transmit it to any possible offspring of the union, and that if he did not want to visit this curse upon "the third and fourth generations" he had best not marry at all.

This ruin of his romance and his dreams for the future naturally affected him keenly. His terrible predicament seemed insurmountable, and his final words to his sister had

67

been: "Under no condition will I marry now that I know all this." But what troubled him above all else, according to Mrs. Jayson, was the fact that he could not give his fiancée a satisfactory explanation for breaking the engagement. There seemed no way out of his difficulty, he told his sister that he felt himself a pariah from society. "I think the poor boy decided to take his life," said his sister.

Possessed of this information, we immediately requested the coöperation of the police in the town near which the missing boy's college was located. We asked them to make a tour of all the drug-stores (most of the druggists knew the student body well) in order to learn whether or not a young man had purchased any poison or deadly drug which might be employed to end one's life. We checked with his intimates at college to learn whether or not he possessed a pistol. Then we made a canvass of steamship booking offices on the theory that possibly he might have purchased a ticket to some coastal or foreign port. Finally, at one office, it was learned that a young man about Loring's age and general description, who appeared to be deeply preoccupied, had bought a ticket for a gulf port, booking under the name of John Morley. He had little or no baggage. We asked for information as to whether or not John Morley had debarked at his destination, and we were then informed that certain of his belongings had been found in his empty stateroom; that they were being held, although of small value, and might have been intentionally abandoned. These articles were later identified as the property of Merton Loring. No one remembered Morley's debarking at the port for which his ticket called.

It was now obvious that "John Morley"—or Merton Loring—had jumped overboard, and every effort was made to recover his body. The Coast Guards along the entire route were requested to be on the watch for bodies floating at sea, but Loring's has never been found.

Later when we were obliged to tell his sister of developments, she was philosophical about it. She conceded that it was a sorry end for a young man showing the promise her brother did but, under the circumstances, she felt that his suicide at sea was perhaps the best solution to the tragedy imposed by his tainted heredity.

The next suicide case I am going to tell about has a hospital setting and concerns a nurse. Her story is a checkered one, and consists of a long record of high jinks indulged in by a girl who could not stand the big city pace. Five years ago, when she was twenty, this girl, whom I shall call Jeanette Martin, came to New York from a small town in Wisconsin. She was convinced that the midwestern town of her birth afforded little opportunity in the way of advancement in the nursing career she had chosen. Jeanette dramatized herself in her profession. She saw herself as a second Florence Nightingale; had visions of being hailed as an Angel of Mercy, who had made great sacrifices for a suffering humanity. So she came to New York, and secured admission, as a student nurse, to one of the leading hospitals. She performed her duties with such enthusiasm and efficiency that she soon attracted the attention of her superiors and the medical staff. Patients, too, were grateful for her efficient ministrations, and her popularity was great.

Comely of face and figure, with an attractive personality, it was little wonder that she won the attention of the young internes. It was not long before she was receiving invitations to dine and go to places of entertainment. The inevitable social drinking played a part in these amusements, and soon the girl was in the full swing of gay city life in its more flamboyant aspects. She danced and went to parties and the theater whenever her duties permitted. Flattered by the attention of the young student doctors and some of her ex-patients at the hospital, she soon became proud of her charm for men, and the influence she wielded over them.

Jeanette realized, with the thrill that only a small-town girl can experience, that she could be selective, picking from a goodly assortment whichever friends were most congenial to her. Her choice was not always wise for her own welfare, but she led a gay life with no responsibilities. She was far from home and relatives; and she was young; so she let herself go and had her fling. The life of the big city was fascinating, and she was not going to be a prude. What did it matter, she argued with friends who tried to advise her, if she did return from an evening at a cabaret a bit exhilarated by cocktails? She had plenty of would-be lovers. At times she may have been more generous with her favors than a woman can afford to be. But what did it matter, she thought. Her life was her own. Why keep in abeyance her natural impulses and desires? Nature's law was older than any man-made law, and had been followed for countless centuries before there was any other rule or law of living.

If it occurs to the reader to wonder how I came to know the thoughts and arguments this young woman advanced to justify her way of life, let me say that all of this information was gleaned during the investigation we carried on after the girl's death. Her friends told us bits here and there until we had pieced together her mode of life and her philosophy.

SUICIDES

Jeanette's pastimes and pleasures were not permitted to interfere with her duties in the hospital. Regardless of late hours and cocktail drinking, she pursued her work with enthusiasm, and eventually graduated with high honors. Her great thrill came when she was entitled to write R. N. after her name. After graduation, she took a small apartment with another nurse, and embarked upon her career. She had few idle moments. About this time a young and promising physician began paying her marked attention. He proposed marriage, and while Jeanette did not accept him, she did not definitely reject him either. She seemed to prefer his attentions to those of her other numerous admirers. About a year after she had graduated, she met with a mishap. In her difficulty she appealed for aid from the young physician who was in love with her. There had never been anything improper in their relations, and yet, strange as it may seem, she did not hesitate to go to him in her moment of need, and he assisted her out of her difficulty.

Another phase of her life was entered upon shortly after this experience. She was called to attend a wealthy young man who had married, about five years earlier, a woman ten years his senior. His wife was a fairly attractive woman, but like so many women of this day and age, she wanted a Career. Her husband had a respiratory ailment which made it necessary for him to go to a climate milder than New York's. His physician recommended Southern California, but his wife did not feel free to accompany him. She had too many local interests, her profession, her clubs and the like. So Jeanette was taken along instead to serve as guardian of his health. His ailment was not so serious that he was confined to bed. He merely suffered from a condition which called for sunshine and balmy air, and the attentions of a sympathetic and congenial companion. Jeanette Martin had all the qualifications for this job. Of course, the obvious happened: patient and nurse fell violently in love. The young husband planned to give his wife a divorce and marry his nurse-companion. He was confident that this could be easily accomplished, and never dreamed that he would be balked in his desire. He wrote his wife, frankly telling her of his infatuation. Feeling that he understood his wife and that she would not condone such behavior, he believed she would at once commence action to free herself of her unfaithful husband.

But the wife, in the perverse way of many wives, was not inclined to take advantage of the opportunity afforded her. She proved tolerant and understanding, much to the dismay of the husband off in sunny California. She wrote that she was sure that he would recover from his temporary passion for the nurse, and be no worse a husband for the experience. As for poor Jeanette, who had fallen deeply in love with her patient, there was nothing for her to do but return to New York when it appeared settled that her romance could lead to no permanent relationship.

For a time she resumed nursing, taking cases as they came along. And, as before, during her leisure hours she sought diversion in night life, and became more reckless and dissipated than ever. One day her roommate, off-duty, returned home to find a note from Jeanette telling her that she had gone out on a case, and did not know how long it would last. A day or two later we received a report from an uptown precinct that a young woman had been found dead in a hotel room. She had registered from Albuquerque, New

Mexico, two days prior to the discovery of her body, saying that her husband would join her in two days. Hotel attendants several times had tried her door, which was locked from the inside, and received no response. Finally the management broke the door down and entered, to find the young woman lying in bed dead. The autopsy performed upon the body indicated that her death had been due to over-indulgence in alcohol. She had simply drunk herself to death with suicidal intent.

As soon as the case was reported to us, we communicated with the police of Albuquerque, and asked if they had any knowledge of a family by the name under which the suicide had registered. We received word that no one by that name was known there, and all further efforts on our part to learn the identity of the dead girl were, for a time, unavailing, and the body went to Potter's Field.

About two months after this a young woman presented herself at the Bureau. She told me she was a resident of Wisconsin, and that she had come to New York for the purpose of learning the whereabouts of her sister, from whom the family had not heard for more than two months. She said that the last letter her mother had written to her sister had been returned marked "Unclaimed." Her sister's profession, she said, was that of a nurse, and she was a graduate of a leading hospital here. My caller also informed me that she had called at the apartment house at the last address her sister had given the family, and had been told that the girl occupied an apartment there with another nurse. This nurse was out on duty, but the superintendent said that all they knew about the matter was that her sister had left word one day with her roommate that she was going out on a case, and that was the last that had been seen or heard of her.

As the young woman related her story, I thought at once of the unidentified hotel suicide. The date of the suicide corresponded roughly with the time of the disappearance of the girl from her apartment. I asked if she had a photograph of her sister, and she immediately took one from her handbag. Almost always people who come to us for assistance in locating missing persons remember to bring photographs. The very first thing a caller does is to pop a picture at us, and naïvely expect us immediately to produce the person by some process of black magic.

This photograph which the sister had brought showed the nurse as young and beautiful, with an animated expression, the vivacious type. I sent at once for a photograph of the suicide taken after death, for all unidentified dead are photographed and fingerprinted, and these photographs and prints are kept on file by us until identification is made. While the cold death mask bore little resemblance to the live and glowing face in the picture, I was certain we were on the right trail. The sister said she was sure that the dead girl was not her sister, and remarked that she saw no likeness whatsoever. However, I noted that certain features, the nose, the ears, the shape of the eyebrows, were identical, and I was confident that the mystery of the girl's disappearance had been solved. Not wanting to shock my caller needlessly, I hesitated to make the assertion until we were positive of identification. I asked her if she would be able to identify her sister's handwriting, and she replied that she could very easily, because the missing girl's handwriting was extremely individualistic. I assigned a detective to accompany her to the hotel where the suicide had taken place, and upon being shown the registry card of the young woman from Albuquerque, she immediately identified the writing as that of her lost sister. As the young woman was anxious to learn, in so far as possible, anything which might disclose a motive for her sister's act, the detective went with her to the apartment which the dead girl had occupied with the other nurse. Little by little they learned from this roommate something of the history of Jeanette's life since she had known her. She said that not infrequently the girl had returned from an evening's outing considerably intoxicated, and that she had been "hitting the high spots" with more and more regularity. Her trunk was opened, and in it was found many bundles of letters from different male friends. Everything was in neat array, for Jeanette, despite her haphazard way of living, was the personification of neatness as to her personal effects. She had preserved all sorts of little souvenirs, dance programs, party favors, bits of lace, ribbon and gift-books. One of the thickest packets of letters came from the young married man she had nursed in California. These letters protested the writer's love for her, and his bitter disappointment at their enforced parting. They were idolatrous in tone, as were the love letters from other men. The girl obviously had possessed great personal magnetism and charm, which had caused many men to fall in love with her. Among the cards was one giving the name and address of the young physician who, early in her nursing career, had proposed marriage to her.

Although everything pointed to suicide, the detective was not wholly satisfied, and felt that here might be a clew to some one who might possibly have caused her death. He visited the physician's office and, hoping to surprise him into an admission if he were guilty, abruptly announced that the girl was dead and that he knew all about it. At once the doctor slumped into a chair and cried out; "My God! is Jeanette dead? When and where did it happen?"

When told the circumstances, he fainted and after he had regained consciousness he related that part of the girl's story in which he had figured. He said he knew that she did not care for him, that she was living at a fast pace and leading a promiscuous life, but regardless of all this, he still retained his love for her.

"Knowing all that I do about her, if she were alive, and willing, I'd marry her tomorrow," he declared.

He said he had not seen her, nor heard from her for months, and had supposed she was probably launched on another love affair, since the flame for one man burned only a brief time. He had heard also that she was drinking to excess, and although he stood ready to help her again, as he had once helped her over a tough hurdle in the past, she had never again sought his aid.

Perhaps I have gone too much into detail in narrating this case history. But it is so typical of the experience that comes to many girls from the hinterland who visit New York only to be swallowed up in the maelstrom, that I could not resist relating it in full. Perhaps it may serve, as I hope it will, to take a bit of the glamour from the romantic picture so many girls have of life in the great metropolis.

The story of a squalid and hopeless life came to light about a year ago when the body of Julia Napier, forty years of age, was found dead in a furnished rooming house in the Bronx. Her death was caused by drinking poisoned alcohol.

SUICIDES

Her relatives were unknown, and we tried to learn if she had ever been reported missing. Her identity too was unknown. She was just a bit of human wreckage cast up on the tide of the big city. But we had to discover, if possible, who was interested in the dead woman. We wanted to know who her relatives were and, what is more important still to the City of New York, who there was to assume the responsibility for her interment.

Questioning of the landlord of the rooming-house and the woman's few acquaintances elicited the information that she was divorced from her husband, who was a machinist. When he was found he consented to view the body at the Morgue, and identified it, but refused to claim it. He said he had been obliged to leave his wife because she drank too much, was guilty of infidelity, and had spent her days in riotous living. The husband added that his divorced wife had relatives living in New Jersey, and he gave the name of an uncle, a well-to-do contractor. When this man was informed of the death of his niece, he refused to even view the remains, or to permit any member of his family to do so. He said, "Bury her in the Potter's Field. Even that is too good for her."

After we had investigated, we were inclined to agree with him. Even the detective on the case used the word "debauchery" in his report, and when a cop employs a word like that the situation justifies it. But, inasmuch as a city cannot take cognizance of one's character when it comes to the matter of burial, her body was interred in the City cemetery in a pauper's grave.

IV. FAKED SUICIDES

FAKED tragedies are the gnats in our day's labors. I can conceive of nothing more reprehensible than an attempt to camouflage a disappearance so as to make it appear a suicide or accidental death; yet there are certain types of men and women who, desiring to drop out of sight for reasons of their own, fake their own demise. Usually the stage setting for the trumped-up tragedy is the ocean or some other large section of water, where the recovery of a body is always problematical.

Disappearances of this kind usually leave an aftermath of shock and grief for some one, and they also cause suspense, that exquisite torture which cannot be measured in terms of the sorrow a person might feel when confronted with a definite and established death. While these "suicides" bring anguish to the schemers' relatives, they also carry in their wake a great deal of extra and unnecessary work for the Police unit responsible for finding those who devise them. The motive in connection with a faked disappearance is always one which stamps the person who engineers it either as a criminal at heart, or else one completely devoid of normal consideration for family or friends. It is a brutally cruel and supremely selfish course of action, to put it mildly.

FAKED SUICIDES

Fate stepped in, neatly enough, and punished the man guilty of the following "suicide." His act did not, in this instance, bring grief to his family.

Early in the bathing season a few years ago, there came a report from a precinct located in the Rockaways to the effect that a man's suit of clothes had been found in a bathhouse when the cleaners were putting it in order one Monday morning after the Sunday rush to the beaches. In the pocket of the coat was a business card bearing the name and address of a man who appeared to be the victim of suicide or accidental drowning. His name was Sam Abrams, and the address was on the East Side in New York City.

One of our detectives was sent to the Abrams' home, and there discovered that the owner of the name, address and suit of clothes, had been missing since the previous day, when he had left to go to the beach for a swim. This information was given by Mrs. Abrams, a stout and typical East Side matron who, when informed of the finding of the suit in the bath-house, at once became hysterical. She displayed all the outward signs of grief, wailing, wringing her hands, and shrieking. Later, when she became more calm, she told the detective that she had been under the impression that her husband had stayed overnight with his brother, who resided near the beach, and therefore she had not been worried by his absence. An alarm was sent to all shore line precincts in the neighborhood where Abrams was supposed to have lost his life. Ordinarily the body of a person drowned at this beach would come to the surface and be washed ashore within a week or ten days. If it does not wash ashore within a reasonable time, it is assumed that the body has been carried out to sea, probably never to be recovered.

79

During our investigation to ascertain whether the death was accidental or a suicide, it was learned that Abrams carried a $50,000 life insurance policy, which was a somewhat suspicious circumstance. Shortly after the disappearance of her husband, Mrs. Abrams put in a claim for it, and appeared much more interested in its payment than she did in the recovery of the body of her husband. The companies carrying the insurance postponed paying the policies until there was some better proof of Abrams' death.

Every case of a disappearance such as Abrams' is carefully sifted by us to determine the possibility of suicide. Now had Abrams' business been poor, or had he been in any other difficulties, the assumption might have been that he actually had committed suicide by drowning. But there seemed to be in his case no logical motive for a deliberate act of that kind. If his drowning was accidental, there were certainly suspicious circumstances to be cleared up.

About two months later, just as I was about to leave my office for the day, a telegram was received from the Police of Montreal, asking if we were interested in one Sam Abrams. The message stated further that a man had been the victim of an automobile accident in Montreal that day, and had been removed, unconscious, to a hospital. A search of his clothing revealed nothing that would serve to supply the name of the victim, except a newspaper clipping which described the finding of the clothing of a Sam Abrams in a bath-house at Rockaway Beach. The clipping contained a description of the man who was supposed to have been drowned. Checking this description against that of the victim of the automobile accident, the Montreal Police were impressed with the similarity of the two. We replied to the telegram, requesting that the Montreal Police attempt to establish the identity of the injured man as soon as he regained consciousness.

He revived during the night, and when he was confronted with the news that the New York Police Department was interested in him as a result of his disappearance two months before, he broke down and admitted his identity. He confessed that he had planned the apparent suicide or "accidental drowning" in order to collect insurance, and that his wife had aided in the frame-up. It was, it developed, the old attempt to swindle insurance companies. He and Mrs. Abrams had worked out the whole scheme, and on the day of his disappearance he had taken along an extra suit of clothes, with sufficient means of identification stowed away in the pocket to make it appear he was a bather who had drowned.

Not quite so plausible was Mary Schwem's similar plot a few months ago. Mary was a sixty-five-year-old peddler of shoe-laces, and she conceived the ingenious method of dropping out of her husband's life by way of faking suicide. He had been a helpless invalid for years, and she was tired supporting him.

On April 8, 1932, Mrs. Schwem boarded a Staten Island ferry-boat at the Battery, taking with her an armful of her clothing which, upon departing from the boat, she left on the seat she had occupied. With the clothing, when it was found, was a leather wallet, seventeen pairs of shoe-laces, a set of eyeglasses, a photograph of herself, and her peddler's license, which gave her name and address. A note, directed to her husband, and found among these belongings, read: "Pray for me, Daddy."

She failed to return to her home that evening, and her daughter, with whom the aged couple resided, reported her to the Bureau as missing. The detective assigned to the case made an immediate check-up of the unidentified dead reported during the past twenty-four hours, with no result. He then referred to the files of Arrests and Aided Cases at the Bureau of Information at Headquarters, but found nothing pertinent. Next he went to the home of the complainant. A person reporting any one missing is always designated the "Complainant," although in the true interpretation of the word, he is not precisely that. Privately I refer to them all as "our customers."

During this visit the detective learned from the daughter that her mother had a sister living in Waterville, Connecticut. He sent a communication to the Chief of Police at Waterville, requesting him to ascertain whether or not Mrs. Schwem was at the home of her sister. The detective had his doubts about the whole affair. The very obvious effort made by the woman to establish her identity, by leaving her clothing, license, a note, her pocketbook, and name and address, indicated precautions which would not ordinarily be taken by one contemplating suicide. Soon word came back from the Waterville Police that Mrs. Schwem, the "suicide," was with her sister. When she was questioned as to the reason for her subterfuge, she replied that she had tired of the burden of supporting her husband, and had decided to disappear in a manner which would lead him to believe her dead.

FAKED SUICIDES

Thomas W. Judson also staged his act with a water setting, although his motive for faking a disappearance was
entirely different from that of Sam Abrams. Judson was an
inveterate sea-bather. It was his almost daily custom to
go to one of the best known bathing resorts at Coney Island
and swim and bask in the sunshine for hours at a time. One
day about four or five years ago Judson went to his usual
bathing resort, and asked for the key to his bath-house,
which he rented by the season. The man in charge called
his attention to the fact that there was a severe storm threatening. At the moment a high wind was blowing offshore, and
rumblings of thunder could be heard in the distance. But
Judson ignored the warning, and said he enjoyed rough
water. As he was known to be a strong swimmer, little importance was attached to his entering the water in face of
the approach of bad weather.

Shortly after Judson entered the water the storm broke,
and it proved to be one of unusual severity. No one thought
about him; probably it was assumed that he had left the
beach with the rest of the scurrying bathers. But later, when
his clothing was found in the bath-house, it was feared that
Judson, strong swimmer though he was, had been caught
at a distance from shore, blown out to sea, and drowned.
The matter was reported by the local precinct as one of
probable drowning.

Two or three weeks later, Judson's daughter, a young
married woman, came to see me. She said she was impelled
to do so by reason of the fact that she and her mother felt
somewhat sceptical about her father's disappearance. She
said that things had not been going so well at her parents'
home for a considerable period prior to his supposed drown-

ing. According to her, Tom Judson was a bit of a Don Juan. The family for some time had suspected him of paying attention to other women, but they had no definite knowledge as to the identity of any of them.

An investigation was made to learn who these charmers were, but nothing definite developed. Some of Judson's acquaintances admitted they had occasionally seen him in company with women not of his own family, but he had always avoided introductions. Two years later, however, we got a tip which led us to a small town fifty miles upstate, where the "drowned" man was discovered living under an assumed name. As for the motive in this case, she would tip the scales at about 130 pounds. She was a plump brunette, and Judson's neighbors and fellow townspeople believed her to be his wife.

The Barton mystery, too, had a bathing beach background, and to this day certain phases of the case are baffling. The principal character figuring in it was James Barton, a successful and well-known business man. He was married, and had a beautiful wife and two children. One June he was staying at Rye Beach with several other summer bachelors, while his wife and family were vacationing in the mountains. Barton was a noted long distance swimmer, and he reveled in rough water and strong tides. It was nothing unusual for him to swim out to sea, and to be gone for an hour or more at a stretch.

Accompanied by several of his companions, he started out one hot day for a swim. There was a strong offshore current, so strong, in fact, that most of his friends hesitated to go very far from shore. Some of them declined even to venture into the water. But Barton, as was usual with him, swam out with bold strokes. He wore a black one-piece bathing suit, which had a wide orange stripe around the center, making him very conspicuous. His friends could see the suit even as he got far out from shore. The last that was seen of him by any of his party was when he was at least a quarter of a mile offshore, apparently swimming with a strong tide current. When, an hour and a half later he had not put in an appearance, his companions began to fear that all was not well with him. Glasses were brought into use, and the water within view carefully scanned for sight of him.

After a vain search of the shore line, the police were notified, and in due time his disappearance was reported to the Bureau. A General Alarm was flashed to all precincts within the water front scope of Barton's disappearance. The United States Coast Guard covering that zone was also requested to coöperate. But time passed without anything being learned of Barton's fate. Of course, it was eventually decided that he had been swept out to sea and drowned. After a time it was agreed that there was no hope of recovering the body, and the executor of his estate offered his will for probate. It was found that Barton had few assets, with the exception of life insurance policies totaling $75,000, made in favor of his wife. Life insurance companies have learned from long and hard experience that it is not wise to pay the face of policies too hastily where there is no evidence of death, and where no death certificate is presented. They took, in this case, every means of protecting their interests.

Barton, however, was of such prominent social standing, and it seemed so apparent that he was the victim of drowning, that after a period of time the companies carrying the policies conceded that they should be paid. They were about to pay them when, in some way which has not been disclosed, an investigator for one of the companies came into possession of a clew or tip, which occasioned a hurried trip to a Florida resort. And there Barton was found, stopping at a hotel, registered under an assumed name.

When charged by the insurance investigator with an attempt to defraud his company of the life insurance, he pleaded that he had no knowledge of who he was, or where he came from. In other words, he contended that he was suffering from amnesia, or loss of memory of his identity and past. He claimed that he could not be accused of an ulterior motive, since he knew nothing of his past beyond the time when he found himself living at the hotel where he was located. He has continued this assertion ever since. "That's my story," in other words, "and I'm going to stick to it."

But confederates he must have had, for so far as can be shown, the last time he was seen, prior to his being found in Miami, he was a long distance offshore, swimming out to sea in a one-piece bathing suit. And he was found in Miami, in possession of baggage, clothing, and money to meet current expenses. And Miami is a long swim from Rye Beach, New York. The reader must draw his own conclusions as to whether or not he wants to accept Barton's story at its face value.

V. AMNESIA CASES

A MNESIA, that mysterious impairment of memory which blots out whole portions from one's life, often causes untold suffering to those afflicted by it. This drawing of a curtain across that portion of the brain which carries within its convolutions knowledge of one's identity and past, is not only fraught with disaster for the victim, but also brings acute anxiety to his relatives and friends.

This mental disturbance, however, is rarer than is generally supposed and but few examples of it have come to my attention in connection with work of the Missing Persons Bureau. In most instances these proved the result of shell-shock received during the World War. The retired Army officer who figures in the following strange predicament traveled for days solely through the promptings of his Sub-conscious, which came to the fore and saw him through when he lost, temporarily, all memory of self.

On a hot afternoon in midsummer, two years after the close of the War, the Chief Surgeon of the Police Department called me by telephone from his office at Headquarters and said that he was bringing "a customer," thus tagged through Departmental usage. A few minutes later he arrived, accompanied by a fine appearing man about thirty-five who was apparently in the peak of physical condition. The Chief Surgeon said that, about ten minutes before, the Chaplain on duty at Headquarters had brought the man to his office, and explained that he had appeared at his desk, and in reply to an inquiry as to what he could do for him, simply said, "I was sent here."

The Chaplain questioned him, but could get no further response. The man only gazed at him fixedly and remained silent. The Chaplain came to the conclusion that the visitor was suffering from some mental disturbance, and had suggested that he accompany him to the adjoining office of the Chief Surgeon. The Chief Surgeon, in turn, asked the stranger several questions, to which he received no reply. The man appeared dazed, and the surgeon believed he was suffering from amnesia, and was a hospital case. Knowing that my Bureau would be called upon to make an identification, and to learn the address of the afflicted man, he brought him to me first.

I asked him some questions, but the man still remained silent. I noticed that he was wearing a handsome wristwatch, and I removed it. On its reverse side was inscribed a name which I assumed was that of the wearer. The inscription indicated that it had been presented to him by the citizens of a city in Illinois, in token of the high esteem in which he was held by his fellow townsmen. I searched his pockets for some identifying information, and found it in abundance. According to one of the papers, he was an honorably discharged officer of the U. S. Army. This paper contained the same name as that appearing on the watch, together with a Chicago address. There were also, among his papers, several cards of membership in various fraternal and social organizations, one indicating that he belonged to the Masonic fraternity. All of the cards were made out for the same name.

Among the effects found in his pockets was a Hotel Pennsylvania baggage check, but when I got in touch with the management, I was informed that he was unknown to them and was not registered there. An ambulance was called, and he was removed to Bellevue Hospital.

We at once telegraphed the police of Chicago, requesting their coöperation in checking up on the data secured from the pockets of the man. About an hour and a half later a reply was received assuring us that the amnesia victim was, indeed, the man his papers indicated, and advising us that a relative of his was leaving for New York to take charge of the situation. Two days later, in company with his brother, our amnesia victim put in an appearance at my office. His memory had returned, and he appeared to be exactly the type I thought he was from his external appearance: a vigorous, mentally alert, and intellectually well equipped man of the world. This is the story he related to me:

During his war-time experience he had been badly shell-shocked. After a long period in a hospital abroad, during which time he had no memory of his identity or any knowledge of his whereabouts, his mind had gradually cleared, and he was finally returned to the United States for hospitalization as a war casualty. After a time he was discharged from the hospital, and informed by the doctors that in all probability he would suffer short recurrent losses of memory, but that each of these attacks would be of lesser severity and frequency, until finally they would disappear completely.

He said that, so far as this recent attack was concerned, the last recollection he had of his whereabouts, prior to finding himself in Bellevue Hospital, was in San Antonio, Texas, where he had gone on a business trip. While in San Antonio it suddenly occurred to him that he was about due for another memory lapse, and that he had better return to his home in Chicago while he was still in possession of his faculties. The last act which he recalled was his purchase of a ticket for St. Louis. Everything that had occurred from that moment was a blank.

It would have been rather interesting to trace the man's movements from then on, for all his actions after buying the railroad ticket must have been subconscious. He had evidently packed, boarded a train, dined, slept and traveled on to St. Louis, to which point he had a ticket. Arriving at St. Louis, his subconscious mind tripped up, and he secured transportation to New York, instead of to Chicago. He had gone about the usual business of bathing, shaving, having his clothes put in order. One thing which had impressed me from the moment the surgeon had brought him to my office was his immaculate appearance. He was an exceptionally well groomed man, clean-shaven, wearing a nicely tailored suit, which evidently had but recently left the hands of a valet. He was newly manicured, and his hair had a neat trim. He was, in short, a well turned out man, from top to toe.

Following his subconscious actions, we must accompany him while he traveled by train to New York, alighted at the Pennsylvania Station, crossed the street and checked his baggage at the Pennsylvania Hotel. Subconsciously our man from Illinois must have realized that he needed help, for he had wisely gone to just the right place to get it: 240 Centre Street. He must have asked directions to Police Headquarters where, even in his extremity, he realized that he would be taken care of.

I do not know precisely the workings of the subconscious mind of an amnesia victim, but I hazard the guess that by the time he reached Headquarters he had come to the more acute phase of his condition. This probably caused his silence and his fixed stares. Concluding his story, the amnesia victim thanked us for our kindness to him during his period of lost memory, and departed for Chicago with his brother.

A piano figured indirectly in the solution of the Alice Breen mystery. Five days before Christmas, 1926, this young woman, who was twenty-five years of age, was reported by her mother as having failed to return from business on the previous evening. According to the mother's description, Alice was five feet, four inches, in height, weighed one hundred and ten pounds, was a medium blonde, and had for years been suffering from a rash on her face. She wore on the last day she was seen, a blue suit, a blue coat with red fox fur at the collar and cuffs, a small black turban, black shoes with common-sense heels, and black silk stockings, for at that time the girls were not yet discarding black hose for the sun-tans of today.

Alice had left her home, on the morning of her disappearance, for her office in a downtown section of New York, where she was employed as secretary to one of the executives of a large corporation. The detective assigned to the case reported to me that he had interviewed the mother, and that she had no idea why her daughter had left home. She felt that in all probability the girl had met with foul play. Let me say, parenthetically, that many a mother is obsessed with this fear when a daughter fails to put in an appearance, even though the girl may be most unattractive. The detective then called at Alice Breen's place of business, and questioned her employer. The information he secured there was that the girl had been in the employ of the corporation for five years, and had risen from the position of office stenographer to confidential secretary. She had been found entirely dependable, capable, loyal to her organization. As the executive she served as private secretary put it, "She was not a clock-watcher. Time meant nothing to her; the completion of the task in hand everything."

Alice's employer said that as she was about to leave for luncheon the previous day, she had asked him if she might have an extra hour in order to do some Christmas shopping. He thought she deserved more time than that, and told her to take the entire afternoon. When asked about his secretary's associates so far as he might know them, particularly among the employees of the corporation, he replied: "Miss Breen seemed to have no interest whatever in the opposite sex. Her work appeared to be the one thing that held interest for her." And he added: "Frankly, my secretary was not exactly a Helen of Troy. It was just as well that she was not fond of young men, for I am afraid they would not have reciprocated her feelings. She was a splendid worker, but not what you might call good-looking."

The executive had no theory which would account for her disappearance, and he was very much mystified. The detective made inquiry at the various stores in the nearest shopping district in the hope of finding some place where

AMNESIA CASES

Alice had been during the afternoon of her disappearance, but he was unsuccessful. When he returned to the Bureau I asked him for a "close-up" of the girl's home surroundings. He said the mother appeared to be the average sort of wholesome housewife; her home was neat and well cared for. He did not present to me a background which would account for Alice's disappearance. But because of a hunch, for which I cannot account, I felt that home and mother might supply the key to the mystery, and therefore on the following day I called upon Mrs. Breen. I wanted to see the home itself, a procedure I seldom have time to follow. I found Mrs. Breen to be just as the detective had described her to me. She possessed the average intelligence of a matron in her walk of life, and was a woman who had mothered a large family of boys and girls, Alice being the youngest of seven.

It was at first difficult to draw from Mrs. Breen the information I sought. I questioned her on the boy phase of her daughter's life, and she said, "Alice has never shown any fondness for the boys."

Then I was amused at the mother's frank remark, which bore out Alice's employer's observation anent the girl's looks: "After all, Alice is not attractive. She has always been self-conscious, too, about a rash on her face."

This second assertion that Alice was short on beauty made unlikely the theory that this case might be one where a vain and dashing girl had skipped off with the man of her choice. By no stretch of the imagination could Alice be visualized as an adventuress.

"What were some of the things Alice liked? Her sports, recreations, hobbies?"

Mrs. Breen quickly replied, "Well, one of her favorite diversions was playing the piano."

I asked her how long the family had occupied the present apartment. She said they had just moved into it, and the day that Alice disappeared was her first in the new place. Glancing about, I did not see a piano, so I said to the mother: "You mentioned the fact that Alice was fond of playing the piano. How could she play if she had no instrument?"

Mrs. Breen then explained that the apartment they had occupied before was larger, and there had been room for a piano, but that they had been obliged to sell it when they moved. She boasted of Alice's "business sense," as she termed it, and described how she had "shopped around" for the purpose of getting the best possible price for the piano. The mother related that on the day they had moved to their new quarters Alice had left for business from the former home, and had returned in the evening to the new one.

"You know, the funniest thing happened that evening," confided Mrs. Breen, smiling a little over the memory of the amusing incident. "When Alice came home, and while she was removing her hat, she glanced around the house and made some comments on the arrangement of the furniture. She complimented me on getting settled so quickly, and then suddenly asked, " 'But where is the piano, Mama?' "

That was my clew! "Evidently your daughter is a bit absent-minded," I remarked.

"Yes, indeed," agreed the Mother. "She was often forgetful. On one occasion she searched for her hat as she was about to leave one day, and all the time she had it on her head."

AMNESIA CASES

Mrs. Breen, although worried about Alice's disappearance, could not refrain from laughing at the thought of what a funny picture Alice presented hunting for a hat that was already on her own head. "Feeling that the joke was on Alice," she continued, "I let her search for it for some time, and then I said: 'You are not looking in the right place, Alice. Look in the mirror.' Alice took it as a huge joke when she saw herself and her hat in the glass."

Mrs. Breen related several similar incidents of what she termed the "absent-mindedness" of her daughter. Right here, it seemed to me, was the key to the whole situation. I believed that Alice's disappearance was probably due to loss of memory of her own identity; in other words, I felt that she was the victim of amnesia. I don't think that Mrs. Breen had ever heard the term, or had any understanding of its meaning, and consequently when she related the stories illustrative of her daughter's absent-mindedness, I laughed with her.

Immediately upon my return to the office, I ordered a General Alarm to be sent to adjacent cities and towns. But several weeks passed, and we seemed no nearer a solution of the mystery of Alice's disappearance. The detective in charge of the case was constantly watching hospital, morgue and arrest records and every other source from which information might come to account for the girl's dropping out of sight.

Then one morning about six weeks later an inquiry was received from the police of a New Jersey town as to whether the young woman, Alice Breen, regarding whom an Alarm had been issued some time before, had been found. When we informed them that her whereabouts were still unknown, they replied that they believed she was in a hospital in their town. They related further that an ambulance had been called to an outlying district fronting on the Hudson River, and that in the shanty of a watchman on a construction job, the young woman had been found in a state of collapse. The watchman, a crippled old man, had given her shelter in his shack, as she appeared to be almost frozen and near starvation.

The young woman, the watchman explained, had appeared at his shack late at night in such a pitiful state that he offered to divide his midnight luncheon with her. She would not accept it, however, but did drink some of the hot coffee which he made on his stove in a corner of the shanty. Then she collapsed. Some time later a policeman patrolling his post in that portion of town was notified by the watchman of the young woman's presence and her condition, and had her removed to the hospital.

I discussed the situation by telephone with the Jersey lieutenant in charge, and found that he knew nothing of the case other than what he had gleaned from the officer who had handled it. I asked if I might talk to this man, and the lieutenant put him on the wire. I questioned the officer about the appearance of the young woman, and he replied: "She looks as though she is in the last stages of tuberculosis. She is emaciated, and her clothing is worn and dirty."

The officer went on to say that the girl appeared dazed, and was unable to reply coherently to questions. He described the efforts made by the ambulance surgeon to secure from her information as to her identity or where she belonged, but said that he had been unsuccessful in this attempt. Following this talk I called up the hospital to which the girl had been sent, and talked with the house surgeon about his patient. He said that she was evidently suffering from exposure and malnutrition, that she seemed to be in a semi-comatose condition, and was very difficult to arouse.

"When she does regain consciousness, and appears to be aware of her surroundings, she looks about her in a confused way," continued the doctor. "She seems to be in a perpetual state of bewilderment, and does not answer any of my questions."

Recalling that piano episode, the forgotten hat, and all the other odd tricks which memory played on Alice in the past, according to her mother's narrative, I asked the doctor, "Is the girl, by any chance, suffering from amnesia?"

The house surgeon replied, "Captain, I wouldn't be a bit surprised if you had made a bull's eye that time!"

From what I learned from the officer and the house surgeon I felt confident that the mystery of Alice Breen's disappearance was about to be solved. I sent the detective who had the case to the home of the girl's mother, with instructions to accompany her to the Jersey hospital for the purpose of making the identification if the young woman proved to be her daughter.

Later the detective related what had happened: "As soon as Mrs. Breen entered the hospital ward, and saw the white-faced girl on the cot she recognized her daughter. She rushed forward, crying out 'Alice!' put her arms around her and asked the usual question, 'How could you go away without letting Mother know about it?' Poor Alice, of course, did not answer; in fact, she appeared not to recognize her mother at all."

The girl remained in the hospital for several days before

she was in a condition for removal to New York. Then she was placed in a New York hospital and remained there for nearly two weeks. It was several days before she was able to take in her surroundings. Even then she was unable to remember her name or address, and it was a week or more before she recognized her mother.

One day as Mrs. Breen entered her daughter's room, the girl cried out, "Mother!" From that moment she gradually regained her memory, and finally was well enough to return home. When she had recovered sufficiently to be questioned, I called at the Breen apartment. Amnesia and its queer manifestations interest me, and I was curious about that blank interval in Alice's life. Did she, I wanted to know, have any memory of her loss of memory? That sounds paradoxical, but what I mean is I wanted to know if, during that lapse of memory, her mind functioned in a way that she could recall. I asked her if she remembered any incident that had occurred after she had left her office for luncheon on December 20, a day important to her because of its being the one when she forgot herself, the world, and her place in it. She said: "All I can remember is that as I started out for luncheon that day, I looked in my purse to see if I had sufficient money to buy all the Christmas presents I planned to purchase for members of my family. Beyond that point, I have no recollection of what happened."

One can only imagine what took place in that long interval of six weeks, during which the girl wandered here and there through Jersey, a stranger to herself, her mind a blank. She disappeared in New York City just before Christmas; she reappeared at a construction shanty in New Jersey one bitter cold night in February. It was evident from her condition that she had been wandering aimlessly during the entire time of her absence.

Two years later Alice had a recurrence of her trouble. She disappeared again, under almost similar circumstances, although this time her loss of memory was of much briefer duration, and less disastrous to her so far as physical suffering was concerned. On this occasion she left her home one morning at the usual hour to go to business, but did not arrive at the office. When she failed to appear, and had sent no word to her employer, he telephoned her home, fearing she might be ill. When Mrs. Breen informed him that Alice had left as usual for the office, the man, having in mind the girl's previous experience, insisted that she immediately report the disappearance to the police, which she did. The usual alarm was sent out, and three days later word was received from a Midtown precinct that Alice had been picked up as she was aimlessly wandering the streets, and had been sent to Bellevue Hospital. She was recognized from the description contained in our alarm.

Mrs. Breen was notified, called at Bellevue, and identified Alice. Two days after being sent to the hospital the young woman regained full memory of her own identity, and returned home. This time it did not require many days for convalescence, and she was soon back at her office again. So far as I know she is still working there, and has had no further attacks of amnesia.

A good bedside manner on my part solved the mystery surrounding a woman who was picked up while wandering the streets in the summer of 1931. Through the usual channels came a report to the Bureau that an unidentified woman, about fifty years of age, had been found and removed to one of the city hospitals. Accompanying it was the physical description, and one pertaining to her clothing. She was reported conscious, but unable to give an account of herself.

A detective was sent to the hospital. After interviewing her, he reported to me that while the woman seemed coherent on almost any subject mentioned, she was apparently unable to remember her name or her place of residence. "She seems to be reaching out for something she can't quite grasp," he said. He told me that at times she grew almost hysterical at her inability to remember who she was, or where she came from. At first I was just a little suspicious of her good faith, suspecting that she was possibly acting a part, and for some reason unknown to us, attempting to hide her identity. A careful check was made on women wanted for commission of crime, not only in New York, but in nearby cities.

The reader may feel by now that police officers are unduly suspicious and sceptical as to the good faith of those with whom they are brought into contact in an official manner. However, experience has taught us to be mistrustful, because of what we have learned of human duplicity and owing to the frequency with which we come in contact with the criminal element who, for their own safety's sake, try to cover their real identity by resorting to all sorts of subterfuges. In the words of W. S. Gilbert's song, "a policeman's lot is not an 'appy one." But we can scarcely be blamed for occasional cynicism.

But this list of women criminals brought nothing to light that would fit this particular woman. The detective was instructed to make frequent visits to her at the hospital, but he found no apparent change in her condition. The case interested me exceedingly, because of the fact that the woman displayed such genuine attempts to reach out into her elusive past.

One afternoon I visited the hospital, hoping that possibly I might be able to deal successfully with the situation. First I observed the woman carefully. From the appearance of her hands, which were soft, with shapely nails well tended, it was apparent that she was a woman from the better walks of life. Evidently she had been accustomed to good living; she was refined and obviously well educated.

After I had been introduced to her, and we had finished shaking hands, I sat at her bedside, and began visiting with her in a casual way. I sensed in her attitude that straining, that intense effort to grasp at a straw.

Apropos of nothing at all, I asked, "Do you enjoy shopping?" She replied, with a smile, "I don't think I'm much different from the majority of women in that respect."

"Which of the stores do you prefer?" I named several of them, mentioning Wanamaker's last. She did not seem to recognize any of them, although the last seemed to arouse her interest a little.

I turned to the subject of religion. "Which church do you attend?" and I named several New York churches of different denomination, but she shook her head. Not one of them was familiar to her.

"Do you like the theater?" It must have sounded odd, from a policeman to a hospital patient.

She told me she was fond of the theater, and said she had seen several of the new shows. I tried to fix a theater which she had attended recently, but without success. She seemed to have no recollection of any plays then on the boards in New York. I touched on some of the points of interest about town, but none aroused recognition on her part.

Then I drifted to shops again, and tried to fix her attention on Wanamaker's, which had at first brought forth what I thought might be a gleam of recognition. Again it aroused some dim spark of memory. I tried to fix the location.

"How do you reach this store—by Fifth Avenue bus, surface line or subway?" I asked her. She could not say, and did not seem to know the streets in the vicinity of the store.

I tried another experiment. I transported her mentally to Philadelphia, the next nearest large shopping center, and mentioned several well-known historical spots there, among them Independence Hall and the old Quaker Meeting House. Her face lighted up, and she seemed to be piercing through the haze of mist that obscured her memory. Her mind seemed fairly clear about these Philadelphia places. I mentioned the Philadelphia location of Wanamaker's. Apparently she understood what I was talking about, and also recognized the names of several Philadelphia streets: Broad, Chestnut, Walnut.

It was evident that we were getting nearer and nearer home. The whole expression on her face gradually changed, and she seemed immensely pleased at being able to recall something from her past. Philadelphia, I decided, was either her home city or was located near it. After leaving the hospital I got in touch with the Philadelphia Police Department, and asked whether or not a woman of her description had been reported missing. A reference to their records indicated that no such case had been called to their attention. I then requested publicity in the Philadelphia papers, news regarding the case having already appeared in the New York press to no avail.

In a few days we received a request from a Pennsylvania town within fifty miles from the Quaker City asking for further information about our hospital patient. We supplied additional data, and after an exchange of communications, we established the fact that our amnesia patient was a resident of that town. Her disappearance had caused her family much concern. We learned that she had boarded a bus in her home town to go to Philadelphia on the day she vanished. Apparently her lapse of memory had occurred while she was on the bus and, as a result, she had come straight through to New York, where she had alighted, to start her aimless wandering.

While every one must concede that amnesia is an extremely trying mental disturbance, albeit a temporary one, I can recall one occasion when it proved a great blessing.

One morning, five years ago, we received a report of the disappearance of a responsible executive of a large financial institution in New York City. The previous afternoon and evening had been devoted by his friends to a search for the man, and when they finally agreed that it was a matter of too much importance for longer delay, they appealed to us for aid.

When the James Randolph case was reported, I received numerous calls from influential people, urging me to do everything possible to find the man. Some people have the idea that when outside influence is brought to bear greater attention will be given to the matter by the Bureau. As a matter of fact, this is not so; each case gets the attention to which it is entitled.

Randolph had wide interests and a great many important friends. He was well thought of in the financial world, and was extremely active in civic affairs in his home town, a small city in New Jersey. He had many club and fraternal affiliations, and every one who knew him spoke highly of him. We immediately set out to discover a motive for his act of dropping out of sight. A man connected with any financial activity is always suspect as to malfeasance in the handling of his trust. So the first question I asked was: How has Randolph been administering his duties? An audit of the accounts and financial matters over which he had supervision was made, and everything was found as it should be.

The story of his disappearance as it was presented to us was that he had left his office to go to luncheon about 1 o'clock the previous day, and from that moment on not a trace of him had been found by those engaged in trying to locate him. Inquiry in his home town disclosed that he was public-spirited, and was devoted to his wife and two children. He was never seen in the company of other women, and every one questioned agreed that Randolph's home life was ideal. The only evenings he ever spent away from his family, we learned, were those given over to his lodge, and we were assured that "Lodge" in this instance meant lodge. In every direction in which our investigation reached out, nothing was found to supply a reason for his disappearance.

Finally I instructed the detective to ascertain where Randolph had been accustomed to take his daily lunch, and to ask the manager of the restaurant whether our missing man had a habitual luncheon companion, as is so frequently the case with the average business man. Many executives, and employees for that matter, welcome the opportunity for confidences with men in lines of activity other than their own, so that they can secure a break in the "shop-talk" of their daily life.

It developed that Randolph did have a luncheon companion. The two men met almost daily, and had come to be looked upon by the restaurant people as inseparable companions—to such an extent that a table was regularly reserved for them. I instructed the detective to find this man and ask him if he had any idea as to what had become of his missing friend. I ventured the comment that he probably would learn nothing from him.

"If he will not talk, ask him if he will be good enough to drop in at my office for a conference," were my instructions. I find it is more effective to "request" than to command. "Explain to him that I am usually very keen on getting social backgrounds and reactions from personal friends of a missing man."

As I had anticipated, Randolph's friend informed the detective that he had no idea what had become of him. When the detective, following my instructions, invited him to drop in and see me, he expressed his willingness to comply with my request. The following day he called at my office. To many people a visit to Police Headquarters is something of an ordeal; often the adventure arouses an uncomfortable feeling, and during the first few minutes they are not entirely at ease. Consequently I feel that the first thing to do is to make visitors relax. It is my practice to set about getting acquainted with them by bringing up subjects which will divert them from the thought uppermost: that they are face to face with the Police. I thanked my caller for the time he was giving me; dragged in the old reliable weather topic; discussed that hardy perennial Business, and then asked him what he thought prospects were for the Giants to win the World Series. After that I handed him a cigar.

By now we had arrived at the point where he had forgotten about the barred windows. He puffed away at the cigar, and I switched to the subject of the missing man. I prefaced my remarks with the reminder that our one interest in the matter was to aid in returning this man to his business, his home, and his friends. I made it clear that we had no desire to assume the rôle of censor of morals, that a man's private life was his own as far as we were concerned. I assured him that it was also not within our sphere—or wish—to make public anything told us in confidence, and that anything he might tell me would be strictly "under the rose." I made the point that his friends had nothing to fear from us in the investigation, that anything short of murder would not be too closely scrutinized.

Thus, after I had convinced my visitor that his friends' private affairs were no concern of ours, he looked at me quizzically a moment, and then asked, "Captain, may I use your telephone a minute?"

"Go to it, old man! The City is paying the bill."

My caller, whose name was Theodore Hale, called a number in a midtown exchange. As soon as he got his party I knew at once that the person at the other end of the wire was not of his sex. A man's voice, perhaps all unconsciously, takes on a bit of a purr when he is talking to a woman.

"You're well? Now that's fine. Busy? Been going places

and seeing things?" The usual telephone banalities were exchanged, judging from what was said at my end of the wire. Finally Hale asked, "Like me to call and bring a friend —a chap I know?" And evidently receiving an affirmative reply, "When can we come up?"

After a moment Hale turned to me, and asked when I would be at liberty to accompany him.

"No time like the present," I said, eager to be on the trail, for it was a good guess that here was a pretty close tie-up with Randolph. We set out at once by taxicab, and our journey's end was an attractive little apartment in the Forties, not far from Broadway. A good-looking blonde, who savored just a little of the theater, welcomed us. Hale called her "Lois." Introductions followed, and then my companion got down to business.

"When did you hear from Jim and Maizie?" he asked. Lois said she had had a phone call from them the evening before. She interjected the comment, "Isn't he a darn fool?"

By that time the trail seemed to be getting hot. Lois went on chattering about Jimmy and Maizie, evidently accepting me as a *bona fide* friend of Mr. Hale's, and one from whom it was unnecessary to hide anything. She and Hale indulged in comments and criticisms regarding the lack of wisdom on Jim's part in doing something which, up to the moment, had been a profound mystery to me. But the mystery was fast clearing up. It developed, of course, that Jim was engaged in taking a little vacation, in company with Maizie, at a pleasant resort not fifty miles from New York.

Having secured the information I wanted, our visit was terminated without Lois' having any idea of who I was, or of the real purpose of my visit.

MISSING MEN

It is always a rule of mine to avoid taking too many people into my confidence. Even my own detectives, who can be trusted to the utmost, are not infrequently kept beyond the outer walls. In an intimate situation of this kind I decided it might be just as well if I alone knew the closing chapter. Therefore, after leaving Lois' flat I set out for the vacation spot where Jim was sojourning.

While I was in the Broadway apartment, Lois had mentioned the fact that Jim was using an assumed name, calling himself Frank Clayton. Upon arrival at my destination, I asked the hotel clerk if Mr. and Mrs. Clayton were in. He looked at the key-rack and said he thought they were.

"Wish me to call the room, Sir, and find out?" he asked.

"Don't bother," I made haste to reply. "I'm his brother, and I want my visit to be a surprise to him."

A bell-hop was called and accompanied me to the room. I rapped, the door was opened, and I stepped in, all of which should prove that I would make a good magazine agent.

"How do you do, Mr. Randolph," I said.

As I spoke, I glanced around the room and saw, standing before the bureau, a tall, auburn-haired girl, in her twenties. She was wearing a light green dress. My habit of noting details seldom fails!

The man who stood before me was well-built, about forty years of age, just beginning to gray at the temples. "I think you're mistaken. My name is Clayton."

"I am from Police Headquarters."

Randolph's face went white. After a moment devoted to pulling himself together, he said: "Hands up—what's the charge?" I replied: "Darned if I know! I am just trying to find you. There are a whole lot of persons interested in your whereabouts, perhaps more than you supposed would be worried about anything you might do."

By this time the seriousness of the situation seemed to dawn on him. Evidently, up to that moment, he had not considered the affair anything but a harmless little adventure. The presence of a policeman is often a sobering influence.

After a short silence, Randolph exclaimed: "My God! How am I going to explain all this?"

"Why try to explain?"

"But what am I going to do?"

"As I see it, the wise thing for you would be to say nothing. Let me do the explaining."

And then I did some quick thinking. Just a short time before this, we had an amnesia case. That was the idea!

"Listen to me, old man," I said. "There is nothing you can say that will explain this mess. So say nothing beyond the fact that all you remember is that you left your office to go to luncheon. From that moment until today you have no recollection of what you did, who you are, or where you belong. You have been suffering from amnesia!"

Randolph listened, as though half dazed, and I continued:

"I can say to those interested in you that our Bureau had been queried by the police of a Long Island town as to whether we had a record of a man who had disappeared from New York, and who answered your description. I can inform your friends that you have been picked up here under conditions that warrant us in believing you a victim of loss of memory. They will all be so pleased you have been found that they will not question too closely this explanation of your disappearance."

Randolph broke in, "You're as human as they make them!

I don't see how I can ever repay you for your consideration of me."

I assured him that my thought was not for him. I was primarily thinking of the ruin that would result from his thoughtless behavior if the facts became known. His position would be lost, his home disrupted, his wife and children the object of commiseration.

My diagnosis of the situation so far as his welcome home was concerned proved correct. Every one interested in Randolph had a part, figuratively speaking, in killing the fatted calf. And the financial group with which he was connected insisted on his taking a two weeks' vacation to recuperate from his "harrowing experience."

There are those who may question my wisdom in adopting this course when dealing with the unfaithful husband. In justification, I must remind them that I was out to find a missing man; I was not called upon to destroy him and his family in the process. Randolph was not a criminal; so far, he had harmed no one but himself. It was only if the facts were divulged that others would be injured. It was my opinion that if Randolph had the intelligence he appeared to possess, he had learned a lesson which would deter him from ever repeating his foolish act.

This man has since advanced in the financial field, and so far as I can learn he has never again wandered from the straight path.

VI. INSANITY CASES

WHEN I describe cases I have handled in which the mentally unbalanced figure, I am reminded of an incident of my youth—one which concerns an inmate of an asylum for the insane. This institution was located not far from my father's farm, and it held much fascination for me. When an opportunity afforded I would loiter around the fence enclosing the big buildings which housed so many odd people. Some of the male patients were put to work on the asylum farm, and I used to peer through the fence and watch them as they planted seed, and cultivated or harvested the crops.

There was one wily little Irishman among them who used to "soldier" on the job. He would hoe his row of potatoes at snail's pace, making an effort to do just as little as he could. Always he kept an eye on the attendant, and it used to amuse me to observe his sly watchfulness. The attendant was not blind to his tactics, however, and one day I overheard him say, in a jocular way, "Johnny, I think you're lazy."

To my astonishment Johnny replied glibly, "Boss, we're all born lazy, only some of us show it more than others."

I am sometimes rather inclined to believe that this same

thing, with the word "crazy" substituted for "lazy," applies to most of us. As far as persons afflicted with insanity are concerned, those I have encountered in my work were exceptionally clever men and women who, although wholly irresponsible in their mental functioning were, nevertheless, in many instances, able to deceive a considerable portion of the normal population before they were recognized as unbalanced. Their extreme cunning in working out their insane schemes, the plausibility with which they spun fantastic yarns and made involved plans, during which process they caused a lot of work for their normal brothers, proved them to be ingenious, to say the least.

One of the strangest cases of this kind that has ever come to my attention was one revolving about the Baroness de Hoven, descendant of a long line of wealthy and titled personages. With her mother, she had been a resident of New York from her early childhood. The Baroness was one of the victims, at least indirectly, of the World War. I recall that it was one summer afternoon in 1920 that this young woman came to the Bureau and requested an interview with me. She gave the name "Baroness de Hoven," and when the desk man announced her he seemed quite impressed with the title. As the Baroness entered I saw at once she was an aristocrat. She gave me her card, which bore an address in an exclusive residential section of the city. The Baroness, whose manner was unassuming, carried a bulging brief case.

She was a young woman of about twenty-five, of medium height, with a willowy figure, brown hair and eyes, and an extraordinarily clear and beautiful skin. I was immediately attracted by her personality. She was frank, and bore herself without any sign of arrogance. The Baroness apologized for what she termed her intrusion, but said she felt there was no alternative for her but to come and see me regarding a matter in which she was vitally interested. This matter, she continued, had, in turn, been taken up by several Federal departments in Washington and each one had, after what was described as an exhaustive investigation, reported inability to do anything for her.

When I asked for particulars regarding the subject which held so much interest for her, she related the following remarkable story:

In the late summer of 1917, a Captain Armstrong, attached to the staff of a certain infantry regiment about to go overseas, arrived in New York with letters of introduction to several prominent families, some of whom were social acquaintances of her mother and herself. While awaiting transport from this port to Brest his newly-acquired friends had exerted themselves to entertain him and make his short stay in the city pleasant. The Baroness explained that at one of the social functions given in his honor, she had made his acquaintance.

At once there had developed between them a feeling which the Baroness described as "love at first sight." During the remainder of his stay in the city, Captain Armstrong had devoted all his available time to her, and she admitted that she had reciprocated his feelings in full. When asked to describe him, the Baroness said, with no small amount of naïveté:

"If you can conceive of a modern Adonis, then you will know exactly how Captain Armstrong looked. He was about six feet tall, and perfectly proportioned. His hair was dark, and his eyes were also dark and lustrous. He was extremely well bred."

When his sailing day finally arrived, she accompanied him on board the transport and remained with him until the last "All ashore" whistle had blown. They parted with mutual protestations of love, and pledged each other to write as often as possible. She said that during the entire time of his stay overseas, she had written him almost daily, and had received from him letters penned with almost the same frequency. His letters usually arrived several at a time. The last one received advised her that he would sail for New York on a certain date. The ship he mentioned arrived at Hoboken exactly one year from the day he had sailed for France.

Captain Armstrong wrote that it would not be well for her to come to meet him, because he did not know what duty might be assigned to him at the last minute, and therefore there was no assurance of their being able to see each other at the dock. He asked her to await his arrival at her home. The Baroness described her excitement and impatience that evening as she listened for the sound of the bell. As soon as the longed-for moment did arrive, the butler came to her in the drawing-room and announced Captain Armstrong. At this point in her story, the Baroness said:

"Imagine my surprise when the butler ushered in a man about five feet ten inches in height, with light, sandy hair, a close-clipped mustache, freckled face and hands—a man who in no wise resembled my Boy."

The Baroness always referred to her fiancé as "my Boy."

She continued: "The shock to me was terrific! I had believed that my Boy was coming to see me, and to my utter astonishment a stranger appeared. It was awful! This stranger said to me: 'Marcia, aren't you glad to see me?'

"I replied: 'Why, I don't know you! Who are you? Have you a message for me from Captain Armstrong?'

"He said, 'Don't joke with me. I have been impatiently waiting for this moment.'

"He held out his arms to me. I was so overcome with disappointment it was all I could do to keep from fainting. I denounced him as an impostor, and ordered him from the house. He protested that he was indeed Captain Armstrong, and that he could not understand my attitude toward him. I rang for the butler, and instructed him to escort my unwelcome visitor to the door."

During the entire recital of this story, the Baroness was cool and collected, although I could see she was exerting considerable effort to keep herself in hand. Her story sounded strange. I observed her eyes closely, but their expression seemed normal. I asked her to continue. She went on to say that the next day "her boy" called her by telephone, and demanded an explanation of her strange reception.

"While it grieved me to be forced to say this to him, I again denounced him as an impostor. I said to him: 'Through some means you have secured information as to my interest in Captain Armstrong. For some reason you are now trying to impersonate him. Do not try to deceive me again.'"

The Baroness said that her problem then was to learn what had become of her fiancé. She continued: "I wrote the War Department, giving them what data I had, and received a reply to the effect that Captain Armstrong had returned to this country on the ship his letter to me had stated, and that the records of that Department revealed that he had been honorably discharged from the service, and had returned to his home in Vermont."

She related that, upon receipt of this information, she had immediately gone to Washington and, through friends, had secured an interview with the Secretary of War. She said he appeared to take a great interest in the case, and had assured her that everything possible would be done by the War Department and the Army Intelligence to discover a solution of the mystery. She had remained in the Capital for weeks, first dealing with the War Department, and when finally informed that everything possible had been done, and no solution of the problem had been reached, she was referred to the Department of Justice.

The Baroness had the same experience there, and was eventually advised there was nothing whatever that the Government could do to help her. About this time she recalled that Captain Armstrong was a member of a certain well-known fraternal organization, so she appealed to its national secretary for assistance. This man, like all the others with whom she had been in contact, appeared deeply interested, and promised the most complete investigation. After several weeks had elapsed, she was advised by the secretary that there was nothing further he could do; that to all appearances the man who had represented himself to her as Captain Armstrong was, in reality, the Captain Armstrong from whom she had parted when he sailed for France. It was at this point, she said, that she decided to come to me.

As she recounted her story, the Baroness took from her portfolio masses of correspondence which she had received from various officials and Departments. Glancing through some of these letters I noticed that the most thorough inquiry had been made by each in turn. There was no indication that the writers of the missives looked upon her story as in any way fanciful. Then I examined the correspondence more closely to see if I could learn why each Government official she had approached had been unable to aid her. There was nothing illuminating. Each informed her that there was nothing more he could do for her, and referred her to some one else, and that person, after a thorough investigation, made virtually the same reply, passing her on to another department.

Without quite knowing just wh.. I could do for her, I promised to look into the matter, and ascertain if there was anything the police of New York City could do in her behalf. At the moment I could see no solution to her problem, since she had already invoked the assistance of precisely the machinery it would be necessary for us to enlist for cooperation, were I to enter upon an investigation for her.

I did check up on the matter, however, writing several Government officials in Washington who had interested themselves in her case. These gentlemen were unanimous in expressing the belief that the young woman was suffering from some form of delusion. I called on the Grand Secretary of the fraternal organization, and he told me that he had been so much impressed with the Baroness' story that he had directed Captain Armstrong to report to him in person, and bring with him all documents incidental to his war-time service, together with such other data as would show what his movements were from the time he sailed from New York up to the moment of his return to his home after his discharge from the Army.

This Captain Armstrong did, and the Secretary was convinced that he was not an impostor. Besides, he had checked with Armstrong's local lodge in Vermont, and had found that he was the person he represented himself to be. His identity had been completely established.

During the interval devoted to this investigation, the Baroness was in almost daily communication with me by telephone, always putting the same question, "Have you learned anything about the fate of my Boy?"

Finally, I felt that in all fairness to her and to myself I must inform her there was nothing more I could do. That same afternoon she came again to my office, and expressed herself as deeply disappointed because the "wonderful police department" had been unable to accomplish anything for her. She expressed it as her opinion that some "malign and powerful influence," of which she had no knowledge, was in a conspiracy to cover up or protect the impersonator of Captain Armstrong.

"Just what is the purpose of this conspiracy?" I asked her.

"I do not know," replied the Baroness.

I then tried to convince her that the man who had called at her home actually was her fiancé. But it was useless. She sounded so plausible, seemed so perfectly normal, that it was difficult for me to believe I was dealing with a mentally unbalanced person. Even her eyes gave no hint to my lay mind that she was in any way unbalanced. It was this fact that, in the beginning, had induced me to carry on, and I had been told by the others who had listened to her story that they, too, had been deceived by her apparently rational demeanor.

She had the most charming manner imaginable, and displayed perfect courtesy even when annoyed at our inability to assist her. After I had repeated that nothing more could be done, she said, quite gently but firmly, that she intended to appeal to my superior officer for aid. She left my office and went direct to him.

He in turn was so impressed with her story that he immediately sent for me, and I had some difficulty in convincing him that the Baroness de Hoven was a mental case. The Baroness, in the meantime, was waiting in the Inspector's outer office.

After we had discussed the matter fully, my superior sent for her, and informed her there was nothing the Department could do for her. She then politely asked who his superior was. We both attempted to convince her that she was laboring under hallucination. She was so gentle that, no matter how annoying she proved to be, no one could treat her harshly.

Directly after she left us, she went to the Chief Inspector, and secured an interview with him. It was not easy to make the Chief realize the Baroness' mental condition, but when he did, he instructed me to dispose of her once and for all, so that she would cease annoying members of the Department.

During my interview in this office, the Baroness was in the anteroom. I decided then to resort to an expedient which I hoped might be effective, without its being necessary to go through with it. I instructed the sergeant in charge of the waiting room to call an ambulance.

"Have it sent at once," I instructed him, as I winked at him without the Baroness' seeing me do so. "I want this lady removed to Bellevue for observation."

The sergeant picked up the telephone and, holding down

the hook, transmitted my message into the mouthpiece. Before he had finished talking the Baroness had vanished!

Before this, after I had become fully convinced that the poor girl was the victim of an hallucination, I telephoned her mother, and informed her of her daughter's visits to my office and their purport. I asked her if there was nothing she could do to restrain her from coming to Police Headquarters and taking up our time. I pointed out to her that her daughter should receive institutional care. The mother frankly admitted that her daughter had been suffering a mental disturbance from the moment Captain Armstrong had called on her after his return from France.

"Up to that time she never gave a sign of being anything but a normal, happy girl," she said. "And, although you may not believe this, Marcia seems to be sane on every other subject. She has only this one delusion."

This I could accept as true because, after I became certain that the Baroness had a disordered mind, I tested her by leading her to talk on various subjects. She had seemed perfectly normal, discussing everything in a most intelligent manner. This odd case interested me, and aroused my curiosity to such an extent that I got in touch with one of the leading psychoanalysts in the city, and told him the story. He said that medical history contained a few examples of that type of mania. At the conclusion of his talk, which was interspersed with medical terms, I asked, "Doctor, might that condition of mind be termed 'Idol Worship'?"

The doctor replied, "Leaving out technical terminology, that is precisely what it is."

He went on to say that, due to the long period of suspense and worry endured by the young woman while her sweetheart was in France, she had gradually elevated him to a pinnacle of perfection. She had come to visualize him as the ideal hero, endowed with faultless mental and physical attributes. When he returned to her, shorn of his idealized personality, she had been shocked into believing he actually was an impostor.

I still find myself sympathizing with the state of mind of poor Captain Armstrong at that moment when the girl he loved turned on him and said: "Who are you? I never saw you before."

There was another young woman who tied us in knots for weeks before we discovered she was a pathological type.

Freda Boreshefsky came to the Bureau one morning. She spoke what sounded like Yiddish, and I called a Jewish detective to act as interpreter. I might say, in passing, that I have attached to my staff detectives representing nearly every European race. Freda was eighteen years of age, petite, dark-eyed, dark-haired, and not unattractive. She was, to all appearances, of foreign birth. She said she spoke no English, had lived all her life in Poland, and had but recently come to this country.

The gist of her rapid-fire story was that, during the World War, when the Germans were over-running Poland and had captured Warsaw, she saw her father killed in a horrible manner. He was struck down, and bayoneted repeatedly until he died in agony. Accompanied by her brother, a year or two younger than herself, she managed to escape from Warsaw and reach New York through the aid of a Masonic friend of her father's. She gave a vivid account of the many vicissitudes undergone by her brother and herself during the period when they were trying to reach the shelter of a neutral country. Her poor brother, she said, had died of exposure and malnutrition, and she herself had almost starved to death several times, and understood well the pangs of hunger.

Freda, pathetic little refugee, said she had only been in this country a few weeks, and was now being cared for by some charitable Polish Jews on the East Side. When asked why she came to the United States, she said that some years before her mother, a teacher before her marriage, had left her father and gone to New York, and from there, to quote Freda, "to a city in the interior, which I think is called Philadelphia." The mother had secured employment there as a teacher; the girl described her as "very brilliant."

"How do you know your mother is very brilliant?"

Freda replied that she had had occasional letters from her. She exhibited the torn fragments of a letter bearing evidence of much handling, which she said had come from her mother. The writing on these scraps was in excellent English, and indicated that the mother was attached to the staff of a Philadelphia school, and eager to see her dear daughter. Freda, tenderly smoothing out the battered note paper, said she had come to this country with the one idea in mind of locating her mother and making her home with her.

Inasmuch as Freda professed to speak no English, the Jewish detective was given the job of attempting to find her mother. Communications were sent to the Philadelphia police, supplying them with what data was available, but after a careful examination of the names of teachers in the Philadelphia schools, word was received that no one by the name of Sophia Boreshefsky could be located.

INSANITY CASES

Freda called at Headquarters every day or two, and on her next visit we conveyed this news to her. She was un-daunted. It was quite possible, she said, that her mother was employing her maiden name Mousshky. The Phila-delphia Police department was then asked to check that name. After a lapse of time, we were again advised that no such person was on the teacher list of the Philadelphia schools. A suspicion arose that our Freda was not all she represented herself to be.

One day when she was in my office, in conversation with the detective, I opened her hand-bag, which was on my desk, and found in it a memorandum book. Glancing through it, I saw that it was filled with writing, not in Polish or Yiddish, but in the best East Side English. I broke in on the conver-sation and ordered the detective to place Freda under arrest, and I charged her with a variety of imaginary crimes. This was like waving a magic wand over her, for immediately the girl, who for weeks had employed nothing but Yiddish in her dealings with us, burst into a voluble sputtering of "New Yorkese."

After she finished imploring us not to arrest her, I asked, "What was the idea of posing as a recent arrival in this country, and unable to speak English?"

She said, "Please, please forgive—ah, do have the great kindness to overlook my harmless little plot. You see, I am *so* eager to become a writer! I thought I would be able to get some unusual material through association with the police."

And I am obliged to admit that she certainly had secured some pretty fair stuff for an essay into literature; for weeks she had succeeded in leading the hard-headed New York police a merry chase. I lectured her on the imprudence of this method of getting copy, and told her that she had set about launching herself on a literary career in a very foolhardy way. Perhaps my reprimand was a little severe, for I was then treated to another surprise.

Freda suddenly turned white, and stiffened in her chair. She became absolutely rigid. I thought this was more faking, until I observed that she was foaming at the mouth. When I saw the white froth on her lips, I realized that this at least was genuine, and that she was probably suffering an attack of epilepsy. An ambulance was summoned, and the surgeon's diagnosis confirmed mine. She was removed to a hospital.

A few days after the epileptic attack staged in my office, Freda returned. She again apologized for her deception, and wound up with the plea, "Can't we be friends?" Like the song, I suppose.

Freda confessed that she had been born in Essex Street, where she was at present living with her father and mother. She said she had been a victim of epilepsy as far back as she could remember, and that her attacks recurred more frequently as years passed. One morning about six months later I found, on reaching my office, a letter on my desk addressed to me, with a note attached saying it had been picked up on the sidewalk in front of Headquarters. I opened it, and found it was from the chronic pest, Freda. It related a lurid tale of how she had been kidnaped from a point near her home and taken to Newark, where she had been held in a house for several days before she had had an opportunity of attracting the attention of a passerby. She had tossed this letter to him from a second-story window, and had asked him to deliver it. She wrote that she had given him a dollar for this service. I at once knew her story was untrue because the letter, although sealed, had no postage stamp on it, and it contained an account of the manner in which it was to reach me, and through what hands. It was almost like those fake archeological finds with the date B.C. carefully inserted!

All of this made it evident to me that Freda was again indulging in some of her fantasies, and exercising her flair for story-telling. In this letter the young deceiver begged me to tell the Newark police of her plight, and enlist their aid in her rescue. Freda evidently had a plan to play games with the Newark police but, of course, no attempt was made to interest any one in her misfortune. And, in a few days, we were again favored with a call from her. When I reprimanded her for her second attempt to deceive us, she admitted that her story was false but said her literary urge was unquenchable.

Eventually Freda became such a nuisance that I sent her to a hospital for observation as to her sanity, first talking with her parents. They were of low-grade intelligence. Her father, a night watchman, said his daughter had been irresponsible since childhood. Freda's parents were not sufficiently enlightened to attribute her conduct to anything but a desire to be "mischievous." Freda was detained at the hospital for a short period, and was then released. The report I received stated that, while she was irresponsible, there were so many of her kind that if all of them were placed under restraint there would be insufficient accommodations for them. Exit Freda!

Two runaway girls were actors in a drama which eventually turned into tragedy for one of them.

MISSING MEN

Five years ago two young girls, Marie Latour, of French parentage, and Frances Campbell, seventeen and eighteen years of age respectively, were students at a select boarding school. One morning they did not appear for breakfast, and inquiry revealed that they had not occupied their beds in the dormitory the night before. The school authorities at once notified the parents and they, in turn, came to see me shortly after the report of the disappearance of the girls had reached me through the usual channels.

One of the girls, Frances, had no mother; the other, Marie, had lost her father. Frances' father was a broker, and Marie's mother was a woman of independent means. The girls had always had everything money could supply, and the parents were at a loss to think of any motive for their dropping out of sight.

We instituted the usual investigation. Detectives visited the school, questioned the teachers and schoolmates and intimate friends of the missing girls. The instructors reported that Marie and Frances were studious, had excellent standing in their classes, and were above the average in general intelligence. It was learned that the two were inseparable, and while they cultivated a few close chums, such friends were always mutual ones. From one of these intimates we learned that our missing girls had often mentioned the fact that they were never obliged to do anything for themselves, that they felt themselves "useless." All of their needs were taken care of for them; they never had to exert themselves in the slightest. They confided that they did not look forward to the future, because the prospects were that they would always be pampered and never given an opportunity to show their real metal. On one occasion they had even expressed the intention of going out into the world "on their own" and possibly making a mark for themselves.

Both girls, at the time they disappeared, had a considerable sum of money, as their allowances were liberal and they had been more than usually economical for quite a period prior to their departure from school; so much so in fact, that their friends had commented on it. Ticket offices of all railroads leading from New York were checked, but without result. Express train conductors were interviewed, and eventually one was found who was certain he had had the two girls for passengers on his train. He fixed this fact because he had noticed the girls in conversation with a prominent business man. The conductor knew this man, because he frequently rode on his train, and he and his passenger had formed a sort of acquaintanceship. His name was secured, and we got in touch with him at his office in Broad Street.

He was a business and social friend of Mr. Campbell, and knew his daughter, Frances. Seeing her on the train he, naturally, had spoken to her, and they had sat together conversing until he reached his destination, a point in the central part of the state. Frances had told him that she and her friend were en route to a city in the western part of the state to visit friends over the week end. He had not thought of the incident since.

A detective was at once dispatched to the city the girls had mentioned, and in coöperation with the local police, he picked up a clew which led to a store where the girls had secured work selling books. They had held this position for ten days, whereupon they had collected the wages due them and departed without explanation. At that point the trail was lost.

MISSING MEN

For two weeks nothing was learned about them or their present whereabouts. At about this time, I received, late one afternoon, a telephone call from Mrs. Latour, mother of Marie. In a very excited voice she told me that she was calling from a department store and that she had just left a shoe shop, where she always bought the family footwear. She thought she had a clew to the missing girls. As soon as she entered the shop, she told me, the manager had approached her and told her that he had an inquiry from one of their branches in a mid-Western city, asking whether a Marie Latour had credit rating with their firm.

Mrs. Latour was so agitated at hearing this that she had not asked when or through what channel the inquiry had come—whether by mail, telephone, or telegraph. I instructed her to return to the store at once, and get all details, particularly the channel and the time of the inquiry, and then report back to me. A few minutes later she called, and said the inquiry had been made by telegraph a few minutes before her arrival at the store. The mother talked on excitedly, and I interrupted, "Please hang up the receiver, and return to your home. I will communicate with you there."

As soon as the line was clear I called the Chief of Police of the city mentioned, and, after briefly explaining the situation to him, I requested him to send detectives to the store in question, and if the girls were there, as I believed they would be, awaiting an O.K. on their credit request, to detain them and advise me. About three-quarters of an hour later the Chief called me, and said he had both girls in his office. That night the mother of Marie, accompanied by one of my detectives, went to the city where Marie and Frances were held, and within the next forty-eight hours they were returned to their homes.

Frances immediately went back to school but Marie, fearing that every one was discussing her escapade, could not be induced to return. She was a hypersensitive girl and her mother, comprehending her nature, felt that in time this embarrassment would disappear, so she permitted her to remain at home, with the understanding that she would return to school the following year.

During this interval Marie, who was a strikingly beautiful girl, a decided brunette of the markedly Latin type, with dark luminous eyes, holding a dreamy expression in their depths, made the acquaintance of a brilliant young Japanese, a college graduate, with whom she fell violently in love. She told her mother that she intended to marry him, and very naturally her mother objected. When she could not prevail upon her daughter to relinquish her Oriental sweetheart, she got in touch with me, asked my advice in this dilemma, and appealed for aid, imploring me to help her dissuade the daughter from taking so fatal a step as marriage to the Japanese.

Marie, as a result of several conversations I had with her after her runaway experience, had come, I think, to trust me. Having no father she seemed to feel that I had a sort of paternal interest in her. She willingly came to my office, and I had a long talk with her, during which I attempted to show her how injudicious was her plan. Her mother had told me that Marie had said she would marry the Japanese as soon as she was eighteen. I stressed very hard the differences of race, temperament, and religion.

But Marie advanced the age-old argument that "love

knows no race nor creed." She was a sweet girl, with a charming personality, but I saw the futility of trying to convince her that she ought not marry the man she had chosen.

At the close of this interview, and as soon as the girl departed, I called the mother and suggested the advisability of moving to her summer home at once. The time was late spring. I felt that if the girl were removed from the vicinity of her Japanese swain she might in time forget him, for she was young, and I believed she might form new attachments among her summer associates.

During the early part of her stay in the country, she seemed to react favorably to her surroundings, according to reports I received from the mother. Mrs. Latour said that Marie had even admitted a number of times that her romantic experience with her Oriental friend had been unwise. From this point on, however, she swung to another extreme: she now felt that her contact with the Jap had besmirched her, making her unfit to associate with her own race. She became almost an "untouchable," acting as though she were a social outcast. Her mother noticed a marked change in the girl. She evinced a total lack of interest in her surroundings and in the everyday occurrences of the summer home. There were long periods of brooding, and after a time Mrs. Latour was convinced that her daughter's mind had become affected.

She consulted me at every step along the way. A well-known psychiatrist was called in, and he examined the girl. He made an intensive survey of her condition, and expressed the opinion that she was in need of immediate institutional care. Arrangements were made to send her to a sanitarium, where for two years she was under treatment. Her condition at the time she entered the hospital was rapidly becoming more and more abnormal.

After two years in the sanitarium, during which she had expert professional attention, for her mother spared no expense, she was pronounced incurably insane, and was removed to an institution for permanent mental cases. Here she now lives in constant communion with what she terms her "shadow friend." With this invisible companion she talks by the hour, and resents any interruption of these "visits." Notwithstanding her mental condition, Marie has a lovely and tractable nature. Her mother told me only recently how fastidious she still is about her personal appearance and how, when she is not communing with her shadow friend, she spends considerable time manicuring her nails and dressing her glossy dark hair.

VII. WHY MEN LEAVE HOME

WHILE crimes of violence, murder, suicide, loss of memory, accidents and mental illness account for a certain number of disappearances each year, other causes predominate. Those cases I have discussed in the previous chapters illustrate the more spectacular reasons why people drop out of sight; the majority of cases coming before us are far less dramatic and are often decidedly prosaic.

It is a popular belief that men and women generally vanish involuntarily; that they are victims of crime, or are held under duress. While this is true in some cases, by far the greatest number of persons who disappear are not impelled by force or fear; they do not leave under compulsion, and are not the victims of a sinister plot. They vanish of their own free will. For a variety of reasons they want to efface themselves from their environment, and although those they leave behind affirm that "there is no motive," we usually find the key when we scrutinize the situation.

Men leave home for a variety of reasons: business difficulties, domestic friction, emotional disturbances, incurable disease, over-wrought nerves, fear of mental breakdown. The motivating forces are too numerous to catalogue, but the largest number who cut loose from their usual moorings come within the first two classifications. Paradoxical as it may seem, there are more adults than juveniles who disappear, in the ratio of about three to two; and men outnumber women in about the same proportion.

Spendthrift and slovenly wives cause some men to vanish. Frigid or too demonstrative ones account for the disappearance of still others. There are also men who have simply grown tired of their wives. The women may have lost, through child-bearing or the passing of years, whatever good looks they once possessed; at any rate, they no longer attract their husbands, who disappear either with new charmers, or to gain freedom from womankind—which often results, oddly enough, in another woman. Not infrequently we find that a man's wife is demanding, and expects him to supply her with the wherewithal for greater social display than his finances permit. Certainly the reasons most often disclosed for husbands' disappearances involve domestic situations and complications, with lack of understanding between husband and wife, and the "other man" or "other woman" figuring as contributing factors.

Often the desire for adventure, which we usually attribute only to the young, is an important element in a man's disappearance. We find cases of wanderlust in no inconsiderable numbers among adults. Life has gone stale for them, and they think that by changing their surroundings and thus relieving the monotony of their days, they will recapture their zest for living.

We discovered a reason more subtle than any of those already mentioned for the disappearance of the man figuring in the following case: On a cold March afternoon the desk officer announced Mr. Armstrong, a lawyer. The man entered, accompanied by a young woman whom he introduced as Mrs. Marsh.

He appeared very much perturbed, and quickly proceeded to tell me he feared that one of his clients, a Morris Belker, forty-eight years of age, and president of a company engaged in the manufacture of men's clothing, had met with foul play. He said that Mr. Belker had left his home on West End Avenue at 7:30 o'clock that morning to take a train at 125th Street to go to one of his factories, which was located about seventy-five miles outside the city. He had with him the factory payroll, as it was his custom to combine its delivery with a visit to his plant. He was described as a considerate employer, interested in his employees' welfare, and one who always insisted upon seeing at first hand whether their working conditions were satisfactory.

About 11:30 A.M. that day Mr. Belker's secretary at the main office in New York had received a telephone call from the factory manager, asking if there was anything the matter with Mr. Belker.

"It's pay-day," the manager said, "and you know this is the day for the ghost to walk."

Mr. Belker's failure to arrive at the factory had occasioned surprise, since he was always punctual on his weekly visits. The secretary immediately called Mr. Belker's home, and found that he had left at 7:30 A.M., with the intention of going to the factory.

The lawyer said that at about 2 o'clock, shortly before his visit to me, there had been received at Mr. Belker's office in New York, among other mail, a letter containing bills of lading and other papers having to do with the business. But, most important of all, there was in the envelope, a pencil-printed note on the back of a telegraph blank, which read:

"He would not do as we wanted him to; therefore we were obliged to bump him off. His body is in the North River. Enclosed you will find important business papers that are of no use to us."

To the casual reader that message might appear a definite solution of the mystery. But to me it indicated a situation which was peculiar, and not at all probable.

As soon as I finished reading the penciled note, I said to Mr. Armstrong: "Let us analyze this. Doesn't it strike you as odd that a confessed murderer should be so considerate of Mr. Belker's business interests and his family as to take the time—and to add to the risk of discovery—to write this note? Isn't it expecting rather too much of such a man to hope that he would disclose Belker's fate to his friends so promptly?"

I continued with the analysis, asking the lawyer to note some of the inconsistencies I pointed out: "You say he left his home at 7:30 A.M. To be sure the hour was a bit early to encounter many people on the streets in the section of the city in which Mr. Belker resided. However, bakers, milkmen and others supplying the needs of customers thereabouts would be in evidence. Servants would be going to basement doors for the rolls, milk and cream, so the chance of a criminal's perpetrating the act of murder without discovery would be mighty slim.

"We will concede, however, that it is possible that Mr. Belker was 'bumped off.' If this were the case, there would be presented the problem of disposal of the body. It would be necessary to employ transportation—cab, car or other conveyance—and by the time the waterfront was reached, waterfront workers, longshoremen, truckmen and so on would be at their jobs. There the chance of discovery would be great, but the most difficult part of the job as described in the penciled note would have been to deposit the body in the North River, which is full of ice."

The early afternoon editions of the papers had described at some length the difficulties surrounding the morning's ferry navigation of the river, due to unusual quantities of ice. One of the Jersey boats, after leaving its slip a short distance, had become jammed in ice, and its passengers were able to return to shore by walking over the frozen river. I called this to the lawyer's attention, adding:

"Under these circumstances, the thoughtful and kindhearted writer of the 'murder' note would have been obliged to push aside heavy ice-cakes in order to make an opening, so that his victim could be dropped into the river as the note states he was. To me, the whole thing looks odd. What do you think about it?"

Mr. Armstrong, whose excitement was slowly diminishing, replied: "Now that you analyze it in this way, it doesn't look so good to me. There is something queer about the whole thing."

Questioned as to the condition of Mr. Belker's business, he said: "As his attorney, I know it is thriving, with assets in abundance, and no large outstanding obligations. There are orders on hand to keep his factories busy for months to come."

During this discussion the young woman, who had been

introduced as Mrs. Marsh, sat quietly, saying nothing. As she was about to speak, the lawyer explained that Mrs. Marsh was Belker's married daughter. She said: "It begins to appear as though my father has not been killed. But why in the world should he disappear?"

While I had my own theory as to the motive, for I was mulling over the possibility of the "inevitable woman," I did not think it wise to introduce that suspicion into the situation until such time as our investigation might warrant doing so. After my callers had departed, I assigned a detective to the investigation, with instructions to visit the office of Belker's firm, look over the organization there, talk with Belker's secretary, and run down everything that might serve to supply a clew to this baffling disappearance. I particularly directed him to learn whether Belker was in the habit of doing any pencil printing of notes or inter-office memoranda. It was soon learned that Belker had this habit, and this discovery, viewed in connection with the lead pencil note sent by the "murderers," confirmed me in my belief that the missing man had written the "murder" note himself.

Following this visit to Belker's office, the detective went into the financial standing of the firm, for I felt that possibly the attorney was not in possession of all the facts. But what we found in this respect served to corroborate the lawyer.

It was my wish to have a talk with Mrs. Belker, but her daughter, during her visit to my office, had informed me that her mother was prostrated at the news of her husband's disappearance, and was under the care of a physician. Until the time when I could see Mrs. Belker, her husband's business and private life were investigated, and we found it unusually exemplary. He was not a ladies' man, not a mixer. He did not even entertain his out-of-town buyers, always assigning that duty to some one in his employ. We learned also that, to all appearances, his home life was perfect. Belker was seldom to be found far from the family hearth, spending few evenings away from home, and then only when unusual circumstances made it imperative for him to do so. Friends of the family emphasized the happy conjugal atmosphere of the Belker home. Mrs. Belker, it seems, was particularly affectionate. She would caress her husband's hair in passing his chair, or seat herself on his knee for a few moments, kissing and fondling him.

After an intensive investigation, we were forced to the conclusion that the motive for the disappearance, in so far as could be discovered, was no more in evidence now than at the beginning. The search continued for several months. A General Alarm had been promulgated, and circulars describing the missing man had been sent Police Departments throughout the country.

Mrs. Belker remained in a state of prostration for about a month after her husband's disappearance. Then one day her daughter telephoned me that her mother had recovered sufficiently to be interviewed, and was anxious to have a talk with me. She came to my office that afternoon. The moment I saw her a possible motive for her husband's disappearance presented itself. Mrs. Belker was an unusually well-preserved woman of about the same age as her husband. She was comely despite the fact that the suspense and anguish through which she was passing had left its mark. At the same time Mrs. Belker impressed me as being an emotional woman, whose nature was anything but cold and unresponsive. She appeared to be the over-demonstrative type, the kind that can easily surfeit a man with displays of affection.

She seemed to know little about her husband's business, and was satisfied that it was prospering. Her vital interest, I could see, centered wholly in the home, and in the relationship existing between herself and her husband, which she described as "ideal." This is a favorite term employed by wives, I have found, when discussing their marriage.

"Our life together for twenty-eight years, ever since we married at the age of twenty, has been almost a repetition of our honeymoon," confided Mrs. Belker, as she dabbed at her tear-filled eyes. The entire period of her visit to me was devoted to rhapsodizing over the bliss of her domestic life. The loss of that was the only thing that appeared to matter to her.

After Mrs. Belker left, I began to wonder if the motive for her husband's disappearance was not to be found in his home life. I speculated as to whether Mrs. Belker had not required a kind of attention from her husband which was incompatible with twenty-eight years of married companionship. My observation has been that after twenty-eight years of marriage, the married state comes to be an accepted affair, not calling for an abundance of emotional display. Honeymoons do wane, I knew, regardless of Mrs. Belker's story of her continuous romance.

Then one day I learned that Mr. Belker, in his younger days, had been a traveling man, and had retained his membership in the Association of Commercial Travelers. It occurred to me that perhaps some of his old associates were still on the road, and by some chance might meet up with him some time or some place. I got in touch with the secretary of this association, and asked if he would distribute, through all branches of the organization, circulars describing the missing man. He assured me that he would be glad to do so, and we immediately furnished him with a sufficient number of circulars to insure widespread distribution.

One morning, about a month later, I received a letter from a man describing himself as a commercial traveler who had come into possession of one of the circulars. He wrote that on the previous Sunday, while attending a ball-game in a Texas city, he was quite sure he had seen the subject of our search leaving the ball park. He recognized him from the photograph on the circular. I might say here that Mr. Belker had a singular type of face; once seen, it would be difficult to forget. My correspondent said that he had made an effort to get close to the man, but in the crush of people leaving the park, he had been unable to do so.

A communication to the Chief of Police of the Texas city was prepared and mailed. Several weeks passed before a reply was received. When it did arrive, it said that the Chief felt confident that Belker, under the name of Jumel, was conducting a small tailoring and dry-cleaning establishment in this Texas town. He said the description and picture contained in the circular tallied exactly with Jumel. I felt that we were now on the right track, particularly because of the fact that the man in Texas was engaged in a business closely allied with Belker's former occupation in New York. Further correspondence between the Texas chief and our Bureau ensued until we were satisfied that the tailor Jumel was our man Belker.

I hesitated to take Mrs. Belker into my confidence, so I sent for her daughter, to whom I disclosed my theory as to the motive for her father's disappearance. Rather to my surprise she accepted it, and said that, as she thought of it now in retrospect, it was unusual for a woman married twenty-eight years to be as demonstrative as her mother had always been. She said that this lovemaking on the part of her mother had been such a common spectacle in their home life that she had never before thought of it as strange until now when it was called to her attention.

I suggested that perhaps it would be wise for her to arrange to see her father, and consult him as to his wishes before her mother was told anything about it. We agreed that it was preferable for her mother to believe that her husband might have been the victim of a mishap rather than know definitely that he no longer cared for her companionship; in fact, desired it so little that he was willing to relinquish business, name, friends, everything to get away from her. Mrs. Marsh was fully in accord with me and arranged to pay the visit to her father without letting her mother know the purpose of her absence from the city.

Three weeks later the young woman called on me, and the first thing she said was: "You were right! Dad put all his cards on the table, and told me the whole story. He revealed to me frankly that he felt he could not continue at home in justice to his health and well-being, and so adopted what means he had to escape from the demands of my mother."

To this day Mrs. Belker is under the impression that her husband's disappearance was due to an outside agency, and has become reconciled to this belief. She does not know that she drove her husband away, to create an entirely new life for himself, because of her too intense and demonstrative love.

MISSING MEN

Many husbands and wives fail to confide in each other. This, I have learned, causes many a domestic rift.

Among the routine reports received one morning three years ago there was one pertaining to Joseph Lamson. He was forty-two years old and before his mysterious disappearance had been engaged in the wholesale paint and contracting business, representing the third generation of his family to conduct the firm at the original address.

Our investigation revealed that Lamson was happily married and living in a suburban section of New York. All his acquaintances believed that his business was flourishing, but the detective assigned to the case found that it was about on its last legs. Lamson's type of business had moved away from the section of the city in which he was located, and he had insufficient vision to see that it was necessary to make a move himself in order to keep in touch with his customers. He felt that the firm name alone would be enough to hold his trade. We found that he had reached such a pass that he was unable to meet current obligations, such as employees' salaries and bills payable.

I sent for Mrs. Lamson, and found her a wholesome appearing woman, but she seemed to know nothing of her husband's difficulties. They had always lived well, and she had done considerable entertaining, giving dinners, bridge parties, and afternoon teas. She had continued up to the present the same standard of living to which she had been accustomed, not realizing that retrenchment was in order.

Lamson was described as a rather quiet, retiring fellow, with an introspective turn of mind. He was not prone to take others into his confidence.

WHY MEN LEAVE HOME

"Sometimes," said Mrs. Lamson, "he is somewhat morbid."

When the true state of affairs was described to his wife, and she was fully acquainted with the facts concerning her husband's failing business, she said she feared he might have committed suicide.

"Why didn't he confide in me?" she wailed. "I would have changed our mode of living, economized, made ends meet somehow. It would not have worked any hardship on me at all."

About six weeks after Lamson's disappearance, we received a report from a downtown precinct that an unknown man had been found in the street unconscious, suffering from exposure and malnutrition, and had been sent to a hospital. His description tallied with that of Lamson. A detective visited the hospital, and found that the patient was, in fact, Joseph Lamson. He had responded sufficiently to treatment so that he was in condition to talk.

"Please," he implored, "don't tell my wife what has happened. I'm a failure in business, and she thought I was a success. It became impossible for me to maintain my home in the way to which she had become accustomed, and which she had the right to expect, and so I thought it would be best for me to drop out of sight—cut loose entirely. Promise me you won't let my wife know all this."

We did not see fit to comply with his request, and Mrs. Lamson was informed of the situation. She hastened to the hospital, and I know that after her talk with him he must have been convinced that he had sadly underrated his wife. She did, I learned, take him to task severely for not having confided in her, but she then hastened to assure him that she was willing to play the game of partnership in the full sense of the word. She behaved, in fact, like a true wife.

Another admirable woman who was brought to grief through the action of her husband was Mrs. Walter Crane, who in 1927 reported to the Department the disappearance of her husband, a druggist. Crane was a graduate of a local school of pharmacy, a man who had been in business for years, and was fairly prosperous. There were three children in the Crane family, a boy of nine, and two girls of eleven and thirteen. Mrs. Crane said that as far as she knew, there was no motive for her husband's act. The only feature of the affair which puzzled her, apart from the disappearance itself, was the fact that when Crane's finances were examined it was found that there was a bank balance of but a few dollars. This was surprising to Mrs. Crane, because she had always believed that her husband carried a substantial amount on deposit.

The disappearance of her husband left Mrs. Crane and her children in an embarrassing situation, but she managed to surmount her difficulties successfully through her own efforts. Crane's business and private life were scanned from every angle; there did not seem to be anything unusual in either which might account for his disappearance, assuming that the act was of his own volition. The druggist's intimates, when interviewed, were unanimous in saying he was an unusually superior type. He had always discussed with them his contentment in his home, and his pride in his wife, his son, and his two attractive daughters. He had often described to them his ambitious plans for his children's future.

He appeared to have no enemies. His health was good. We

were thus confronted with what seemed to be an act without a motive. The usual course was followed in a survey of the records of the Department covering accidents, sudden illness, or other circumstances which might render it impossible for the victim to make known his identity or his whereabouts. But there were no results.

After weeks devoted to a bootless search for Crane, it was learned from a confidential source that the druggist had been attentive to a handsome widow. This woman's history disclosed the fact that she was a notorious vamp, the type who plays on men's vanity and their baser passions, and secures a stranglehold on them through their affections, all for material ends.

Such women are often accomplished "gold-diggers," and they are encountered in many of our cases. They employ finesse while securing their loot; many times their victims never suspect them of ulterior motives or designing ends until the cupboard is bare and the bankroll gone, whereupon the ladies also vanish. The men ensnared by the wiles of women of this caliber usually feel that the gifts of money which they make their inamoratas are entirely voluntary on their part. But the pathetic helplessness of the male in the toils of feminine disingenuousness is a classic theme and needs no embellishment from a policeman.

We learned, in tracing the life history of this adventuress in Crane's life, that she had come to New York from a Pacific Coast state. Through the police of the city of her birth we learned that she had behind her a lurid past. Inasmuch as Crane would probably want to get as far away from his wife as possible under the circumstances, it was quite likely, according to our reasoning, that he might head for a section of the country where he thought he would not be caught. At any rate, we decided to extend our search to this Pacific Coast city.

Since Crane was a druggist, and probably not qualified to take up any other calling, I decided that wherever he might be he would undoubtedly follow his profession. On this assumption, I wrote to the Board of Pharmacy of the State in question, giving his name and the school of Pharmacy of which he was a graduate and requested that we be advised whether or not he had applied for registration under the laws of that State.

In due time a reply was received advising us that Crane had registered in December of 1927, and had intended engaging in business in one of the large cities of the state. I communicated with the police of that city, asking whether or not Crane was in the drug business there. I received assurance that he was, with information as to his local address, and the further fact that he was residing there with his wife and a three-year-old son.

At the time of Crane's disappearance in 1927, and three years prior to this discovery, Mrs. Crane, left practically destitute, was disturbed by the feeling that she would be the subject of gossip in the section where her husband had for years engaged in business, and consequently she had closed out his drug store and moved to a suburban town. She took up dressmaking, and in this way managed to support herself and children, sending them to school and keeping them well dressed and happy in their new environment. I recall the day when the mother, proud of the progress her boy and girls were making in school, stopped in at my office to show me the graduation picture of the eldest girl, who was attired in an attractive frock her mother had made.

During all this time Mrs. Crane had heard no word of or from her husband. As soon as Crane's whereabouts were definitely established, Mrs. Crane, on my advice, brought the matter to the attention of the District Attorney of the county in which she had resided at the time of her husband's desertion, and secured an indictment. A bench warrant was issued, and through the process of extradition Crane was returned to this city, where at this writing he is awaiting trial for deserting his wife and children. But no process of law can punish the woman in the case, who has no doubt found another victim by this time.

VIII. WHY WOMEN LEAVE HOME

WOMEN depart from their own firesides, abandoning their household gods, their husbands, and often their children, for many of the same reasons which prompt men to decamp, with but this one obvious exception: business difficulties seldom supply the answer to the mystery of a woman's disappearance.

The largest number of disappearances of women is directly attributable to some phase of their emotional nature. A woman may become satiated with her husband's love, and drop out of sight either because of a desire for a change of scene, or because she has found the society of another man more interesting than that of her spouse. The other man really "understands" her, she tells herself. Perhaps she is disappointed in her husband and his treatment of her. He is cold and unresponsive, and she is hungry for the kind of affection he lavished on her in their courtship days. She never imagined that his love-making would not continue in as fervent a manner as before their marriage. Some men grow markedly matter-of-fact and casual after they have settled down to domestic life, and the habit of taking things for granted frequently piques a wife.

More married than single women drop out of sight; in

fact, comparatively few unmarried women disappear. This is provocative of thought. The numerical difference can, I think, be explained by the fact that younger women, living at home, have not the same opportunity for direct action nor the same initiative that the married woman has, for the latter is more experienced and is her own mistress in the bargain. As for the emancipated business girl, out on her own, she finds her work and her social interests so satisfactory, as a rule, that she has no particular reason for pulling up stakes and departing for parts unknown.

Oscar Wendt was brought to my office by the Reverend James Braun. The minister reminded me that he had met me two or three years before at a church affair, and at that time had learned something of my work. He was "presuming on that acquaintance," as he put it, to bring me a problem and asked for my assistance. The clergyman then explained that Wendt was one of the trustees of his church. He said that, a few days before this call, his trustee's wife, together with her two daughters, Natalie and June, thirteen and fifteen years old, had disappeared in company with another trustee of the church, Ferdinand Cole, a prominent business man, who was also married. Cole had drawn five thousand dollars from the bank, taken his automobile, and had left a brief note for his wife, which read something like this:

> "I find that my married life is not affording me the happiness I expected, and so I am going to leave. I shall establish myself elsewhere. I suggest that you continue the business. I intend beginning life anew in a part of the country far from here.
>
> FERD."

149

Doctor Braun explained that the problem of the moment was to locate Mr. Wendt's wife and young daughters. Wendt impressed me as being a clean-living man, a devoted husband and father. He seemed dazed that such a thing as this could come into his life. As for the home of the Wendts, the minister described it as one where everything had been provided for a woman's comfort. She could have everything within reason she asked for, and the husband had been financially able to gratify her every wish. Cole, on the other hand, was pictured as a man many people considered a hypocrite. He was a pillar of the church, but it was suspected that the pillar had flaws.

Were it not that this elopement would tend to impair the morals of the two young Wendt daughters, this was a case which ordinarily we would not have handled. Under the circumstances, however, it was our duty to attempt to locate the missing family. So the usual police agencies were enlisted, and about three weeks later we found the couple, with the girls, at a comfortable hotel in the Adirondacks.

I sent for the deserted husband, and told him where his wife and children could be found, suggesting that he go to them.

"I do not dare," he replied.

"Why not? Are you afraid of the other fellow?"

"No. I am only afraid of myself. I'm afraid I might kill him."

The expression on his face as he spoke convinced me that his fear was well founded. Physically and mentally he was of the type who could do violence under the stress of intense passion. It was then incumbent upon us to induce the runaway wife to return, with her children, to her husband.

I got in touch with the sheriff of the county in which the Adirondack resort was located, and talked with him by telephone. I suggested that he call upon the couple, and advise Mrs. Wendt to return to her home, stressing the unlawfulness of her act in taking with her, on this escapade, her two children. Further, I told him to point out to the erring wife that, after all, her two daughters were of an age where, even though they did not grasp the full significance of the situation, they would probably understand something of the impropriety of her act. I also urged him to assure the wife that her husband would welcome her without reserve if she came back. Those who have scant sympathy with an outraged husband who condones his wife's infidelities must pause and realize that the vagaries of human nature are many, and few of us comprehend why individuals behave as they do.

The Sheriff evidently did a persuasive job, for the following morning the deserted husband called at my office, and told me that he had just received a long distance call from his rival for the affections of his wife.

"What did Cole say?"

"He asked me if I would take my wife back."

"And you said—?"

"Why, I was so astounded by the call that all I could reply was 'Yes.'"

I told him the only thing he could do now was to await results, and I asked him to let me know when his wife returned. He promised to do so. I heard nothing from him for about two weeks, and then one day he called to thank me for what I had been able to do for him. I asked him when his wife had returned, and he told me it was on the day following the telephone call from Cole. When I questioned him as to why he had not notified me before this, he looked a little sheepish and said:

"Well, Cora seemed a bit tired out, so I thought it would do her good to take a little trip. We have been on a tour and only returned yesterday."

This, I took it, was a reconciliation jaunt. But Wendt did not seem completely happy. He finally expressed the fear that his wife might have a recurrent attack of fondness for the other man, who had also returned to his home, and that she might decide again to leave him. He asked me if I would have a talk with her; we made an appointment for the following morning.

Wendt brought his wife to my office. When she entered the room I had a good picture of what the Amazons of old probably looked like. She was a tall, broad-shouldered, full-breasted vision of health and vitality, and appeared capable of handling a household or any other problem. I asked Wendt if he would wait in the outer office while I talked alone with his wife. He withdrew, looking as though he would like to sit in on any disclosures or admissions Cora might make.

As soon as the door closed behind him, I asked the woman why she had left her husband for the other man.

She answered briefly, "Because I love him."

"I've had a chance to get pretty well acquainted with your husband. I consider him a splendid man. In what way is Cole your husband's superior?"

The wife was silent a moment. Then she said: "Well, he's more showy, for one thing. He has more pep. He is socially inclined, enjoys having a good time. So do I."

"Briefly, you think Cole is a fine playfellow."

She nodded in agreement.

"Has it ever occurred to you that life is not all a game? And did you ever take into consideration the fact that more essential qualities go to make a good husband than the ability to stage some fun? Your husband has always furnished you with a good home, hasn't he? He has always been kind to you and the children?"

Again she nodded. "Oh, he's a good provider," she agreed, with a little note of irony in her voice.

Then I said, "Madam, how you can fall in love with a man of Cole's type is more than I can understand!"

"You do not know what kind of man he is. Have you ever met him?"

I replied: "No! And I don't want to. Any man who would permit the woman with whom he was eloping—and whom he stole from her home and husband—to take with her her two adolescent daughters, is a scoundrel."

Mrs. Wendt lost her composure, her head drooped, she even blushed a little. But I continued: "When I think that you actually left a loyal, kindly husband for Cole, a man who deserted his own wife, I just wonder if you are wholly responsible for your acts."

There are times when straight talk by a disinterested stranger will have more effect upon a love-blind woman— or man—than all the arguments of friends and family.

Mrs. Wendt broke down, admitted that everything I had said about her husband was true. "I wonder if my husband can ever trust me again?" she murmured.

"He's just the kind who will if you will only offer him proof you are entitled to his confidence. Shall I call him in now so that you can say to him what it never occurred to you to say before? I think you see him in a new guise. Let him know that you appreciate him and his magnanimous conduct toward you."

I called in Wendt and left them together for a few minutes. When I returned I found them with their arms around each other, both their faces tear-stained. This may sound rather like the happy ending in a sentimental movie but it is precisely what happened. I have witnessed many another similar domestic reconciliation in my office, which at times takes on the functions of a Family Court.

Since this episode I have had assurances from the minister who first enlisted my aid that the Wendts are living together amicably and are apparently happy.

Strategy sometimes plays a part in our work; most of my detectives are first-class strategists. In the case I am about to describe I was the one forced to employ artifice in the search for a missing woman.

James X. Watson, member of a well-known law firm in New York, came to my office at Police Headquarters one day in 1923, and said his visit was in connection with the disappearance of the daughter of Frank Cheston, a client of his. The young woman, he said, was twenty-seven years of age, and had disappeared from her home three weeks before. He had been authorized by her father to spare no expense in his search for her. Representatives of two private detective agencies had been working on the mystery, supplemented, as he said with modesty, by his own "poor efforts." They had had absolutely no success, and therefore he had come to me.

Watson's air indicated he considered that everything possible for human ingenuity to conceive of had already been done by the private detectives and himself, and that this last step was a mere gesture. He was the opinionated, arrogant type, with a mouth cut straight across his face, and lips so thin they were scarcely in evidence. He had an air of perfect confidence in himself, and a domineering manner.

When I asked for particulars, he said: "There aren't any beyond the fact that the young woman was of a studious turn of mind. She had many interests, all of a wholesome nature. After leaving college she was for several years interested in literature. One afternoon about three months ago she, with some friends, visited the studio of an artist, a man about fifty or fifty-five years of age. This artist has earned a degree of appreciation in the art world due to his unusual concepts; he is interested in and an advocate of a new school of art."

Mr. Watson finally condescended, after being prodded by me, to reveal more about this friendship between the errant daughter of his client and the artist. It seemed that Miss Lucy Cheston had appeared deeply interested in the works displayed in the studio. A few days after this visit she returned alone, and secured an interview with Gruere, the artist. She asked permission to become his pupil, and he consented. At once she began her studies which she pursued with every indication of profound interest in her teacher's original technique. Miss Cheston spoke with admiration of him and his methods on all occasions. But as time passed she lost her rounded face and figure, and began to look wan and haggard. Her friends suspected that the intensity with which she pursued her art studies was beginning to wear on her both physically and mentally. And then suddenly the aspiring art student disappeared, and simultaneously the artist vanished from his studio and his usual haunts.

Gruere was married, and his wife was proprietor of a bookshop. When questioned regarding her husband's whereabouts, she professed to know nothing about them. She was the kind of woman, said my visitor, who would have very little interest in anything not pertinent to herself, since she was a completely self-centered individual. Mr. Watson went on to say that Gruere had exhibited in London and New York under the patronage of a well-known collector of art objects and antiques, who was considered a connoisseur in his particular line and, incidentally, had accumulated a considerable fortune. This man was described to me as an Armenian by birth, named Arnim Takatyan; he was forty-five years old and an extremely dapper dresser.

It was not easy to draw this information from Watson, who had the weary air of one wasting his time. I asked him, step by step, precisely what had been done by his private detectives, and I laid special stress upon the rôle played by the art connoisseur.

"Oh, everything possible has been looked into in that direction," he said, with a shrug. The Armenian, he maintained, simply had an interest in the artist's success; undoubtedly this interest was increased since he had created a demand for the works from Gruere's brush. Further, as his patron, he had been instrumental in widely advertising his protégé, and had sold many of his pictures. Both artist and dealer thus contributed to each other's financial success.

"Have you considered the possibility of the artist being in contact with the Armenian?" I asked Watson.

"Yes, yes, we considered all that, and we have exhausted

every possibility in that direction, I can assure you. Nothing to that phase of the case."

As for the artist, he had been described to me by the lawyer as a man who "lived for art alone." He would go for days without giving any attention to his personal appearance. Even food was often forgotten by him unless a meal was brought to him. He was on these occasions completely absorbed in his work. When, later, we interviewed his wife, she told us that when Gruere came out of his trance long enough to eat he appeared to be entirely unconscious of what he was eating. It was this phase of his character which had seemed to capture the imagination of his eager pupil.

When reviewing the case afterward, I decided that Miss Cheston was probably impressed by what she thought were manifestations of genius. She had been heard to say that the relations between Gruere and herself were far more than those of teacher and pupil. According to the girl, the artist declared she was an inspiration to him. Thus she basked in reflected glory, for, mediocre or entirely lacking in talent herself, she maintained that she was fully recompensed for any sacrifices she might make in behalf of her teacher, by the knowledge that she fanned the flame of genius in him. The two, seemingly, lived in their own imagination at least, on a very exalted plane, in a rarefied atmosphere, far above all mundane things.

So far as I was concerned, I felt certain that the connoisseur was the one person who would be apt to know the whereabouts of the pair: the enthralled "genius" and his handmaiden. The art dealer was the one channel through which the artist could dispose of his work, and having no means other than those derived from his brush, he would be obliged to market his products. When I suggested this aspect of the matter to Mr. Watson, he was unimpressed. He repeated that there was nothing to the idea. By this time I was a little exasperated by his attitude, and his apparent boredom at being questioned about a matter which he felt had been so thoroughly gone into by himself.

At length, I said to him: "If this case has been so thoroughly covered by men as capable as you have described your private detectives to be, supplemented by your own efforts, why come to us? Why bring us a job you consider impossible to work out? Is it because you wish to impress your client that you have left nothing undone? I think that is your only purpose in coming to us. You do not think it possible for the 'stupid' police to secure results when you and those guided by you have failed. I cannot see why you waste your valuable time—and mine—asking me to listen to a story that has no point. Why give me details of a case as hopeless of solution as you seem to consider this one to be?" And I arose to terminate the interview.

Then the lawyer changed his manner. It was apparent from his attitude that he had undergone a change of viewpoint regarding the police. Since I, a mere police officer, had been able to read so easily his purpose in visiting us, the police in general, he doubtless figured, were not as obtuse and slow-witted as he had always thought them to be.

Watson said: "Let me apologize. I admit your criticism is justified. I did come to you, not expecting that you would be able to solve this mystery, but to satisfy my client that I had left no stone unturned in my efforts to find his daughter. But now I am commencing to feel that perhaps your experience in dealing with problems of this sort may carry you farther than my amateur efforts did me."

After this apology, he continued, "Now, Captain, will you do the best you can in this matter, and forget my previous attitude?"

After this I secured from him a more accurate and detailed description of the missing young woman and her probable companion than had at first been given me. I told the lawyer I believed the Armenian art dealer was the wedge that would split the case. From among my detectives I selected a man who, before joining the Department, had been in the employ of an art collector, and was familiar with the conduct of that line of business. I instructed him to devote his attention wholly to learning everything possible regarding the Armenian, his business methods, his private life, how he was looked upon by others in the same line of business. I wanted anything and everything that would shed light on the man Takatyan. Since Takatyan had been successful in business to an unusual degree, I was confident that, among his competitors would be found men envious of him, who would welcome an opportunity to disclose anything unfavorable they might know regarding him. If we unearthed something that was discreditable to the Armenian we then had a weapon which might enable us to force him to reveal what he knew of the whereabouts of the missing pair.

Two or three days later the detective brought to my office a man whom he introduced as "Mr. Gray," one-time private secretary to Mr. Takatyan. According to Gray, Takatyan had summarily and without cause dismissed him from his service. We welcomed Gray, for here, we felt, was a possible well of information. Our surmise was correct. Gray had been in Takatyan's confidence for a long period. He was in possession of much information regarding the private life of the art dealer. He told about the many young women with whom Takatyan associated, and described the ruthless manner in which the Armenian flung them aside when he tired of them. As for his business life, he was just as inconsiderate of others as he was in his dealings with women. Customers, associates, and inamoratas were all accorded the same kind of treatment.

Gray described one incident typical of many. Takatyan had sold what purported to be the original model from which had been built, over six hundred years ago, a temple in a certain city of Persia. From a rich and credulous spinster who prided herself upon being a collector of antiques, he had secured fifty thousand dollars for this "model," which, in actuality, had been constructed in the basement of Takatyan's place of business by a clever Armenian craftsman. All of this information was invaluable, because it supplied me with the necessary lever to pry from Takatyan any information he possessed regarding the whereabouts of the missing pair.

After Gray had taken his departure, I instructed the detective to call on Takatyan at his place of business. "Ask him if he can throw any light on what might have become of his one-time protégé and friend," I told him. "He will probably say that he does not know where he is. In that event, ask him if he will kindly call at my office, as I desire an opportunity of securing from some one who has known Gruere as intimately as he must have through their long business relationship, an intimate picture of the man."

I felt quite sure that Takatyan would refuse to call on

me, that he would probably instead ask me to come to see him. This, of course, I would not do, except as a last resort. I am a strong believer in the old adage, "A rooster always crows loudest in his own yard." At Mr. Takatyan's place of business I would be just one more policeman; in my own office, surrounded by the machinery of my job, I would have the appearance at least, of being a somewhat important individual. I knew the atmosphere would impress Mr. Takatyan in spite of himself.

The following day the detective reported that he had met with no success in his talk with the Armenian. Takatyan said he had no information, and as for visiting me at my office, that would be "out of the question," because he was such a busy man. However, he said, he would grant me ten minutes of his valuable time, were I to make an appointment to see him at his office.

After securing the art dealer's telephone number I called him. I introduced myself as the superior officer of the detective who had visited him, and then courteously expressed my regret at his inability to call at my office. We did a great deal of Oriental verbal bowing and scraping, each endeavoring to outdo the other in unctuous tone and oily politeness.

"I am deeply grieved to inform you that I am a very busy man," he said. "Otherwise I should be most delighted to have the pleasure and the great honor of visiting you."

Then it was my turn: "While I would be more than pleased to call and talk to you, Mr. Takatyan, it is with great disappointment I am obliged to inform you that I, too, am an exceedingly busy man. Unfortunately a public servant is not permitted to leave his duties, as he owes a definite obligation to the community."

I went on to say that I felt the public also had a definite obligation to assist the slaves in its service, and added that, after all, my desire to see and talk to him had a slight humanitarian motive. I then confided that, during our investigation of this baffling disappearance of the Cheston girl, we had heard numerous rumors regarding those who were known to be friends, acquaintances or business associates of the artist. "And you, too, my dear Mr. Takatyan, have come in for a share in the stories. Doubtless, most of these tales are slanderous, emanating as they do from competitors in business, and I place little faith in them."

I then told him that our efforts in the case had met with so little success that the father of the young woman was becoming a bit restive, and that were he, in his impatience, to appeal to the prosecutor of the county, possibly that prosecutor might not be as mindful of the reputation of Gruere's friends, nor as anxious to protect them from unpleasant publicity, as I had been. I then guardedly hinted at some of the stories that had come to my attention regarding his business and private life.

His voice and attitude changed immediately. "When do you wish to see me, Captain? Now that I think of it, I may be able to spare a little time."

I fixed an hour the following day, and assured him that I would not detain him more than a few minutes.

Sharp on the hour set Takatyan appeared. He was a man about five feet six inches in height, well proportioned, and dressed in the latest mode and best of taste. He had a sallow complexion, a smart black mustache, waxed at the ends, and carried gloves and a cane. After salutations were exchanged in the most approved diplomatic manner, suave talk began to flow. Sometimes it is necessary to impress our visitors with the fact that, after all, policemen can be as polite and mannerly as persons in other walks of life, thus establishing us on an equal footing; the visitor does not then adopt the high and mighty attitude of one who talks down to the "cops."

I immediately got down to business. I asked him as to his business relations with the artist, his patronage, the way in which he disposed of Gruere's pictures. We surveyed, in a general way, the relations existing between them from the purely business standpoint. He said that, as far as he knew, the artist had no agent other than himself for the disposal of his pictures; also, that he had no other source of income. Since he claimed he had no idea of the artist's whereabouts, I asked him if he could explain how Gruere now disposed of his paintings if they were out of touch, because dispose of them he must if he were to earn a livelihood. He was all at sea on this point.

Then I brought up what I expressed as the "imminent danger" of the young woman's father taking the case out of our hands, and placing it with the district attorney of the county. I was relying on my visitor's lack of knowledge of the mechanics in matters of this kind.

I continued: "Were that to happen, I am very much afraid that some of the stories I have heard regarding you might be made public, for instance the one that has been circulated to the effect that you have imposed upon some of your patrons by selling them articles which you represented as antiques but which, as a matter of fact, were manufactured, at a recent date, by yourself. Of course, I know that you would not jeopardize your standing as an art connoisseur in a shady enterprise of this kind but, nevertheless, the story, if it got out, might hurt you."

Takatyan denied that he had ever practiced deception of this sort. He was highly indignant. He had never been guilty of unethical practices.

Then I hinted at some of the stories concerning his private life, and of the scandal that would ensue if such things were made public. Again he was emphatic in his denials.

During all this time his face was expressionless, a perfect poker face. The Oriental is adroit in covering his own feelings, and concealing the operations of his mind behind an impassive mask. But I knew when I touched a tender spot. Each time I made a hit he would change the crossing of his legs. He had forgotten that faces are not the only portions of one's body that express thoughts. His legs were talking loudly, although he was not aware of it.

He remained more than an hour. When I felt I had got him in the right frame of mind to be coöperative, I thanked him for his courtesy in giving us so much of his valuable time. He, on his part, assured me that if at any time in future we felt he could assist us, it would be his great pleasure to do so. We parted with mutual expressions of regard. I was quite certain, however, that I had inoculated him with the virus I had intended: a fear of evil consequences to himself.

Two days later I had evidence that I had pursued the right course in my dealings with him. Shortly after my arrival at my office that morning, Mr. Watson, the lawyer, telephoned me.

"Captain, I think you are a wizard."

"How is that?"

"My client, Mr. Cheston, received last night a telegram from his daughter requesting that Mr. Takatyan be not annoyed, nor in any way exposed to peril, as he had had no part in her or the artist's disappearance. Lucy also disclosed their whereabouts in Novia Scotia."

Within a week the artist was back in his studio, and the young woman in the home of her father. I thought then, and I still believe, that the relations between teacher and pupil were platonic. Possessing little or no talent herself, and being of the hero-worshiping type, the girl considered that in her artist friend she had discovered a man of genius, and was content to be a satellite. He, on his part, flattered by her admiration, looked upon her as a spiritual influence which would aid him to accomplish great things. She was a fool-hardy girl, and he, judging by what I knew of him, was too inspiration-ridden to be preoccupied with sex.

IX. JUVENILE CASES

UNSATISFACTORY home conditions are responsible for most cases where young people disappear. They are maladjusted to their environment, as the sociologists put it. Often the runaway's mother has earned the reputation among her neighbors of being a wonderful housekeeper. Her home is so spick and span at all hours that she is prepared for any emergency—that is, for any except the one where her son or daughter brings in a friend or two. She cannot have the orderly arranged furnishings disturbed by young intruders; her own children see "Keep off the Grass" signs all over the premises. This type of home is not a pleasant abode for young members of the family; it necessitates too much restraint; their young animal spirits demand greater outlet.

It is not always the mother who is at fault. Not infrequently the male parent constructs a pedestal for himself, mounts it, and insists that the family bow down and adore. That kind of father is self-conscious, fearful that were he to display interest in the things that bulk large in the lives of his adolescent children they might think him undignified, and fail to respect him. He can never bring himself to ask Bill or Tom or Jack how the baseball club is coming on, or what positions they are playing on the football team; to reveal an interest of that sort would, he believes, make him appear ridiculous.

A parent should be friend, confidante, adviser. But all too often young boys and girls who have escaped from their unhappy homes only to be brought back by a detective of the Missing Persons Bureau tell me that theirs were the kind of parents who thought that when shelter, food and clothing had been provided, they had done their full duty toward their offspring.

With the boy, perhaps the second most important reason accounting for his disappearance, is his spirit of adventure—the desire to see the world beyond the horizon of his daily life. To him it is a mysterious place; he is eager to know what it has to give him. Always it has been the prerogative of Youth to build castles in Spain, and such structures necessarily have to be erected beyond the skyline of everyday existence.

Sometimes school-work plays a part in the disappearance of the young, and this applies to both sexes. They despise school; the desirability of acquiring an education is not always properly understood or valued; it is considered a waste of time that could be employed to better advantage. So comes the desire to secure a job, and the money resulting from it. Boys and girls realize they must remain in school if they stay at home, and to dodge that necessity they go out into the world where they are unknown.

Boys seldom come to harm as a result of this experiment. The lad who runs away is almost always a worthwhile youngster, possessing a good square chin and a firm jaw. He has the confidence in himself which will prove a valuable asset later in life when leadership counts. But while it is rarely found that the boy is endangered through a runaway experience, the girl of tender years strikes the snags.

Sometimes it is Romance that lures Youth from home. This proved to be true so far as Becky and Dominick were concerned, and I will tell how this affair began and—ended.

Mrs. Rose Blumenstein, a resident of the lower East Side, came to the Missing Persons Bureau in great excitement one day. She insisted on seeing "The Boss," as she termed its commanding officer. We saw her, and this was her tale of woe:

Her daughter Becky had run away from home. She said she was very much afraid that the girl's reason for doing so was because she had been forbidden to marry Dominick Isola. Becky, sixteen years of age, had been for some time keeping clandestine company with Dominick, aged seventeen, an Italian youth who had gone to school with her, and who lived in the same neighborhood. The mother learned of the affair, and forbade her to continue it. When the matter was put up to Becky in these terms, Mrs. Blumenstein said her daughter insisted that she had a right to go with whom she pleased; Dominick was a nice boy, she loved him, and therefore it made no difference to her whether he was Jew or Gentile.

"You might as well say 'Yes' and be through with it," Becky had declared, angrily, "because we're going to marry anyhow."

We took Becky's description. She was five feet seven inches; weighed 115 pounds, had dark hair, brown eyes, and wore, the day she disappeared, a tan dress and brown hat. A detective was put on the case and the search for Becky commenced.

JUVENILE CASES

The day following the visit of Becky's distracted and irate mother, Dominick's equally incensed mother appeared upon the scene. She requested the assistance of the Bureau in locating her son, Dominick, who had run away from home two days before. She said she had discovered Dominick "keeping company" with a Jewish girl, and when she charged him with it, he had asserted his right to associate with whom he pleased. Becky was a nice girl, and simply because she was Jewish did not alter the situation at all. He loved her, and that was that, and what was his mother going to do about it?

Mrs. Isola related the story of this unreasonable conduct on the part of her son, with Latin tragedy of voice and gesture. "I'd rather see my Dominick dead than married to that Becky!" she said at parting.

As both runaways were from the same neighborhood, the same detective had both cases. The usual course of questioning companions ensued; in most instances those quizzed were mutual friends of the pair. It was learned that Dominick had thrown up his job as packer in a shipping room; he had told friends he was going to get work elsewhere. The detective succeeded in tracing him to his new place of employment in another section of the city where he was working as a loader for one of the large department stores.

Dominick was approached by the detective and gruffly asked where he had hidden Becky. Detectives have a way of making a startling approach to boys of the age of Dominick. After the boy had at first denied any knowledge of her whereabouts, he finally admitted that he and Becky were living together in a furnished room in a street remote from their respective homes. When asked if he did not know he was doing wrong, he guilelessly declared that he loved Becky and she loved him, and that inasmuch as their parents had denied them the right to marry, they took the one course possible for them: they decided to live together without the formality of marriage until they were of an age to marry without the consent of parents. They did what many older people do and term "living their own lives."

Dominick led the detective to the furnished room where Becky was waiting. Both young people were brought to my office, and their parents summoned. The Blumensteins were asked if they desired the prosecution of Dominick. It was explained that it would be necessary, in that event, for Becky to be taken before the Grand Jury to tell her story; and if an indictment of Dominick were secured, she would be forced to appear in open court to testify against him. In other words, their daughter's impulsive act would become so widely known it would probably ruin her future.

The Blumensteins wisely decided that in Becky's interests the matter should be dropped. I was guided, in this instance, by the wishes of the girl's parents. The young couple was brought to my private office and warned of the consequences that would follow a repetition of their act: Dominick would, in all probability, be sent to a reformatory, and Becky to an institution for incorrigible girls. Both appeared deeply impressed with the ease with which they had been found, so it was not difficult to convince them that it was next to impossible to successfully hide away from the police for any length of time. Dominick appreciated the predicament from which he was escaping, but of Becky's like reaction I was not so sure. She was sullen and resentful, and I did not think it was a propitious time to try to make her see the folly of her ways. I, therefore, asked her mother to bring her back the following day.

Mrs. Blumenstein arrived the next morning with Becky. When closeted alone with the girl, I discovered that she was a most interesting type. As is my custom, I began talking *at* her, because I have learned that we must erase from the juvenile mind the natural fear they have of the Police, especially after they have done what their elders, at least, believe to be wrong.

At first Becky looked at me resentfully, a hard expression on her face, her lips pinched tight, hatred in her brown eyes.

I said to her: "Becky, I am not going to scold you for what you have done. From experience, I know it to be unwise, but I don't blame you for it because, after all, you were just following your natural impulses. You like Dominick, and you did not see any reason in the world why you should not do what your fondness for him prompted you to. But, nevertheless, it was the wrong thing to do, because if you had the right to do it, every one else would have exactly the same right. And if the rest of the world did what you have done, there would be a whole lot of confusion. Few of us would even know who our fathers were."

As I talked to Becky along this line, the stubborn look gradually disappeared from her face. Her eyes lost their resentfulness, and took on an expression of understanding; the moment that happened I knew we were on a sympathetic basis. Then I brought up the matter of Dominick in a more definite way. Before I was through talking with her, she agreed with me that it would not do at all for her to marry a boy alien in religion and race, particularly when the parents of both Dominick and herself objected to the match. I reminded her, too, that after all neither was old enough to form an enduring attachment, since they were both little more than children.

With the keen perception of her race, Becky seemed to comprehend at once, and to be rather impressed by the fact that I had not "bawled" her out, as she later told me she had expected me to do.

She asked: "Are you going to send me away?"

I might say here that the business of "sending away" is the bugbear of many children of the congested East Side. Their parents use that term so often that the youngsters come to fear the phrase, and many times run off to avoid being "sent away." I assured Becky there was no thought in my mind of sending her away, and told her that I felt sure she was too sensible a girl to make it necessary for me to do that. Becky had a most attractive smile, and she flashed it on me now. She had rather a large mouth, filled with excellent teeth, but they had been woefully neglected.

By the time we had reached the confidential stage I felt that I could safely advance some suggestions as to her personal appearance. I complimented her on her teeth, and said that it was really too bad she was neglecting them. Then I read her a lecture on their care: "Becky, when you go home, I want you to get at those fine teeth and scour them. If you cannot afford to buy toothpaste and a brush, you can do this: get some of your mother's kitchen salt, put it in a little strip of cloth, wet it, and work it over your teeth and gums. It is the best dentifrice I know of, and it will whiten your teeth, clean them, kill germs and harden your gums."

Doubtless, manufacturers of dental preparations will not

thank me for this gratuitous advice. And I dare say that many people will feel that dental advice is a strange function for a policeman to take on himself.

Becky, by this time, was listening to everything I said with an expression which convinced me that she considered me a friend. I had wiped from her mind the belief that policemen take delight in annoying and interfering with people—a view, I may say, which is held by many much older persons than Becky. To her I had become a human and understanding person, one trying to be of help to her. We had reached a basis of mutual sympathy.

Mrs. Blumenstein had said that the family needed Becky's financial assistance, and that she wanted her to go to work as quickly as possible. I suggested that she be given a few days in order to rest, and, in the meantime, we would see what we could do in the way of securing employment for her. A few days later I was able to supply Becky with a job in a department store, through the manager who was a friend of mine. When I sent for her to come to my office, so that I could tell her about the work, and give her a letter of introduction, I tried again to impress her with the fact that we were friends, and that she must not hesitate to keep in touch with me.

"I really want you to do that, Becky," I told her, but I also disabused her mind of any idea that I might, in a sense, be placing her on probation. I felt certain that she left me feeling we were friends, and flattered at the privilege (for I made it appear a privilege) of calling me up. I reminded her that our communication would necessarily have to be by telephone, since her working hours and mine were about the same. This all happened in midsummer and, except for an occasional telephone call, I did not hear from her until a week or two after the Christmas and New Year holidays.

Then one day the desk man in the outer office announced that a young woman wanted to see me. He was instructed to show her in. A real vision entered the office. She was tall, well dressed, attractive, with a gleaming smile. She came toward me with her hand outstretched, and until she said: "Why, Captain, don't you know me? I'm Becky," I did not recognize her. It was evident that she had accepted my salt formula, for her teeth were dazzling. She would have made an excellent dentifrice advertisement. She was attired in excellent taste, and looked like a young débutante who had just alighted from her limousine.

Becky had gained several pounds since I had last seen her; the angularities of her lank five feet seven had filled out. I asked her how she had been getting on, and she reverted to East Side parlance:

"Swell! Simply swell until yesterday when they gave me the gate."

"How is that, Becky? Have you been misbehaving?"

"No, sir. Everything was going along fine until I was canned."

Becky added that she was not at fault. "I guess it was because business slowed up after the holidays. They let out quite a few of the other girls, too."

I got in touch by telephone with my manager friend. He did not know of Becky's dismissal, and I asked him if he would reinstate her if she had been dropped for no other cause than a reduction of staff. He requested a few minutes in which to check on Becky's record, saying he would call me back.

While waiting for his call, I asked Becky how she had been behaving herself in the matter of keeping company with boys. She promptly replied that she wasn't wasting time in that way; she felt that it did not pay for a girl to go around with them until she was old enough to pick one she could marry and, anyhow, she did not think a girl should select a boy her own age.

"He should be old enough to have a business," said the now sagacious Becky. "He should be able to support a wife, without making it necessary for her to work in a store." Here she revealed the practicality of her race.

The manager then telephoned and informed me that Becky's record was all right. "Send her back," he said. "Don't worry about her job; she can have this one as long as she makes good."

Becky evidently behaved herself, for she remained with this store for almost two years longer, advancing in responsibility, and getting several raises in salary. When she did leave it was of her own accord, in order to marry a man of her own race. The one she picked was "in cloaks and suits." Today Becky is riding in just the kind of car I had pictured her in that day she called at my office.

It is now several years since Becky's marriage occurred, and she and I are still friends. The thing that pleases me most about this case, aside from the fact that my interest in the girl has been repaid in results, is that Becky, after the birth of each of her children (she has four) brings them to my office in turn to exhibit them to me. Her life is happy, if her face and what she says are any indications.

On one of her recent visits to me, she said: "Captain, you

are really responsible for my happiness. You were so kind to me you made it possible for me to leave the gutter."

I appreciated that little speech. Sentimental? Why "cops" are full of sentiment!

Little Peter Spargo was a rascal! We knew that the moment we saw a snapshot which his mother brought to us as an aid toward finding him.

One day his parents, Mr. and Mrs. Peter Spargo, rushed to the station house of the precinct where they resided in the Hell's Kitchen section, and excitedly told the desk officer of the disappearance of their son, Peter, ten years old. They were certain that he must have been kidnaped. As a matter of fact, the ten-year-old runaway is rather unusual. Boys of that tender age seldom take the bit in their teeth and decide to go it on their own, so that the police of the precinct were not altogether sure that Peter had not been kidnaped, or become the victim of some degenerate or pervert, nor were we at the Missing Persons Bureau, when the case was brought to our attention a few minutes later.

The detective to whom this job fell was ordered to make a thorough search of the neighborhood. Cellars and roofs were combed, and inquiries were made in all directions. Peter's playmates were questioned, but without result; his friends shrugged their shoulders with the expressive gesture of the gamin, a movement which said, "We don't know nothin'." Assistance of the uniformed force was called in to make the hunt a thorough one. Coal-bins, boxes, and barrels were peered into; in fact, everything that could shelter a body the size of Peter's was searched during the following two days.

JUVENILE CASES

Finally our detective projected himself back through the years to the ten year old period of his own life, and attempted to visualize what, at that time, he might have done were he a particularly assertive youngster of the type Peter was described as. Some of the children had said Peter was "de boss of de gang." So the detective, scouting outside the immediate neighborhood of the boy's home, climbed to the roof of an eight-story loft building several blocks away, one with the usual water tank towering above it, on the theory that that would serve as a good hideout, and one which would be least expected to shelter a boy of Peter's age.

Sure enough, under the protection of that big water tank Peter had established a den—what to him was a regular camp! Some old pieces of carpet had been utilized as sides for the "tent," as he called it. Soiled comforters were used for a bed, and when the detective found the ten-year-old rebel in his "secret camp," he was the central figure of a most amusing scene. All around him were empty milk bottles, and pieces of dry rolls, with the most succulent parts eaten out. The boy had on a cap four sizes too large, with a big visor which came down over his eyes, dirty overalls intended for a boy years older than he, the slack taken up with suspenders, and his face was wearing an expression, which he no doubt thought in keeping with his desperate character.

It was quite evident that Peter was the type that could well be designated as "de Boss." When he was questioned about his friends, he gave the names of several of the boys who had been interviewed by the detective and who had denied all knowledge of his whereabouts. When asked how he got his supply of food, Peter said that "de gang" had "swiped" the milk and rolls from doorways in the early morning hours, and that sometimes they had even brought him cake stolen from stores in the neighborhood, or food filched from their own homes. Peter explained that the quilts and blankets had been "lifted" by the gang from clotheslines on the roofs of tenements in the vicinity.

"De Boss" would let down a rope, after dark, to which would be attached a small sack, and after his henchmen had filled it, he would haul up his supplies. When asked how he got to the roof of the loft building, which was occupied by sweatshops, he said, "Sneaked by de boid at de door." After successfully passing the elevator man he had scurried up the stairs, and ducked through the scuttle door on to the roof, where he pitched camp. He had been there for more than a week.

When the detective interrogated him as to his reason for leaving home, Peter said, "De old man he beat me if I ain't in de house by ten o'clock."

He was ten years old, but tough as they come, in fact, so hard-boiled and difficult to handle that his own mother did not want him in the home once he was found. She said that he frequently broke open the gas meter and stole quarters it contained, to say nothing of performing other acts of vandalism.

We were much interested in this case, and the detective working on it was particularly impressed by what, even to him, inured as he was to these happenings, appeared to be an unusual situation. It was remarkable in that it involved a very young gang leader, for he was "de Boss" in quite the same sense that Capone, in the adult realm, was the monarch of his kingdom. Peter, too, had henchmen who

were willing to obey his slightest whim or order, young out-
laws in one sense, because they had not hesitated at the
petty larcenies necessary in order to supply their chief with
nourishment. They were willing to serve him in any way
in his time of need.

Eventually Peter, a true type of incorrigible, who could
not be restrained at home, was committed to a reformatory.

The trail of Marietta Gonzales, who disappeared from
home, took us far afield. Manuel Gonzales, a cigar manufacturer, with many flourishes of the hands and a look of
anxiety in his eyes, stood before the desk officer in an upper
East Side precinct one afternoon about 3 o'clock and reported the disappearance of his daughter Marietta. He said
she had been sent by him to the bank about 2 o'clock to
deposit $460.00 which had been received from customers
during the day. It was his habit, he said, to send her to the
bank each day to make deposits, and when she failed to
return after the usual interval, he got in touch with the
bank, but was told she had not been there. Hurried inquiries
were made in the immediate neighborhood of the factory,
but no one was found who had seen her.

Gonzales described his daughter as a beautiful girl, seventeen years of age, five feet five inches in height, weighing
one hundred and eighteen pounds; brown eyes and dark
brown hair. She was wearing a blue, two-piece dress, rather
youthful in style, and a blue hat. He was positive the girl
had met with foul play for, as he explained, she had been
his bookkeeper and messenger to the bank for a long time,
and had always been faithful to her job.

MISSING MEN

Search for the girl was instituted. Some credence was given to the view of the father in the matter of foul play, for the reason that he had noticed a group of young fellows, whom he described as "tough-looking" and strangers in the vicinity, near his factory early in the day. Cellars, roofs, alleyways and backyards of houses for blocks around were searched for the girl. Neighbors were questioned. Suspicious strangers in the neighborhood were summarily queried, and made to account for themselves between the time the girl left the factory for the bank and the hour when she should have returned. Following this thorough, albeit fruitless, search of the neighborhood, we began to speculate as to what a girl of her age and her Latin blood might do. She was mature for her years, and was said to be extremely attractive. But Marietta, we learned, was not at all interested in boys. She had been heard to express the opinion that young men were "boobs" and not worth wasting time on.

Having exhausted all possibilities which the immediate vicinity might yield, we turned our attention in a new direction, on the assumption that the girl might have tired of the humdrum office work which formed her daily routine and decided to adopt some more congenial occupation, such as going on the stage, becoming a screen star, or the like. There was some ground for this theory, since she had often been heard to express great admiration for movie stars. In fact, she did possess some of the necessary qualities for the films. She was handsome, had a good figure, and was young and vivacious. What, then, would be the first step taken by a girl motivated by that ambition? The answer, naturally, was: make herself as attractive as possible, by dress and otherwise. Fine dresses she did not possess, but she did have her father's four hundred and sixty dollars. Expensive clothes were thus procurable.

So the dress departments of the nearest stores were visited until finally, in one well-known shop, a wide-awake saleswoman recalled having waited on a girl of Marietta's description, who had told her a story which, doubtless, she had spun in order to account for the fact that a young girl was spending money so lavishly on her own initiative. She had told the saleswoman that she was much older than she appeared to be, but that her parents wanted to keep her looking as young as possible. This had annoyed her, and she had decided to take the bit in her teeth, and buy some clothes in keeping with her real age.

After purchasing several dresses, she asked to be directed to the baggage department, saying that she wanted to buy a bag in which to carry her purchases home, and that in any event she would need one shortly when she paid a visit to friends out of town. After getting a detailed description of the dresses which the girl assumed to be Marietta had bought, the detective went to the luggage department, and it was not long before he had located the salesman who had sold the girl a bag, and had helped her put her bundles in it.

At this point the trail was lost, only to be picked up again at one of the ticket offices of the New York Central Railroad. Here a ticket agent recalled a girl purchasing a ticket for Chicago. He remembered her because of the fact that she appeared to know nothing whatever about traveling, evidenced by her asking his advice as to whether or not she should have a Pullman seat, and how long it would take to reach Chicago. It seemed evident that the girl was Marietta.

Our search then shifted to Chicago, and the coöperation of the Chicago Police Department was asked. It was suggested that Marietta would probably apply to the Y. W. C. A. for shelter, because we had learned that she had at times frequented one of the branches of this organization in New York City, and was probably familiar with the fact that "Y's" were often chosen by unaccompanied girl travelers. We also asked the Chicago police to visit hotels, rooming houses, and all likely places which might shelter young women.

After about a week Chicago learned that Marietta had stopped at one of the branches of the Y. W. C. A., but had checked out the day before the discovery was made. She had registered under the name of "Dolores Florentine." Then began a systematic check-up of Chicago employment agencies, and it was finally discovered at the office of a well-known railroad restaurant chain that a girl answering her description, and giving the name of "Dolores Florentine" had appeared at their office and had been accepted as a waitress for one of their branches at a station well on toward the Pacific coast.

As I did not want to take a chance on the efficiency of the police force in a place where the population was so small that probably its police needs were supplied by a single constable, I wired the manager of this restaurant direct, asking him regarding "Dolores Florentine" and describing her possible costume. Here accurate description was of value, and the detective had, of course, secured details of the dresses and other apparel she had bought in the New York store, and which she would probably be wearing at this time.

About two hours later a reply to our wire was received to the effect that Dolores Florentine had the day before drawn her week's pay, and had left with the expressed intention of going to Los Angeles. Now we did some computing, and also some guesswork. When we checked with the store in New York we found that Marietta had used up the major portion of the cash she had been supposed to deposit, and that she probably had only fifty or sixty dollars more than enough to buy her ticket to Chicago. Then, after paying her expenses for a week in Chicago, we knew she would have very little money left. The restaurant company had supplied her with transportation to the Western branch, since the employees of this restaurant chain were given passes.

Our search shifted to the Far West. Surely Hollywood would be her final goal. Dolores Florentine of Hollywood! Potential cinema material, according to the dreams of Marietta. At any rate, we took a chance on it, and got in touch with Hollywood. By a fortuitous circumstance a detective of our Department was in Los Angeles at this time. We wired him the full history of the disappearance, and suggested that possibly Hollywood might have been the Pied Piper for Marietta Gonzales, alias "Dolores Florentine."

This detective did some fine work. Within two days he had succeeded in tracing the girl to the home of a well-known woman motion picture star. Here Marietta had applied for a position as maid, and had secured it. It might appear that she was getting into motion pictures by the back door but that literally was just what she was attempting to do.

She later confessed to the detective: "I knew nothing of the movie game, so I thought I'd try learning through ob-

183

servation. I felt I could get all the inside stuff by working and living in the home of a movie star."

The detective took her in custody as a runaway, and when he left for the East, as he did the following day, Marietta accompanied him. She was received with open arms by her family; the money she had taken was entirely forgotten.

Our investigation had shown that Marietta, young and unworldly as she was, had come through her experience uncontaminated. All of her contacts had been wholesome ones; her only desire had been to reach Hollywood and a glamorous career. She had wisely taken shelter under proper auspices, and when she was finally returned to her home, she was no worse for her experience, possibly even a little enriched by it.

This next story concerns a boy who made two attempts to escape from the stuffy confines of city life to the wide open spaces, in pursuit of a life of freedom, one which would permit a boy to do all the things he had ever dreamed of doing: hunting, fishing, adventuring.

We will start with the first time he ran away. John Brewster was the fifteen-year-old son of a civil engineer. One morning he failed to appear for his toast and coffee, and his mother, surprised at his absence from the breakfast table, went to his room to arouse him, thinking he had overslept. She found his bed empty, with no evidence of its having been occupied the night before. Excitement prevailed in the household. Johnny was missing! Hasty telephone calls were made to the homes of chums, but they elicited no information; John had not gone visiting. Then the disappearance was reported to us. A detective went to the boy's home, and talked with his parents. John's background was sought. What was his favorite type of reading matter? His sports? His pastimes? Had his school work been satisfactory? Had there been any punishment for lapses from the standard to which a son should conform?

All of this was discussed for the purpose of finding a motive for the boy's disappearance. His home life, it developed, had been perfect; his school work was beyond criticism, and his monthly reports had always shown him in excellent standing. It was found, however, that he was extremely fond of out-of-door life and all kinds of sports. When the detective visited his room he discovered it littered with books of adventure, stories about the boy who lived in the open, and which gave vivid descriptions of hunting and fishing exploits.

Among the boy's belongings was a map of North America. On it was traced, in red ink, a line running from New York up through Canada to Hudson Bay. At the moment, the significance of that red line did not appear, but later when the detective interviewed some of the boy's schoolmates, it became clear that it had a real bearing upon his disappearance. John had often talked over with some of his pals the idea of running away from home, so that he could live as he liked, earning his own living by hunting and trapping. The boy had expressed a conviction that the Hudson Bay section of North America was the ideal place in which to put the plan into practice.

Wires were sent to the police of border towns in northern New York, requesting that a lookout be kept for John, and three or four days later we received a message from Rouses

Point that John was being entertained by the police of that town. Two days he was back in the bosom of his family.

We thought we had finished with John Brewster, but about two years later, on the seventeenth of March, the second anniversary of his last adventure, he again failed to appear at the breakfast table. And again an investigation was commenced with the view of rounding him up or heading him off. A hasty examination by his parents of his belongings disclosed that a rough hiking suit, a change of underwear and shirts, and a twenty-two caliber rifle, which his father had recently given him, were missing.

It was at first assumed that John was making a second attempt to put into execution the plan he had conceived two years before. Steps similar to those taken at that time were repeated. His description was again sent to towns along the Canadian border. After a reasonable time had elapsed without results from those efforts, we decided that the boy had succeeded in making his way past the Canadian barrier, and was probably well en route toward his Eldorado, Hudson Bay. The police of cities and towns through which he might be likely to pass on that journey were communicated with; circulars describing the boy were prepared and mailed, with the request that they be posted at likely points along the route.

Later we learned from the boy's father that he had devoted all his evenings to mailing out circulars independent of those sent out by us. He admitted this in a rather shamefaced way, since he had frequently assured us he was confident everything was being done by the police to find his son. Mr. Brewster repeatedly declared that he had no fear for John's safety; he was confident that his son was able to take care of himself wherever he might be. But he con, fided to us that his principal worry was for John's mother, who was terribly upset by the boy's unaccountable absence. As he said this, the chin of Brewster, Senior, trembled, in proof that his boy's absence had occasioned *him* no worry.

When everything possible had been done to round up the boy, the situation settled down to a routine of watchful waiting. By this time Mr. Brewster had got into the habit of dropping in at my office about twice a month, just to make sure that nothing had been heard from the boy, although he had been told that the moment any information of his whereabouts was secured, he would be notified.

Then one day in midsummer, when he dropped in to see me, I asked him, more for the purpose of making conversa- tion than anything else, since we had already discussed many times all angles of the case, if there was any favorite reading matter of his son's which he had failed to mention. He asked me if he had ever spoken of a certain magazine which de- votes most of its space to stories of outdoor life, and I replied that he had not. Knowing something of the make-up of this publication, and that it carries a page devoted to Personals, I expressed the opinion that we might employ that medium of communicating with John, particularly in light of the fact that Brewster said the boy could scarcely wait for the magazine to be placed on the newsstands before he bought it. I had in mind a "Personal" addressed to him, one which would inform the boy that his parents desired only to be assured of his safety and well-being. Brewster approved of the idea.

I at once called up the editor, and explained to him our vital interest in this matter, asking him if he would give our Personal right-of-way in the next issue, which he readily promised to do. Then things settled down again to the business of waiting.

One morning in October at about 10 o'clock Mr. Brewster rushed into my office. I knew something unusual had happened. His eyes held an entirely different expression from any I had seen there before. He almost shouted: "We have heard from the Boy!"

"Good! Tell me about it."

He drew from his pocket a bulky envelope which contained a letter from his son, an answer to our Personal. I asked him where John was.

The father replied: "Buenos Aires, Argentina."

He proceeded to read to me portions of the letter, a small volume which recited a history of the boy's experiences after leaving home eight months before. Instead of starting for the Canadian wilds, as we had guessed he would, John had gone to Boston because he wanted to see Bunker Hill Monument, the Common, and other historic points. He had taken along his rifle, with the thought that later he might have the opportunity of doing some hunting. Boston, however, quickly consumed his small savings, whereupon the rifle was taken to an "Uncle" of the three gold balls, and pawned. It required but little time to exhaust the proceeds, and then one morning, empty of stomach, he was down near the docks when he heard a shout from a schooner tied up nearby, and he was asked, "Want to sign on, Buddy?"

That was precisely what he desired. A job meant food, and food was what he wanted at that moment most of all. So he became a sailor on board a lumber schooner. The boat was about to sail in ballast for its home port of Halifax to take on a cargo of lumber consigned to Buenos Aires, where in due time it arrived with John on board.

At the time of writing the letter, John stated that the boat was taking on a cargo of bones. Argentina, as we all know, is a great cattle-raising country, and the bones, after the flesh has been turned into "canned Willie" and other beef products, for consumption all over the world, are articles of export, to be made up into "ivory" ornaments, bone-handled knives and the like.

This cargo was consigned to Philadelphia, where it was expected shortly before the holidays. Mr. Brewster, after reading this letter to me, left my office apparently walking on springs. Two or three days before the following Christmas, he called me up one evening at my home, and told me his son had arrived. The ring of his voice amply repaid me for all the efforts made to accomplish this reunion.

Mr. Brewster reported that his son had gained several inches and pounds, and was almost a man. He asked if he might bring him in to see me and, of course, permission was granted. Between the Christmas and New Year holidays, John and his father called one day. It could easily be seen that young Brewster's experience had not been harmful; he had become a big, broad-shouldered young man, radiating self-confidence and possessing the grip of a blacksmith.

I had the idea that his experience on the return voyage might have cured him of any penchant he might still have had for a sailor's life, and I asked him regarding the condition of the ship, loaded as it was with green bones, particularly during the period when it passed through the tropics.

He laughingly assured me that he had become accustomed

to the odor. "But," said he, "there was one thing I didn't like so very much. I couldn't stand the darn maggots; they were all over the boat."

This experience, I thought, should have curbed the desire for roving but, much to my surprise, John showed no distaste for continuing the life of a sailor. He expressed it as his opinion that a sailor's life was the only kind of existence for a "he-man." A little later, and not in John's presence, I discussed the situation with his father, and suggested that, inasmuch as the boy had a strong predilection for a life at sea, it might be wise not to oppose it.

"Don't go against your son's wishes," I urged. "I feel it is your duty to help him, as far as you can, to realize his desire. Why not give him a course at the State Nautical School?"

Mr. Brewster acted on the suggestion, and his son was sent to this school. He was given credit for one term's work as a result of his experience at sea, and was entered for the winter term. Two years later he graduated with a certificate of proficiency that entitled him to a mate's rating. Today John Brewster, twice a runaway, is First Officer on board one of our Transatlantic liners.

X. MISCELLANEOUS CASES

THERE are cases in the files of the Missing Persons Bureau that defy classification. Since so many of these give illuminating slants on human nature and the strange quirks in the make-up of men and women, I am going to outline a few of them here, and entitle them "Miscellaneous."

This one, for example, constitutes a drama in which loyalty, deception, cruelty and vicious temper are blended. A woman played the star rôle in it, and the case came to our attention in the summer of 1924. At that time Mrs. Laura Spencer, a wealthy woman of some social prominence, came to the Bureau and reported that her ward, known as "Grace Spencer," due to her long residence with the family, had disappeared one evening six weeks before.

Mrs. Spencer told us that, fearing publicity might result if she reported the girl's disappearance, she had employed a firm of private detectives to make a search for her. But, continued Mrs. Spencer, after she had paid them several hundred dollars for a fruitless hunt, in which not a single clew to Grace's whereabouts had developed, she had finally decided to appeal to us.

Asked for a description of the girl, Mrs. Spencer said she was seventeen years of age, five feet four inches in height, and weighed one hundred and twenty pounds. The girl had a fair complexion, light-brown hair, and blue eyes. Mrs. Spencer said that five years before she had taken her from an orphanage, and, since then, had treated her as a member of the family.

When the society matron was asked to describe the clothing worn by Grace at the time of her disappearance, I observed a noticeable hesitation on her part. At length she replied, saying that the girl probably would not be wearing the same clothing, for she was vain of her appearance, and, doubtless, would have availed herself of the first opportunity of securing different apparel. The reason for Mrs. Spencer's hesitancy when questioned about the girl's clothes was later made clear.

Mrs. Spencer was one of those energetic, restless women, and she appeared to be about thirty-eight or forty years of age. She had bright red hair and brown eyes. I judged her to be a termagant, a woman of ungovernable temper, and one difficult to please.

I summoned a detective available at the moment, and asked Mrs. Spencer to give him all details of the girl's disappearance. According to her, Grace had few, if any, friends or acquaintances. She was a bit vague as to her attendance at school, saying that her ward had suffered so much from illness that she had been unable to go to school with any degree of regularity, and that, as a result, she had been forced to account to truant officers for her absence by producing a doctor's certificate. She had, therefore, permitted the girl to receive instruction from the governess engaged for her own young daughter.

As Mrs. Spencer described Grace's place in the family

one would gather that it was very nearly perfect. It appeared that she had given the orphan every advantage one would ordinarily bestow upon a daughter.

As soon as Mrs. Spencer left the office, the detective checked the Departmental records of Arrests and Aided cases, the latter covering all cases in which public ambulances are employed. He also searched the Morgue records, thus clearing the slate, as it were, of the possibility of an accident accounting for the girl's disappearance. These records showed nothing that might have any bearing on the case, so he then got down to the business of tracing the girl. Tradesmen in the vicinity of the Spencer home were questioned, and this inquiry disclosed the fact that Grace was quite well known to them. Several of the storekeepers described her as the family slavey, for she seemed to be continually occupied in running errands, carrying market supplies, and bringing bundles to the Spencer home. The tradesmen said the girl always appeared scantily clothed, regardless of how the thermometer registered.

Through a clerk in one of the stores, the detective succeeded in tracing Grace. This man had a cousin who had, at one time, worked with him, and who knew Grace, from having seen her in the store. Since that time he had secured a better job in another section of the city, and one day a short time time ago he had noticed, much to his surprise, the girl standing among a group of customers, and he had spoken to her. She appeared startled and disturbed at being recognized, and hurriedly left without having made any purchases.

He watched her as she went down the street, and saw her enter the home of one of the customers of the store.

He forgot the incident until, several days later, he was reminded of it when he met his cousin, who told him the story of the girl's disappearance. In this roundabout way the incident reached the detective, who then called on the store clerk who had learned the girl's whereabouts and was directed to the house.

He rang the bell, and a young woman opened the door. Grace herself stood before him. The detective recognized her at once, from the description Mrs. Spencer had given him.

"How do you do, Grace. What are you doing here?"

He then explained who he was. Grace seemed greatly taken aback, and quickly stepped outside the hall on to the porch, half closing the door behind her.

"Please don't speak too loudly," she implored. "Miss Baker is ill, and, in any event, I don't want her to know that the police are looking for me."

"How old are you, Grace?"

"Twenty-four."

The detective, as soon as he saw her, had observed her appearance of maturity. She certainly looked twenty-four, and he was inclined to believe the girl's estimate.

But he said to her, "Mrs. Spencer says you are only seventeen."

Grace, a well-mannered, rather gentle appearing girl, spoke up resentfully: "Mrs. Spencer has told you a lie. She knows exactly how old I am. I am twenty-four, and I can prove it!"

At this point he asked her if she would be kind enough to accompany him, because it was necessary for her to establish the fact that she was over twenty-one years of age;

otherwise he would be obliged to turn her over to Mrs. Spencer.

"I am twenty-four years old," insisted the girl. "And neither Mrs. Spencer nor any one else has any right to interfere with me."

This, of course, was true if her age was actually what she claimed it to be, and the detective believed she was telling him the truth. However, to avoid assuming all responsibility, he induced her to accompany him to the corner drug-store, from which place he called me by telephone, and relayed the story to me. I instructed him to persuade the girl to come to my office, after assuring her that if she were the age she claimed, we would protect her against all interference.

She consented to go with him, and within half an hour they arrived. A glance at her convinced me that she was, in all probability, twenty-four years of age, if not older. She was embarrassed and nervous in her present surroundings, and I knew that it was probably the first time she had found herself in a Police Department office. After reassuring her, I asked her to tell me her story, how it happened that she had gone to live with Mrs. Spencer, and about her experiences there.

She said that in 1910, when she was ten years of age, she had been taken to a convent by her mother, and left there until 1912, when Mrs. Spencer, with the permission of the Sisters, took her into her home. She had at once placed her in charge of her infant daughter, who was then about six months old. Her rôle from that time on had been that of nursemaid to the baby. Grace took her for airings in the carriage and later, as she grew older, for daily walks in the park. She was held responsible for the child from the moment she left her crib in the morning until she was tucked away for the night.

Grace went on to relate that Mrs. Spencer had a violent temper, and often treated her with extreme cruelty. When questioned as to her illness, and her inability to attend school, as stated by Mrs. Spencer, she said her health was perfect, but that she had not been permitted to go to school, because Mrs. Spencer had insisted that she needed her constant help at home. Her foster mother had, in some way, secured a certificate from a doctor to the effect that Grace was in poor health and unable to attend school. Sometimes Mrs. Spencer, in her frequent rages, had beaten the girl brutally, she claimed. In proof of this Grace pulled up her sleeves and showed me scars on her arms where she said she had been struck by Mrs. Spencer at various times. The girl also leaned toward me, parted her hair, and displayed a well-defined scar which she said was the result of having been struck by a plate thrown by her foster mother.

It was obvious that, if the girl's statement that she had been in a convent in 1910 at the age of ten were true, she must be twenty-four years of age. I asked her if she knew in what convent she had been placed, and she gave the name of one on Long Island. I referred to a telephone directory, got the number of this institution, called up and asked to speak to the Mother Superior. When she answered the telephone, I told her who I was, and explained that I wanted information regarding a child who had been placed in her care in 1910.

She at once asked, "Is the child little Grace?"

Receiving an affirmative answer, the Mother Superior said she remembered all about her, because at that time she was only a Sister in the convent, and the little girl had been her particular pet. The nun explained that the convent did not make a practice of taking in children for shelter, and it was only at the earnest solicitation of the child's mother, who brought her to them with the statement that she wanted her daughter to be properly brought up in the Catholic faith, that they had been induced to depart from their usual rule and receive her. The mother had agreed to pay a stipulated sum monthly and, at the time of her visit, had paid down a month's maintenance.

"That was the last time we saw her until July, 1912, when she reappeared at the convent, and informed us she had come for her daughter," she concluded.

You can readily understand how interesting this information was to me. After the Mother Superior had inquired about the girl who had once been her charge, and I had assured her of her well-being and thanked her for the information, I hung up the receiver and turned to the girl.

"Grace, why didn't you tell me that Mrs. Spencer was your mother?"

At first the girl was nonplussed, but at last answered, rather reluctantly, "I had a reason for not telling you."

"But why did you deceive me, when your every impulse should have been directed toward justifying yourself? If your mother was cruel to you, as you stated, why didn't you tell me all the facts?"

The girl's attitude was puzzling. Her explanation is one of the strangest stories of filial loyalty to which I have ever listened. Any one would naturally assume that she would have been delighted to reveal the true relationship at the first opportunity, but this young woman's fancied duty toward her mother kept her lips sealed, even in face of persecution.

Grace told me that her father had died when she was eight years old, and that her mother had been obliged to go to work to support herself and her child. Feeling that the burden was too heavy for her as the girl grew older, she placed her in the convent. Shortly afterward she became acquainted with a wealthy man, and after a few weeks married him. During their brief courtship, her fiancé had told her that he would never marry a woman who had been married before. He had even declared that he would leave any woman if he found she had been married before and had deceived him. All this time Grace's mother had been posing as a single woman, keeping her widowhood a secret. After hearing these pronouncements by her prospective second husband, she was more determined than ever to prevent him from discovering her status and deserting her as a result of it.

"It so frightened my mother that she never disclosed to him that she was a widow," explained Grace. "She impressed me with the importance and necessity of keeping our real relationship secret, for she told me she was positive her husband would leave her if he ever learned about it. I promised her never to say anything regarding my true identity."

For a while after her marriage, Mrs. Spencer had ignored the little daughter in the convent, but after the birth of her second child, she schemed how to get the girl back. She told her husband she was going to take in an orphan to look after the baby. From the moment Grace entered her mother's home she was instructed to call her "Mrs. Spencer," and from

then on had continued to play her unique rôle. Grace said
Mr. Spencer had treated her with much more kindness than
her mother had. Two or three times when her mother, in a
fit of rage, had driven her from the apartment and out into
the hall, on a cold winter night, with the remark, "That's
a good enough place for you," Mr. Spencer had smuggled
out blankets to her to protect her from the cold.

She had continued to live with Mrs. Spencer up until the
time she ran away, which was about two months ago. The
"last straw" had been the injury she received when her red-
haired mother, in one of her fits of anger, had hurled a plate
at her, cutting her scalp. The girl, unable any longer to endure this abuse, decided to secure a job, if possible. Then
one day she read in the "Help Wanted" column of a morning
paper an advertisement for a companion to an invalid.

Hurriedly leaving the Spencer home, without disclosing her
purpose, she called on the advertiser and secured the position. Her new employer, a Miss Adelaide Baker, told her
that she was a retired school-teacher and had become a
chronic invalid as the result of an injury. Miss Baker said
that in return for her services, she would house, clothe, and
educate her, and also pay her a small salary. This was indeed
a haven to Grace, as contrasted with her mother's home,
where she received no education nor money, and where she
was obliged to wear the cast-off clothes Mrs. Spencer gave
her, and undergo a generous supply of abuse. Her clothes
had been so shabby that often she was ashamed to appear
on the street.

While I was listening to Grace's recital, the detective telephoned Mrs. Spencer to inform her we had found her ward.
She at once wanted to know where she was, and when he

told her that the girl was at the Missing Persons Bureau, Mrs. Spencer demanded to know by what right we had taken her there. The detective, to avoid entering into an argument with her, replied that he had been acting under his Captain's orders. She at once asked to speak to me. The detective requested her to hold the wire, hurriedly repeated to me the gist of their conversation, and then the request was made to the switchboard operator to cut in on my wire.

Mrs. Spencer opened the conversation by asking, "By what right was Grace brought to Police Headquarters and not delivered at my home as she should have been?"

Her tone was belligerent. I told her the girl had said she was twenty-four years of age.

"The girl is a liar! I guess I know how old she is because I've been supporting her for the last five years—ever since she was twelve years of age. Therefore, she couldn't be twenty-four according to my mathematics."

"But the fact remains, Madam, that this young woman claims to be twenty-four, and she has every appearance of being that age. Under the circumstances, it will be necessary for you to come to the Bureau so that the matter can be threshed out to our satisfaction. If the girl is the age she claims to be, she is a free agent as far as you are concerned, and you would have no control over her."

Mrs. Spencer angrily retorted, "I will come down, but you may rest assured your superiors will know all about this, and you will suffer for it."

During my conversation with her mother, Grace seemed nervous, and kept glancing at the clock. I asked her if she was afraid to encounter her mother.

"Yes, I want above all things to avoid meeting her. I never

want to see her again. I am slowly coming to realize what a cruel and inhuman parent she is, and that she is unworthy of any loyalty."

However, I still felt that the glances at the clock had a different significance. I asked her how she would explain her absence from the Baker home. She replied that Miss Baker usually slept through the forenoon until luncheon time, and if she were there at noon to bring her her tray, she would not show any curiosity as to where she had been.

I told the girl that we had her interests at heart and would protect her; that if she did not wish to see her mother she was within her rights. I also assured her that we did not want to cause her any embarrassment in her new home, adding, "If you will give me your word that, if necessary, we can reach you at the Baker residence, you may leave at once."

She promised to be available, thanked me profusely and left, after asking me not to tell her mother where she was. About half an hour later Mrs. Spencer arrived. I was well aware who it was, for I could hear her strident voice demanding of the desk man, "I want to talk to the Captain who refuses to send my ward home."

She was shown in. The moment she appeared in the doorway—and she certainly loomed large in that setting—I noted that her red hair fairly stood on end, a bristling blaze of color, fitting index to her fiery temperament. She started to give off sparks at once.

"By what right do you make it necessary for me to come to Police Headquarters to get my ward? And where is she?"

I asked her to sit down, but she replied: "What I have to say to you—and it's plenty—I can say standing up."

My calm demeanor seemed only to anger her the more,

and she strode up to my desk, her eyes blazing, shaking her finger at me as she said, "I am going right down to City Hall the moment I leave here, and tell the Mayor about it, and you will not last long, I assure you."

By this time patience had ceased to be a virtue, and in a tone she could not misinterpret I commanded, "Sit down!"

Perhaps the expression in my eyes added emphasis to the order. At any rate, she seated herself.

"Madam, your ward has stated to me that she is twenty-four, and I am satisfied she has told the truth. Therefore, neither you nor I nor any one else has any control over her movements."

She immediately broke into a tirade of abuse directed at Grace. She accused her of ingratitude, and lack of appreciation for the many kindnesses showered upon her. She painted herself in the guise of a philanthropic woman who had taken pity on a helpless orphan, bringing her into her own home only to be rewarded for her charity by having the ingrate run away from her as soon as she could secure employment.

"Perhaps I'm well rid of the creature!" she cried.

Then she told some unmentionable stories about the girl and her character, accusations which, after talking to Grace, I felt sure were untrue. It was time to play my cards.

I looked her straight between the eyes, and said: "What a despicable thing for a mother to say about her own daughter! I know the whole story. I have talked with the convent where you abandoned your child fourteen years ago."

Instantly she crumpled. She became a different person, a beaten woman. And there was then enacted one of the most emotional demonstrations that has ever been staged in my office, and I have witnessed many of them.

She fell upon her knees and begged me to listen to her story and, above all, never to reveal to her husband what I knew about her.

"I have always had a violent temper, and have displayed it even toward those I love most. Everything Grace has told you about me—my treatment of her, our relationship, and the reason it was kept secret—is true. But although you may not believe it, and I admit I have not shown it, I love Grace. If she will only return to me, I will make up to her for everything she has suffered at my hands."

She pleaded for an opportunity to speak to the girl, so she could implore her forgiveness. "Please tell me where I can find her."

While refusing to give the girl's address, I did agree to get in touch with her, and ask her if she cared to see her mother.

"But it rests entirely with Grace," I reminded the woman. "If she wants to see you again, you can meet here and discuss the matter of what your future attitude will be toward each other."

When I communicated with Grace, she refused to see Mrs. Spencer who, a week or two later, called to see me again, this time in a different mood, and bringing with her her youngest daughter, a pretty child who had been reared in luxury. She also had with her a thick letter for Grace.

For several years thereafter my Bureau was a sort of post office through which the mother sent letters and Christmas and Easter cards to the girl who adhered to her decision never to see or communicate with her unnatural parent again.

MISSING MEN

Once, searching for a missing nurse, our hunt encircled the globe and wound up, oddly enough, at the point whence it started.

Several years ago one of our Deputy Commissioners called me to his office and introduced to me a priest, a Father Murphy who, he explained, was a member of a Catholic Order and had been sent by his superiors in Rome, Italy, to visit branches in the United States.

The Reverend Father Murphy was a fine appearing man, with black hair, olive complexion, and snapping black eyes. He could easily have been mistaken for a son of Italy until he spoke, acknowledging the introduction and revealing a rich, round Irish brogue. The Deputy Commissioner said that Father Murphy wished to talk to me about a missing girl, and asked me to do everything possible for him.

We returned to my office, and the padre explained that while en route to the United States, he had visited his home in Ireland. Here an old woman, a neighbor of his parents, upon hearing he was about to visit this country, requested him to make an effort to learn the whereabouts of her granddaughter whom, she explained, she had never seen because the girl's father had "gone out" from Ireland when he was a young man, and had settled in Melbourne, Australia.

This aged neighbor told him that she had frequently heard from her son, and received news of his growing family. He had written her often about one of his daughters, who had graduated from a Melbourne Hospital, and who held the degree of registered nurse. On one occasion five years ago he wrote his mother that this daughter had gone to San Francisco, where she had immediately secured a position in a hospital. For three years thereafter the family in the Antipodes had heard from her at regular intervals, but the father of the nurse eventually confided to his mother, by letter, that he was greatly worried about his daughter, for he had not heard from her now for about two years.

The family received no more letters, and all their efforts to get in touch with the young woman had failed. He was of the opinion that harm had come to her, or, perhaps, she might even be dead. San Francisco was a long way from Australia, and he was at a loss to know how to go about seeking the girl. When Father Murphy arrived in Ireland bound for the United States, the grandmother selected him as the one to help solve the mystery.

The priest told me, in reply to my questions, that the girl's parents had repeatedly written to her at her old address, but their letters had been returned marked "Unclaimed." They had written the superintendent of the hospital, and he replied that he had no knowledge of their daughter's whereabouts after she left the hospital. Father Murphy said that the old Irish neighbor of his family had wept, and begged him to learn the facts concerning her granddaughter's long silence. The priest shook his head rather hopelessly, as he said, "The poor auld woman thinks the gurrl is dead."

After explaining to Father Murphy that it was out of the question for the New York police to conduct a personal investigation on the Pacific Coast, I said that we would, however, do everything possible for him through correspondence. He assured me that he would not expect us to give greater attention to a matter which he clearly understood was not within our jurisdiction. He supplied me with the name of the nurse, which was Moira O'Brien, and said she was a young woman in her late twenties. I wrote the Police of San Francisco, supplying them with what data we possessed regarding the young woman, requesting them to make whatever investigation was possible toward checking her movements after she left the hospital.

About two weeks later I received a reply to our letter, advising us that the San Francisco police were unable to learn anything about Moira O'Brien beyond the fact that she had terminated her employment at the hospital about two years before and had advised no one of her plans for the future. Apparently, as an afterthought, the Chief of Police added a postscript to his letter to the effect that he had been unauthoritatively informed that Moira O'Brien had friends residing in Sacramento, and he supplied the name and address of these people.

A letter was at once addressed to the Chief of Police of Sacramento, with the request that he investigate the information supplied by the San Francisco Chief. His reply was that the information from San Francisco was correct, that the people in Sacramento did know Moira O'Brien and they had, in fact, but recently received a letter from her from New York City, where she was employed on the staff of a well-known hospital.

As soon as I received this news, I called up the superintendent of the hospital, who chanced to be a friend of mine, and asked him whether he had on his staff a nurse by the name of Moira O'Brien. He replied that he had. I asked if I could speak to her, and was connected with the ward in which she was on duty.

After telling her who I was, I asked, "Do your parents live in Melbourne?"

206

MISCELLANEOUS CASES

She replied in the affirmative, whereupon I delivered a short lecture on filial duty, and told her that a daughter owed it to her parents, when a long distance from home, to write at least occasionally about how she was faring, and I suggested the advisability of communicating with her home at once.

The nurse admitted her neglect, and promised to dispatch a letter to Melbourne immediately. "People at a distance sort of fade out of memory," she said in an effort to explain her long silence.

Distance does not always lend enchantment. More often than otherwise it fosters forgetfulness. New contacts are made, and familiar figures of the past grow dim with the years.

As for Moira O'Brien, we had followed her around the world in an effort to trace her and determine her whereabouts. The last place where she had been was San Francisco, and we traced her there, the farthest point she could get from New York and still remain in this country. Through a casual clew she was found in the city from which our hunt began, although the request to find her came from Ireland and, in the first instance, from her parents in the far Antipodes.

No wonder people employ the trite saying, "The world is a small place after all."

When Father Murphy was informed of our success in finding Moira O'Brien, he was so delighted that one of his missions in this country had turned out so well, that he suggested we go out to luncheon and "celebrate." This we did, and the good padre voted American spaghetti quite as tasty as any he had ever consumed in Italy.

MISSING MEN

In June, 1921, Henri Dietz, a Swiss, reported to us the disappearance of his seventeen-year-old daughter Camille. He said that the girl, employed in a Brooklyn women's specialty dress shop, had failed to return home from the store the previous Saturday night. On Saturdays Camille worked until 10 o'clock, and it was sometimes her custom to spend the night with a girl friend, employed in the same store with her. Her parents at first believed that she had stayed over night with this friend, but when she did not return home reasonably early Sunday they telephoned her supposed hostess, and learned that Camille had not been there. This girl said she had last seen Camille when they both left the store together shortly after ten o'clock the evening before, saying good-by to each other at the door.

Mr. Dietz described his daughter as about five feet four inches in height, with brown eyes and long brown hair. She wore a green dress, severely tailored, a small black hat, and black gloves. The detective working on the case followed clews assiduously, but after a week had elapsed we still had no definite line on the girl. About this time her father, a pleasant, well educated man, came to the Bureau and asked to see me personally.

After some hesitation he said: "There is something I ought to tell you about my daughter. It may help in your search for her. Captain—she—my daughter is—well, Camille is one of the world's unfortunates. Nature played a trick on her. Camille is a member of the intermediate sex."

Her father then sketched an outline of the tragedy of the girl's life, saying, "There was some doubt in our minds as Camille advanced from childhood to maturity whether to deal with her as a boy or a girl. There was a certain masculinity about her and yet, on the other hand, she was feminine, too. Her mother and I finally decided that the girl rôle would more properly fit her, and as she grew older we almost came to believe that we had made the right choice.

"Nevertheless, a shade of masculinity was evident in her face and figure. Her arms were muscular, her hands looked like a boy's. Sometimes there was something in her walk, her gestures, which ill became a girl, although in other ways, she was completely feminine. So far as we knew, there was for a time no conflict in her own mind; she never rebelled at feminine attire, and appeared to live the life of any normal young girl.

"However, when Camille was about fourteen years of age, a growth of hair appeared on her face, as is the case with the adolescent boy. After a time it became very noticeable, and from then on Camille was obliged to shave with regularity. We realized that this humiliated her, and set her apart from other girls. The very fact that she was obliged to shave made her realize that she was different from her acquaintances in that one respect, at least. Sometimes, when in haste or through oversight, she failed to shave, the fact was apparent, and the sight of the stubble on her cheeks and chin, embarrassed her.

"Camille did not, however, complain much about her predicament, or the grim jest nature had played her. It is quite possible that she did not thoroughly comprehend the significance of it all. She is young. We have never discussed the subject with her. I am certain that it has never influenced her emotional life. She has never formed any strong attachments for members of either sex. It has been difficult for me to tell you all this, but I thought you ought to be informed of it.

We are eager to find Camille. She is our favorite child. We have five other children, but I think Mrs. Dietz and I are more fond of her than of the others because we realize that 'third sex' element in her makeup is something of a tragedy, and may lead to future unhappiness for her."

As soon as Camille's father had made this revelation, I instructed the detective to cease hunting for a girl, and direct his attention to finding a boy of Camille's general physical description. The search was taken up from that angle, and three days later the detective secured a clew which led to a drug-store.

Here, behind the counter, attired in white jacket and trousers, was Camille in the act of serving a customer with a sundae. The girl-boy was deftly mopping up the counter with firm, boyish hands, when the detective quietly approached her. When he convinced her that he was aware of her identity, he telephoned me, and I instructed him to bring "Harry Black" to my office, for this was the name she had assumed.

While the detective and Camille were on their way to Headquarters, I telephoned Mr. Dietz at his place of business, and he arrived about the same time his daughter did. As soon as he saw her, he put his arms around the boyish figure and embraced her. It was evident that father and daughter understood each other fairly well.

I questioned Camille, in his presence, about her reason for leaving home, and asked her to explain her movements from the time she left the dress shop Saturday night.

Camille, without embarrassment, and with complete frankness, replied: "For quite a long time I have realized that by nature I am more boy than girl. The fact that I wear girl's clothes and am supposed to be a girl, and yet have a growth of hair on my face like any man, and am forced to shave regularly, has embarrassed me a great deal. What is more, I have felt that I am masquerading when I wear dresses. It seems to me I should dress as a boy, and do a boy's kind of work. All of this has been confusing to me. I did not know exactly how my parents would look upon this shift on my part from one sex to another. Because I cannot be happy as a girl, I decided that I must make the necessary change, and in order to do it, I ran away from home.

"After leaving work Saturday I went to a men's clothing store, and bought a complete outfit of boy's clothes. I told the proprietor that I was buying the clothes for a twin brother as a birthday present, that we were the same size, and that anything that would fit me would fit him. My purchases were wrapped up, and I went to Prospect Park, which was almost deserted at that late hour. Behind the shelter of a clump of bushes I changed my clothes, hiding my girl's outfit in the shrubbery. Then I cut off my hair with a shears I had brought from home. Pulling my boy's hat down over my head, I went to a barber shop, and had the barber give me a real hair cut. Then I went to a rooming house section and rented a room. I stayed there until Monday when I started out to hunt a job. I decided that, while I knew nothing about serving behind a soda fountain, it would be a good job to seek at the start. I have watched soda clerks enough to be able to do pretty much as they do, and it didn't take long before I landed work. This job lasted but three days. I guess I wasn't so clever at serving up cream and soda as I thought I would be. At any rate, the druggist fired me. But very soon I lined up a job in another drugstore —the one where your detective found me."

At the conclusion of her story, Camille, still wearing her boy's outfit, and looking and acting very much more like a boy than a girl, asked, with a tragic look clouding her brown eyes: "What shall I do? I am more boy than girl. How shall I live my life?"

After a long conference, Mr. Dietz, Camille and I decided that, since nature had been so indefinite about establishing Camille's sex, we would determine it according to her own inclinations and temperament. Camille, we agreed, should remain Harry Black, and no longer have a conflict within herself as to which rôle she should assume in life. Since Mrs. Dietz did not know that her daughter had been found, and because both Mr. Dietz and Camille felt that the mother would not agree to this changing of sex, she was not taken into their confidence.

Camille Dietz was still Harry Black the last time I heard from her father, and as "Harry" she is far happier, better adjusted, and more reconciled to her fate as a member of the "third sex" than she would have been as Camille, who had to shave every morning before applying her powder and rouge.

About six years ago the representative of a taxicab company reported to the detective squad of an Uptown precinct the disappearance of one of the cabs of the corporation. Frank Collins, the driver, had failed to bring his taxicab to the station at the end of his tour of cruising. It was suspected, of course, that the driver might have stolen the car. A description of it, together with that of Collins, was broadcast through the usual channels, not only to the local but also to out of town police departments, and detectives were on the alert for the cab and its driver.

Two or three days subsequent to this the wife of the driver of the car reported to our Bureau the disappearance of her husband on the same day that the taxi was not returned to its station. Mrs. Collins said that her husband had always been regular in his habits, and had seldom failed to return home at the close of his day's work. So the efforts of a detective of the Missing Persons Bureau were augmented by those of other detectives of the Department in the search for a missing man and his cab.

A day or two after the matter was brought to the attention of the Bureau, a clew was picked up on the upper East Side of the city, one which led our detective to a certain speakeasy. Here definite information was secured that Collins, accompanied by three other men, had visited the place late in the evening of the day of his disappearance. From the story told it was evident that the four men had been drinking, although not to the point of intoxication. Then, step by step, or rather, mile by mile, the progress of the taxicab and its occupants was traced down through the East Side, where stops were made from time to time at other thirst-quenching establishments, until finally it was definitely determined that the party had crossed Queensboro Bridge.

At Long Island City the cab's course was traced by the detective from resort to resort until he found that the cab had made its way in the direction of Astoria. It was then learned that a taxi of a similar description, with several occupants who were singing and shouting, had been seen on a certain Astoria street in the early hours of the morning following. Nothing could be ascertained of its further progress beyond the point where it was last observed, traveling along a street leading directly toward an open dock. At this point all trace of the vehicle was lost.

Finally, after a conference with our detective, the conclusion was reached that it was possible that the taxicab had been driven off the end of the dock, probably as a result of the inebriated condition of the driver. Due to the murky state of the water at the foot of the dock, eyesight was of no service in determining whether or not our theory was sound.

The captain of a dredge tied up nearby volunteered to drop a grappling hook at the end of the dock, and after it was dragged backward and forward several times it hooked into an obstruction. Upon being hoisted to the surface, it brought with it the taxicab and its four drowned occupants.

Thus ended tragically, one busman's holiday.

Several years ago, Max Huber, residing on the lower East Side, reported the disappearance of his wife Olga. He said she had been missing for several days, and intimated that another man had had something to do with his wife's dropping out of sight. Huber was a night watchman and man-of-all-work in an East side abattoir, where his duties commenced at six o'clock in the evening, and continued through the night until the day force came on in the morning. In addition to making the rounds of the building at intervals during the night, the remainder of his time was devoted to clearing up and disposing of unmerchantable fat and bones that had accumulated during the previous day. He collected this waste matter and put it into the hopper of a grinding machine, from which it emerged in a thoroughly minced state, dropping into a large bin on a floor below, later to be disposed of to manufacturers of fertilizer and soap.

Huber was a squat, stolid man of foreign birth, with a low, overhanging forehead, and small, animal-like eyes. He was about thirty years of age. Reduced to readable English, this is the story he related of his wife's disappearance:

"I went on duty at six o'clock the evening my wife disappeared. Every night at about ten-thirty I go to my home near the slaughter-house to eat lunch. Many times lately when I went home for my evening snack, I found that Olga was not there. When I asked her where she had been, she said she had dropped in on a neighbor for a visit.

"But when this went on for a long time I didn't believe her any more. I started asking questions of my neighbors, and learned that my wife had been seen with a certain Jack Porter at the movies in the neighborhood. I don't know anything about this man, who he is, or where he lives or works. I only know that he is a good-looking fellow, for people who have seen my wife and Porter together told me this."

On the surface it would appear from the husband's story that this was just another case of a wife deserting her husband for another man. An investigation was commenced. The detective, in an effort to check up on the story told by Huber, made inquiry at a number of moving picture theaters in the vicinity, but was unable to find any of the employees who knew of Mrs. Huber's alleged visits to those places of amusement.

Several of the persons questioned knew Mrs. Huber, but they knew her merely as a resident of the neighborhood, a drab sort of woman, always poorly clothed in worn calico dresses. She was described as a household drudge. No one could visualize her as the gay companion of another man, one who went around to picture shows with him in the absence of her husband. Mrs. Huber was the mother of a nine months' old baby and, according to the neighbors, divided her time between attending the infant, and caring for her home, scrubbing, washing, baking, cooking and mending. No one had ever seen her with any man other than her husband.

A door-to-door inquiry in the tenement house in which the family resided disclosed that neighbors had overheard frequent quarrels in the Huber home. Huber was often heard abusing and threatening his wife. The investigation, carried a little further, brought to light that Huber had frequently been seen in the company of a pretty, black-eyed girl with not too enviable a reputation. She was a hanger-on at speakeasies in the neighborhood, where Huber had been seen with her at various times.

This girl had been heard to boast, "Max Huber is my future husband."

It was discovered that on the night of Mrs. Huber's disappearance the neighbors occupying the apartment adjoining that of the Hubers had overheard a violent quarrel between the pair. Mrs. Huber was heard upbraiding her husband for his attentions to the other woman, Huber retorting, "Sure I'm crazy about Lil! What are you going to do about it?" After this defiant speech Huber was heard to leave the apartment, slamming the door behind him.

Shortly after he left, his wife, it was learned, called on one of the neighbors, bringing her baby with her. She asked the woman if she would take care of the infant for a few minutes while she went to the delicatessen store on the corner. She failed to return, and two or three hours later this woman, fearing that something had happened to Mrs. Collins, went to the abattoir to tell her husband about it. Huber asked her if she would take care of the baby, saying that as soon as he got through work in the morning he would report the disappearance of his wife to the police.

Inquiry in the neighborhood of the slaughter-house revealed that a night watchman of a nearby building had seen a woman, whose description tallied exactly with that of Mrs. Huber, standing across the street from the abattoir entrance at about eleven-thirty on the night of Mrs. Huber's disappearance. He attached no particular importance to the incident, although the neighborhood was not one frequented by women late at night. This was the last that was seen of Mrs. Huber.

There were many possibilities open to account for her disappearance. She might have walked down to the waterfront upon which the slaughter-house abutted, and thrown herself overboard because of her unhappy life with an unfaithful, abusive husband. She may have accidentally fallen in. She might have entered the abattoir itself, and her husband, desiring her out of the way, could easily have made away with her in the same manner that he disposed of the slaughter-house refuse of bones and fat—through the grinding machine. To remove the chance of telltale portions of her clothing being found among the refuse he could have disrobed her and thrown the clothing into the fires under the boilers.

We took the precaution of searching the ashes for possible buttons or pins. Unfortunately for the success of our search, women's clothing in recent years call for few, if any, buttons or pins. We subjected Huber to a series of grillings, but he persisted in his story that the last time he had seen his wife was when he left the house the night she vanished.

Is this a voluntary disappearance or a homicide? We never learned.

XI. UNSOLVED MYSTERIES

MOST mysteries—and every case brought to us is a mystery—lose much of their malign quality as soon as they are solved. It is only when a mysterious disappearance remains unexplained that the evil aspect continues to harass relatives and friends of the person who has dropped out of sight. Although only two per cent of the total cases which reach us remain unsolved, still that two per cent represents about five thousand cases in the past fifteen years, since, as I said before, approximately a quarter of a million disappearances have been handled by my department during my time as commander. These unsolved cases are thorns that occasion us much vexation and worry.

Perhaps no case of disappearance in recent years has aroused as much interest as that of Supreme Court Justice Joseph Force Crater, who dropped from sight on August 6, 1930. Literally a world-wide search has been conducted for him, and every bit of machinery that could be made available has been employed: Municipal, State, and Federal, together with the most complete coöperation from representatives of foreign Governments whenever it has been found necessary to appeal to them for assistance. Innumerable clews, or what at the moment were considered clews, have been followed, but always up to the present without success.

MISSING MEN

Some of these leads took us to Canada, but when run down they amounted to nothing at all. Others led to Cuba, while still others turned the hunt to various far places of the globe. The missing Judge has frequently been seen on the decks of outgoing steamers, at quaint hostelries in Italy, in touring cars in the West, and in the lobbies of palatial hotels here and abroad. He has been "found" in various parts of the West Indies, in a monastery in Mexico, at race tracks in different parts of the United States, and sometimes in a number of widely separated places simultaneously. He has been observed driving automobiles at many different points, and yet the Judge could not drive a car! He was "positively" seen on a certain steamship, and his photograph was identified with "certainty" by deck stewards, room stewards, and the dining room help of this ship.

Little peculiarities of the Judge, as noted by those doing the identifying were, oddly enough, in many cases typical of him. Yet when these "clews" were run down it was found that, while those who offered the "tips" were sincere and believed their own stories, all were on the wrong track. Several times it was found that a man some one took to be the missing Judge actually did bear a striking resemblance to him so far as contour of face and similarity of figure were concerned. Often a man so closely resembled Judge Crater that it was easily understandable how a stranger to him, having only a photograph and a description as a guide, could be mistaken.

But, skeptical as we might be regarding a rumor or a tip, we could not overlook a chance of finding our man, and accordingly we ran them all down. We worked on each piece of information until we were convinced that the person in question was not Judge Crater, and had definitely established the true identity of the "double." And doubles of the missing Judge existed, as I have said, in many places. For example, on one occasion we received a letter from a woman stating that she had traveled from New York to a South American port on one of our well-known steamship lines, and that a man she believed, from pictures she had seen of him in the papers, to be Judge Crater had the deck chair next to hers. She gave the name of this man as it appeared on the passenger list and his stateroom number. She said she had observed him closely, for her attention had been attracted to him by the fact that he was accompanied by a very attractive woman, whose name and stateroom number she also supplied. She wrote that the couple seemed most devoted to each other, and that their attitude was precisely that of couples "vacationing together."

An investigation was made. Photographs of Judge Crater were displayed to various members of the ship's personnel who had been brought into contact, during the two weeks' voyage, with the man supposed to be he. All were unanimous in declaring the photograph was that of the man they had served. This lead looked good. The reservations held by this man were looked into, and it was learned that he had not made them himself. They had been arranged for through a representative, but eventually the man himself was reached in a certain New England city. There a little comedy entered the situation, although the joke was somewhat on the "double."

When the detective, after much difficulty, finally traced the man to his place of business, and questioned him regarding his trip, he at first denied it. The detective, in a way detectives have, convinced him, however, that after all denial in the face of overwhelming proof to the contrary, was useless. The man thereupon held out no longer, and admitted making the journey, winding up with the plea: "For God's sake, don't tell my wife! That was the first vacation I have ever been able to take where I felt I could do as I damn well pleased without danger of criticism."

When the detective assured him that he was not in the business of endangering a man's domestic happiness, the man seemed somewhat relieved, but still could not banish entirely his fear of an exposure, and asked, "Does that go for your Commanding Officer, too?"

Although he was assured that it did, he went to the length of making a trip from his home down to New York to see me at Police Headquarters. He desired to secure from me personally the assurance that his escapade would not be given publicity. When he walked into my office I was struck by the close resemblance between his face and that of Judge Crater as it appeared in the photographs. Judge Crater has a peculiarly shaped nose and his mouth is wide and mobile. Looking at this stranger from New England, I was not at all surprised at the many "identifications" made by members of the ship's staff: he was the perfect counterpart of the missing Judge, and I think, under similar circumstances, I too would have been confident he was the man sought.

I had considerable correspondence with a woman in New Jersey, who said she was certain the Judge had come to a roadside refreshment stand which she conducted and made some purchases. She described a man about the same height, weight and build as Judge Crater, and said that he drove to her place almost daily, and stopped there while he ate a sandwich or drank a glass of soda. She said he wore blue glasses and a peaked cap, the costume still sometimes worn by men driving open cars, one of which this man operated. The woman also described certain mannerisms typical of the Judge, but when the clew was run down, and the identity of the man in question learned, it was found he did not fit into the picture. It was only one more mistake on the part of a person honestly endeavoring to be of assistance. These episodes are but a few samples of scores of "tips" received by us from all parts of the world, all of which were run down.

Checking these "clews" involved hundreds of letters, innumerable telegrams, and many long distance telephone conversations, all in the hope of finding the one missing man. Wherever the trail led we almost invariably met enterprising representatives of the New York papers working on the story.

It occurs to me to wonder how many of those who read this necessarily incomplete story of a mysterious disappearance will pause to conjecture about the tremendously powerful motive which must have existed to occasion it. Picture a lawyer coming to New York from a small country town to enter into competition with those long established there in the same profession. Then contemplate his entry into politics in rivalry with astute local politicians, handicapped as he was by the jealousy of those with whom he would necessarily be in competition. Observe him at length overcoming, through sheer force of character, and legal acumen, these very real handicaps. We next see him as a man whose highest ambition (and we have his own statements to that effect) was to reach the Supreme Court Bench, and once arrived there we find that he suddenly dropped out of sight.

MISSING MEN

Was the disappearance a voluntary act? If so, what was the motive? And if it was not volitional, then what could have impelled another, or others, to cause his disappearance? That was the problem presented to the Police when Judge Crater first disappeared, and which still confronts us.

We will turn from Judge Crater to another baffling disappearance. A report was received by us one morning, five or six years ago, that James Jerome had, on the previous day and in company with a stranger, left his boarding and rooming house, which was conducted by two spinster sisters, and not returned. He had left word he would be back in a short time, and his intention of absenting himself for only a brief period was evidenced by the fact that he had not worn an overcoat, although it was cool, early spring weather.

Jerome was reputed, and upon inquiry found to be, a man of independent means, a bachelor about forty years of age, with no regular business, who occasionally engaged in speculation either in Wall Street or in modest real estate deals. He was a native of a Western state. The report of his disappearance was conveyed to us by one of the sisters who conducted the boarding house. Their roomer, she said, had informed them he was about to visit a certain bank. The stranger with whom he had left the house was described as a man about six feet in height, thin, angular and clean-shaven, with what the landlady termed "a Yankee twang." This description, particularly that of the voice, proved very important later.

Our informant knew little of her tenant's background beyond the name of the city which he claimed as his home town. The detective I put on the case made an examination of Jerome's home life, or rather, boarding-house life, and learned that he was very regular in his habits, spending most of his evenings reading, sometimes devoting an hour or so to visiting with his landladies. He went, like Pepys, "early to bed," was an early riser, and usually took a constitutional before breakfast.

In view of this very regular schedule there seemed scant probability of any private entanglements which might account for the disappearance. The detective called at the bank which Jerome said he was about to visit, and, upon securing an interview with the manager, learned that the missing man was a depositor and had always carried a sum of several thousand dollars in a checking account. The detective also found that on the previous day Jerome had drawn a check for three thousand dollars, payable to Frank Smith, the name by which he introduced the man who accompanied him, and who, judging from the description given, was the same man with whom he had left his boarding house.

Jerome, in the presence of the manager, had turned over the check to Smith, who had requested that it be certified, stating as his reason that he desired to use the money in a real estate transaction, and in that form the check would be equivalent to cash. This still left us up in the air as to the identity of Smith. The problem now was to discover through what channels the check was turned into cash. This necessitated setting in motion machinery which eventually brought to light the bank in which the check was deposited. Right here entered a peculiar angle of the case.

Inquiry at the bank of deposit developed that Smith had attempted to have the check cashed but, due to the fact that he was unknown to the teller, his request had been refused, and he was told that it would be necessary for him to be identified by some one known to the bank. He replied that he was a total stranger, but that the manager of the bank on which the check was drawn had been present at the time, had certified it, and would be able to identify him. The teller called up the manager, and the manager, while admitting that he saw the check prepared and had certified it and that he had seen the man to whom it was given, said that nevertheless he knew nothing about him, and could not vouch for him beyond saying that he had been in his presence for a short time.

Eventually the matter of the check was arranged in this way: Smith was told that he might deposit it to his account, and that any draft against it over his signature would be honored. The usual arrangement for opening an account was made, and Smith became a depositor to the extent of three thousand dollars. I naturally felt that sooner or later Smith would draw against this three thousand dollars, and to make certain that this was not done without our knowledge, I assigned a detective to remain at the bank each day during banking hours. I believed that Smith was the key to the Jerome disappearance.

Months passed, until finally I began to fear that Smith might have come to an untimely end, or else for some reason had decided it would be unwise or unsafe for him to attempt to secure the money on deposit. Then one day the manager of the bank came over to the detective, and informed him excitedly that a sight draft for almost the entire three thousand dollars had just been received from a bank in a certain Canadian city. We requested the manager to delay honoring it until an opportunity was afforded us to get in touch with the police of the Canadian city. This we at once did, supplying them with the necessary information to enable them to locate and detain Smith.

In a few hours we received a wire from our Canadian fellow policemen that Smith was in custody. Now another knotty problem arose. We had a prisoner in a foreign country, but we had no indictment; nor could we in all probability secure one because, up to the moment, we were unable to present any facts to a Grand Jury which would constitute necessary evidence or proof of the commission of a crime on the part of Smith. However, a policeman's job is one which sometimes calls for ingenuity, and this quality was employed to create a situation which would enable us to return Smith to this side of the border, where an arrest could be made on the reasonable grounds that he had played a part in the commission of a serious crime.

I at once sent a detective to Canada, where the police believe that a spirit of coöperation, especially with the New York police, is a virtue. When our detective reached his destination, and went into the details of the situation, he was told: "All right! We won't waste time with red tape in ths matter. We are convinced that Smith is an undesirable resident for our country. You may pose as an Immigration Official, and we will see to it that your man voluntarily accompanies you across the border."

After a short interview with their prisoner, in which they explained to him the situation as it might effect his future in Canada, he was more than willing to accompany the "Immigration Official" across the border. He even supplied the transportation, because he was the owner of a car of ancient

227

vintage. The detective wired me as soon as he had crossed the border, advising that he had disclosed his true identity to Smith, and had placed him under arrest. He had told his prisoner that he could drive his car to New York in his custody or, if he refused, he could abandon it and be brought to New York by train. Smith elected to drive the car.

They proceeded on their way that same evening, driving all night and arriving at Police Headquarters in New York City at 8 o'clock the following morning. Both the detective and Smith had gone twenty-four hours or more without sleep. Smith was thus in splendid condition to be taken in hand for a course of questioning. I chose to present a sympathetic front, telling him how I regretted the necessity for entering immediately upon an effort to solve the mystery of Jerome's disappearance before permitting him proper rest after his' long and tiresome journey. Although Smith disavowed any desire for breakfast I insisted that he have this meal, and sent a detective with him to a restaurant.

After his hasty meal, Smith was returned to my office, and I had an opportunity of observing him closely. He impressed me as being a man of considerable mental agility, resourceful, sly, with a veneer of frankness which was disarming. He possessed plenty of native wit, but was evidently a weakling, one who might easily be led to engage in any act planned and engineered by a stronger will.

I began by questioning him as to his antecedents, remarking, "It is evident that you are not a New Yorker." This he admitted. With an appearance of friendliness I proceeded to make an attempt, which I am satisfied succeeded to a certain extent, at securing the confidence of our prisoner. I explained that it was necessary for the disappearance of Jerome to be accounted for, and convinced him that his connection with Jerome, up to the point of his leaving the bank upon which Jerome's check was drawn, had been definitely established. I said that we knew of his attempts to have the check cashed in another bank, and that eventually he had been obliged to deposit it.

After outlining the situation to him up to that point, I said: "Smith, this calls for an explanation. Now it's up to you. I feel convinced that Jerome has been made away with by some one. You are the man last seen in his company. Now tell us about it."

He replied: "You have treated me kindly, and, somehow, I feel I can confide in you. I will tell you how I came to know Jerome. I had been told by a friend, a man by the name of Richardson, that Jerome was a man of means, and that he was likely to be interested in any scheme giving promise of a quick turnover on an investment."

I asked who Richardson was, and what his business might be. Smith said Richardson was a man who had come from California to New York, that he was a bit of an adventurer, willing to take a chance in almost any sort of shady venture if it showed any prospect of making money for him. At the time Smith approached Jerome, Richardson had been engaged in bootlegging. Richardson had conceived the plan of employing the subterfuge of a story of a quick turnover in liquor to induce Jerome to place in his hands, through Smith, three thousand dollars in cash, which would be given to a certain man in New Jersey who was running liquor for Richardson.

When I asked Smith how he had convinced Jerome that the turnover would be speedy, he said he had explained to him that the moment Richardson had received and paid for the liquor all arrangements had been made to transport it to a certain nearby point where it was to be placed in the hands of a distributor of bootlegged liquor, who would pay a considerable advance upon the price at which Richardson had secured it. According to Smith, Jerome had immediately fallen for the plan, and had accompanied him, after the final transaction at the bank, to a point on a river near a city in New Jersey, where he met Richardson and introduced Jerome to him.

Richardson informed Jerome that in a short time a boat with the liquor would dock at this point, that he had a truck waiting a short distance away, and that as soon as it was loaded it would be driven to a place where the consignee would receive it and pay cash. Richardson said he desired Jerome to be on hand in order to receive his portion of the profits, together with the three thousand dollars advanced. Smith then pretended to turn over the certified check to Richardson, who made some excuse to speak privately with him, apologizing to Jerome for so doing with the statement that he wanted to give him some instructions regarding work to be done in New York.

During this private conversation, Smith was instructed by Richardson to return at once to New York and have the check cashed, or deposit it to his account, so that the money might be available the following day. He said that he would "take care" of Jerome, and see to it that there was no further annoyance from him.

Smith stated that this was the last time he had seen either Jerome or Richardson. Richardson, at parting, had agreed to call him by telephone the following day, and fix a rendezvous for a division of the three thousand dollars. Smith, according to his story, did return immediately to New York, and attempt to cash the check, eventually depositing it as described.

When I asked him as to the agreed meeting with Richardson on the following day, he said he had remained at the furnished room where he lived, reading and awaiting the telephone call, but had not received it either that day or the following one. Then, fearing that something had happened to Richardson, that he had perhaps got in trouble with the police or other authorities, he became frightened and decided to go to Canada, where it would be difficult to find him.

Smith said he had occupied his time while in Canada doing odd jobs for garages, for, as he put it, he had always been "handy with tools." After the lapse of several months he began to feel that he could, with safety, secure the money on deposit in New York, and that was the reason he used the sight draft which had led to his apprehension.

Every effort was made to secure an indictment against Smith. An Assistant District Attorney questioned him at length, supplementing our efforts in the most whole-hearted manner, but it was impossible to break down Smith's story. Under the circumstances Smith's statement could not be employed against him; there was no complainant, for the reason that the only person, according to his story, who had been wronged by him was Jerome, and Jerome could not be found, although the most diligent efforts were made to locate him. The assistance of the New Jersey police was enlisted in making an exhaustive search in the vicinity of the point to which Smith said he had taken him, but the search proved fruitless.

MISSING MEN

The mystery of James Jerome's disappearance still remains unsolved.

A man leaves his home in New York City to accompany an invalid sister of his wife to a health resort in a Far Western state. He places his sister-in-law in the sanitarium and, realizing that he is almost within hailing distance of the Pacific Coast, which he has never visited, he decides to take advantage of his proximity and go on to Los Angeles, and thence north by slow stages to San Francisco. This new, to him, part of the country, with its beautiful scenery and celebrated climate, is of absorbing interest to him, as his frequent letters to his wife testify. Then, after about a week in San Francisco, he checks out of his hotel, wires his wife that he is starting home and—drops completely out of sight.

This is the story, in brief, of Theodore Barthwell, who vanished twelve years ago, and has never been seen nor heard of since. Twelve years ago his wife, Mrs. Louise Barthwell, came to us in great distress, and related in detail the circumstances of his disappearance. She began with a recital of her sister's illness. Physicians had advised her to go to a dry climate, and a sanitarium in Arizona was recommended. The family at first could not decide who should accompany her, since she was not in a condition to permit traveling alone. Finally Mr. Barthwell was selected as the logical companion for her on her way West, and they started on their journey.

Barthwell left behind him his wife and two young daughters, Dorothy, aged ten, and Ethel, twelve, in their comfortable New York home. Mrs. Barthwell heard daily, either by letter or telegram, from her husband, who described the progress of the journey and informed her of her sister's condition. He sent loving messages to his young daughters of whom he was inordinately fond. Realizing that perhaps another opportunity of visiting the Pacific Coast might not present itself again for many years, Barthwell decided that the present chance was too good to lose, and he wired his wife to that effect. He asked whether she approved of his plan and, if so, he requested that she send him additional funds.

She fully approved, and the necessary amount was wired to him at once. Barthwell proceeded to Los Angeles, and then on to San Francisco, continuing his practice of communicating daily with his wife en route, writing her long letters describing the novelties of his journey. He remained a week or ten days in Los Angeles and its environs, and then proceeded slowly by short stages up the Pacific Coast to San Francisco. He remained there a week, sending as usual daily bulletins to his wife, who was delighted that her husband was realizing a long cherished dream. The final communication was a telegram, informing her that he was checking out of his San Francisco hotel to begin his homeward journey, and giving her the time of his arrival. That was the last word she has ever had from him, the last intimation of his whereabouts.

When Barthwell did not arrive on the expected day, Mrs. Barthwell made due allowance for delays. After several days had elapsed, and he had not arrived, and no message was received from him, she naturally became worried. She consulted her family as to what should be done, and it was decided that she ought to appeal to the Police for aid. Hence her visit to the Missing Persons Bureau.

MISSING MEN

I questioned Mrs. Barthwell as to the domestic situation. Nothing could have been more tranquil and agreeable, she assured me. She said that her husband was devoted to her and their two children. Barthwell was voted by all his friends an extremely likable man, and the last one in the world capable of intrigue or impropriety, and not at all the sort of person to abandon his wife and children.

During the investigation I visited two uncles of Barthwell, who had employed him since his boyhood. His father had been in partnership with them in the business of importing and distributing teas and spices, and had died about a year before Barthwell's disappearance. It seems that it never had occurred to Barthwell that, as an only child, he had inherited his father's interest in the business, because he had continued in the same status in the firm that he had occupied prior to his father's death. So far as I was able to learn the question of his rights in the business had never been even discussed by the trio.

When I interviewed his uncles, two close-fisted, crusty old men, I discovered that they seemed to hold considerable animus toward their nephew. They immediately launched into a long recital of dishonest acts on his part. One of Barthwell's duties was to make collections, and one of the old fellows said testily: "We find, in going over the books, that he failed to turn in over two hundred dollars which he had collected from time to time."

The straitened circumstances in which Barthwell had left his family seemed to have no interest for them whatsoever. When I asked if it were not possible for them to do something for their nephew's wife and children, one of the old men spoke up quickly: "I don't see why. She's no relative of ours. Why should we do anything for the woman, particularly after her husband mulcted us out of so much money?"

Further digging into the affairs of the absent Barthwell disclosed that his small earnings were insufficient to permit him and his wife to indulge in even modest social activities, and from time to time he had borrowed small amounts from friends, sums varying from ten to fifty dollars. The total of these obligations amounted to slightly more than one thousand dollars. Probing still deeper, we found that Barthwell's father had died intestate, at the time of his death having a one-third interest in the firm, and that his only son, as his sole heir, should have been on an equal footing with his uncles.

We learned further that the uncles were fully aware of their nephew's legal rights, but had never referred to the interest he had in the income of the business, and it is probable that Barthwell had never known that his father was an equal partner in the firm. In any event, the money which they alleged he had "held out" on his collections was but a small fraction of the sum to which he was legally entitled from the earnings of the firm.

At our request search was made for Barthwell by the San Francisco police, and every means was employed to trace him from the moment he left his hotel in that city. The hotel management confirmed the information contained in Barthwell's last telegram to his wife, in which he informed her he was about to check out. Inquiries at the transcontinental railroad stations in San Francisco disclosed that every transcontinental railroad ticket purchased on that day had been accounted for. All casualties in the city of San Francisco on that day and for many days afterward were satisfactorily established. The railroad officials of all lines by which he might have traveled East were unable to give any information that would help us. Points of interest which a tourist might visit en route were investigated, but no untoward incidents involving the death or illness of any of their visitors were brought to light.

When everything possible had been done toward solving the mystery of this disappearance we were forced simply to await developments. From time to time during this interval of twelve years we have checked on what appeared likely clews to his whereabouts. On one occasion a newspaper account of the accidental death of a man of the same name appeared in a dispatch from Mexico City. When that story was run down, we found it was not the man we were searching for. On still another occasion a railroad accident in Canada supplied a list of several injured persons, and among the names appeared the surname "Barthwell." This clew was followed to the point where the identity of the person was determined. He was not our man.

During all these years Mrs. Barthwell has never lost hope of ultimately finding her husband, who she is convinced is still alive. She feels that some day he will return and explain in a satisfactory manner his long absence. If this should ever happen, he will come back to find himself a grandfather, for both his daughters have married in the interim and have children of their own. Both girls married well-to-do men, and are living in the West.

"Perhaps some day they will accidentally encounter their father," says Mrs. Barthwell, unable to relinquish hope of one day being reunited to her husband.

As for the motive, if Barthwell's disappearance was a

voluntary one, I can attribute it to only one cause, and if we accept this, we must also hold that Theodore Barthwell was a moral coward. It may be, and 1 think the theory plausible, that during the period of Barthwell's visit to the Pacific Coast, he had an opportunity of reviewing what, to him, appeared to be the heavy financial obligations he had incurred as the result of borrowing from friends. To a man of narrow financial vision, who had never earned nor spent much money, the sum of one thousand dollars might appear colossal. He may have feared the embarrassment which might result if his creditors should press him for a settlement which he felt it impossible to make. Then, too, he may have feared that his uncles would take criminal action against him for his failure to account for some of the sums he had collected for the firm. Who knows?—perhaps he will some day read this book in some library and learn that he has nothing to fear by returning. Stranger things have happened in the annals of the Missing Persons Bureau.

XII. KIDNAPINGS

THE Lindbergh kidnaping is the outstanding one of its kind in this century. Fortunately for the peace of mind of the Police of New York City there has never been within their jurisdiction any case of child-stealing of similar importance.

On the night of March 1, 1932, Col. Charles Lindbergh's baby son was stolen from the nursery of his parents' home in the small town of Hopewell, New Jersey. Utter heartlessness marked this atrocious act, which had its culmination seventy-two days later, when the body of the infant was discovered in a section of waste land, overgrown with scrub, at a point not far from a lonely road about five miles from the Lindbergh home. To all appearances the murder of the child occurred shortly after he was removed from his crib, and his death was caused by a blow from some blunt instrument. The brutality evidenced in the murder alone marks the perpetrators of the crime as deserving of no consideration. No one but an unusually inhuman criminal— or a psychopath—could be capable of such an infamous thing.

New York City, in proportion to its population, has perhaps fewer cases of kidnaping than any other large city in the United States. During my time in charge of the Missing Persons Bureau there have been not more than a dozen cases of alleged kidnaping. People usually associate the thought of kidnaping with one of ransom, but none of the child-stealing cases in New York City held the element of extortion or attempted extortion. It obviously played no part in these crimes for the reason that the parents of the children were extremely poor. They were scarcely able to maintain their families, to say nothing of furnishing ransom money.

What kind of person steals a child from his home and parents? In most instances the one guilty of kidnaping is of the pathological type. When money does supply the motive for the crime, the kidnaping becomes what may be termed a "racket," and the same impulses motivate it as those which figure in every unlawful act for gain.

One of our outstanding and well established kidnapings occurred on Sunday, June 3, 1928, when Grace Budd, ten years old, disappeared from her home at 406 West 15th Street.

Grace was described as four feet in height, weight sixty pounds, large blue eyes, dark brown, straight bobbed hair, sallow complexion, apparently anemic and undernourished. The little girl was dressed in a light gray coat, with gray fur at the collar and cuffs and down the front, and she had a pink rosebud pinned on the lapel. She wore a white silk dress, white pumps, white silk stockings, and a gray felt hat, with a blue ribbon streamer hanging down the back. She carried a small brown pocketbook, and wore white pearl beads around her neck. The white frock was her communion dress, for Grace was a Roman Catholic, and just a Sunday or two before the kidnaping, had made her first communion.

The last seen of her was about one o'clock in the afternoon, when she left her home in company with a man who gave the name "Frank Howard." This man had asked her parents if she could accompany him to a birthday party on Washington Heights, the occasion being his sister's anniversary. This was the report transmitted to the Missing Persons Bureau from the precinct in which the Budd family lived, and it launched a country-wide search which resulted in many curious developments. Incidentally, it was one of the most baffling cases of its kind that has come to my attention.

As for the man "Howard," the parents of Grace had made his acquaintance when he appeared at their home about a week before the kidnaping in answer to an advertisement Mrs. Budd had put in a Sunday newspaper. This advertisement had been inserted for the purpose of securing a job on a farm for her eighteen-year-old son Edward. On May 28, the day after the advertisement ran, a man dressed in a well-worn suit of clothes, and giving the name "Frank Howard" arrived at the Budds' modest basement home. Mrs. Budd was janitress of a tenement house, and in return for her services received her own apartment rent free.

Howard said he had a farm at Farmingdale, Long Island, according to Mrs. Budd, who was the only one at home when he arrived. He appeared to be about fifty-eight years of age, had blue eyes, mixed gray hair, a thin face, and wore a dark suit, black shoes and a black felt hat. He had three protruding upper teeth, and was a smooth talker. When Mrs. Budd answered his ring at the bell, he explained that he had seen her advertisement and wanted to hire a boy to work for him on his farm. His visit occurred at about three o'clock in the afternoon, and it so happened that Edward Budd was not home at the time.

Mrs. Budd informed her caller that she expected him at about four o'clock, and suggested that he wait for him. During this interval little Grace returned from school, entered the kitchen where the "farmer" was seated, and called out, "Mama, I'm hungry. I want something to eat."

Mrs. Budd gave her a slice of bread and butter, and she returned to the street and her playmates. Howard, during the child's stay in the kitchen, apparently scarcely noticed her presence. He entertained Mrs. Budd with a description of his home at Farmingdale, spoke of his Swedish woman cook, his chickens, cows, and the crops he cultivated. He impressed Mrs. Budd as being a man of means, a successful farmer, and one to whom she could entrust the welfare of her son. Shortly after four o'clock Edward appeared, and after Mr. Howard had had a short talk with him, he expressed himself as satisfied that he was the type of boy he wanted. He went even farther than that, and exhibited a willingness also to employ a companion of Edward's, a boy about his own age, who also wanted to work on a farm.

After hiring the boys he described the route to be taken to his place at Farmingdale, and said that, were it not for the fact that he was obliged to go over to Jersey on a matter of business, he would take the boys to his farm that evening. But since he was obliged to be in the city the following Saturday he would call for them then. On Saturday they eagerly awaited the arrival of their employer, but in the afternoon a telegram was received from Howard, informing

Mrs. Budd that he found it impossible to call that evening for the boys, as agreed, but would come for them the following day.

Sunday he called at the Budd home about eleven o'clock in the morning, and announced that he had come for the lads. Mr. Budd was just about to sit down to his frugal breakfast in the kitchen, and hospitably invited the visitor to join him. Howard made the excuse that he had just had a hearty beefsteak breakfast. He then presented the Budds with a little gift, a pail filled with cottage cheese and a loaf of sponge cake, explaining that his Swedish cook had made the cheese and baked the cake, and that he thought his city friends would like to taste a farmer's favorite dishes. This thoughtful act further impressed the Budds with the fact that their son was indeed lucky to secure employment with this kindly man.

Just at this point, while the family was sampling the cheese and cake, Edward and his chum appeared. Howard explained to the boys that he was planning to take advantage of being in the city to call at the home of his sister in Washington Heights, as it was her birthday, and he wanted to help her celebrate it. During this conversation Grace several times ran in and out of the kitchen. Howard paid little attention to the child, except once when, turning to her, he commented admiringly on the white communion frock. She had just returned from Sunday school and was still wearing it.

Howard, on this occasion, apparently had on his best clothes, and was freshly shaven, ostensibly all dressed up for his sister's birthday party. The "farmer" apologized to the boys for the delay in getting away, and assured them that he would not remain at the party very late, and would call for them that night. As he spoke, he took from his pocket a roll of money, and peeled two one-dollar bills from the outside, handing one to each of the boys, saying: "Go to a movie, and enjoy yourselves while you are waiting for me."

Not only did the roll impress the Budds and the lads, but it also seemed to fascinate Grace. She had never before seen so much money. As Grace's large blue eyes fixed themselves on it, Howard turned smilingly to her, and asked her if she would like to hold it. She said she would and he handed her the roll and assisted her in counting it. It amounted to about ninety dollars, an enormous sum to the child and possibly to the parents also.

This was about the only attention Howard had given Grace up to this point. But when he again mentioned his sister's birthday party, the little girl spoke up: "What's a birthday party? I never heard of that before."

Then, with apparent spontaneity, Howard turned to the girl's mother: "Why not let Grace go with me to my sister's home this afternoon? She can play with my sister's children, while the grown-ups enjoy themselves in other ways. I can bring her home when I come back for the boys."

Mrs. Budd, flattered by this invitation to her little daughter from her son's employer, at once gave consent. So it came about that early that afternoon Frank Howard left the Budds' basement apartment with little Grace clasping his hand, and that was the last time that the child's family ever saw her.

The Budd family provided us with the foregoing information when the matter was brought to our attention. We started our investigation in the vicinity of the Budd home: neighbors, and the children who had been playing in the street at the time Grace and Howard had departed, were questioned with a view to determining the direction in which the pair had gone after reaching the corner. Many admitted having seen them on their way to the corner, but few agreed as to the direction taken thereafter. Some were positive they had entered an automobile, others that they had gone toward the nearby "L" station, and still others, that they had taken exactly the opposite direction. As a result of these conflicting stories, little reliance could be placed in any of them.

Our next step was to check on the Farmingdale situation. Residents of long standing would all be known, and Howard had said that he had conducted his farm there for a number of years. The local police at our request made a thorough canvass of the entire Farmingdale section, but not even the oldest inhabitant had ever heard of Howard or his farm.

Descriptions of the victim and the kidnaper were sent out, and the coöperation of police authorities throughout adjoining states was enlisted. Circulars descriptive of the child, and carrying a history of her disappearance, were hurriedly struck off, and mailed to towns, large and small, within a radius of hundreds of miles of New York City. In the meantime, the search in the city was pressed.

The kidnaping was not reported until the day following its happening. Grace's mother had not been particularly worried when the child did not return that night, for she had assumed that the party had continued until a late hour, and that Grace and Howard had remained at the sister's home overnight. It was only when the pair did not return the following morning that she grew suspicious.

KIDNAPINGS

We traced to a Harlem telegraph office the telegram which Howard sent to Mrs. Budd on the day before the kidnaping. Inquiry was made in that immediate neighborhood to ascertain if Howard frequented the section. Milk and butter stores and bakeries in the vicinity were visited in order to learn the source of the cottage cheese and cake which the kidnaper had claimed were the handiwork of his Swedish cook. Finally a pushcart peddler was found who remembered selling the tin pail to a man of Howard's description. He recalled the sale because it was the last pail of that kind in his stock. The proprietor of a nearby dairy store remembered ladling a quantity of cottage cheese into the pail. A girl in a bakery shop recalled selling the sponge-cake to a man of Howard's description. But all these leads proved of no avail.

Due to the widespread newspaper publicity given this crime, we received, a few days after the kidnaping, a communication from Brooklyn to the effect that some time prior to this, a man whose description resembled that of Howard, had attempted to adopt a young girl who was ward of a certain charity society of that borough. In keeping with its custom, this society required testimonials of character and standing before turning any of its wards over for adoption. The man who wanted to adopt a little girl had given the name "Dr. Edward Corthell." He said that he had been a resident of Brooklyn only a short time, and that he originally came from Florida. He gave, as reference, the name of a man who was warden of a prison in Florida. The society communicated with the warden, and by return mail the information was received that Dr. Edward Corthell was, indeed, well known to the writer by reason of the fact that he at one time had been confined in the prison of which the writer was warden. The criminal record of Corthell, who was, among other things, a forger, was forwarded to the Brooklyn society as evidence of his "fitness" for foster parenthood of a young girl!

This criminal record was accompanied by a photograph of the man, showing him in prison attire, his head shaved, his number—14918—in plain view across his chest. There was also a complete physical description. The similarity of the description of the Brooklyn applicant for child adoption and the Budd kidnaper impressed us at once. We were then confronted with the problem of establishing the fact that the man in both cases was the same person. Corthell, in his prison garb and haircut, would not, of course, be recognized by those who had seen him as Howard, the prosperous farmer.

I gave the convict's photograph to an artist and instructed him to dress it up, substituting for the prison garb, clothing, shirt, collar and tie as near as possible like those worn by Howard. I also asked him to supply a luxuriant growth of hair to cover the clipped skull of the convict, combed as the Budd family had described Howard's hair. The result was that the reincarnated Corthell bore an appearance of eminent respectability.

This retouched photograph was then re-photographed, and placed among several other pictures of men of about the same age and appearance. These were submitted to the Budd family one at a time. Mrs. Budd and Grace's brother, Edward, unhesitatingly picked out the picture of Corthell as that of Howard. They were brought before the Grand Jury of New York County, and on the strength of their testimony Corthell, alias Howard, was indicted for the kidnaping of Grace Budd.

Circulars were prepared showing a cut of the Florida exconvict, Corthell, as he appeared in his prison dress and as he was conceived by the artist, giving his prison description and fingerprints. The circular read:

CONFIDENTIAL

———

WANTED FOR KIDNAPING

DESCRIPTION—Age, about 45 years; height 5 ft. 10 inches; weight 160 pounds; gray eyes and hair; sallow complexion; medium nose; medium build; large mouth; good teeth, medium lips and neck; protruding chin. Born in Springfield, Illinois; Home, St. Petersburg, Florida. Occupation, a physician.

We hold an indictment warrant charging Corthell with the kidnaping of a ten-year-old girl. If located, arrest and hold as a fugitive from justice, and advise Detective Division by wire.

Copies of these circulars were forwarded to every State prison in the United States, and to Police Departments of all large cities. Weeks and months passed. Then one day word was received from a woman living in a small town in New Jersey that her husband, who had deserted her a short time prior to this, was the kidnaper of the Budd girl. She said that he had confessed to this shortly after the crime, but had refused to disclose what disposition he had made of the child.

She embellished the story by saying that he had told her he had kept the girl in an unused shack a few miles from their home. She said she had no knowledge of the present whereabouts of her husband.

The shack was searched at once. Among the rubbish were found several articles of a child's wearing apparel, a portion of a shoe, a white silk stocking, and a few small trinkets. None of these articles, with the exception of the stocking, bore any resemblance to the Budd child's clothing on the day she disappeared from home. The stocking was somewhat worn, and had been darned; Mrs. Budd was not sure whether it was one belonging to Grace.

Space forbids going into the full history of the search which was made for this runaway husband. Suffice it to say that he was eventually found, and brought to my office at Police Headquarters. The moment that he was ushered in, I was impressed by his resemblance to the "touched-up" photograph of Corthell. My belief that he was the same man was confirmed by others who saw him, and the man himself admitted that the photograph bore a striking likeness to his face.

"But I am not the original of that picture," he stoutly maintained.

It was not until his fingerprints were taken and compared with the fingerprints of Corthell that we were convinced we had the wrong man. Later, however, this man was identified by the mother of the Budd girl as the one guilty of stealing her child. At his trial disclosures were made which provided a perfect alibi for the unfortunate wife-deserter. He was found not guilty and released. He had simply been the victim of a spurned woman's wrath. His wife later admitted that she had concocted the story solely out of malice, and a desire for revenge for his desertion of her.

After his discharge by the Court we found ourselves just where we were before, and again the hunt for the real kidnaper was got under way. One morning we received a wire from the Police of St. Louis, informing us that they had in their custody our very much wanted Dr. Edward Corthell, alias A. Edward Corthell, alias Albert E. Corthell, alias James M. Bradley, alias Frank Howard.

A detective was at once dispatched to St. Louis, and in due time returned to New York with his prisoner, who had waived extradition. Again the Budd family was called in and Corthell, as he admitted himself to be, was stood in a line with a number of other men about his age and general appearance. Mrs. Budd, upon being asked whether the kidnaper of her daughter was in the group, somewhat hesitantly pointed out Corthell.

"There ... there's the man," she said.

Other members of her family were not so sure he was the one, but they did believe that he bore a general resemblance to Howard. After this somewhat uncertain identification, the Budd family was dismissed. Then I devoted some time to questioning Corthell as to his antecedents.

"Are you a physician, Corthell?"

"I am."

I asked him from which medical school he had graduated, and he mentioned a well-known one in Boston. I inquired the date of his graduation, the name of the hospital in which he had served his interneship, where he had entered upon the practice of medicine, and numerous other questions relative to his professional life. He gave clear-cut, definite replies, in well chosen language, to all of my questions. I asked him if any of his classmates were practicing medicine in New York.

He said: "Yes, indeed; a number of them."

I asked him why he had selected an office in the section of New York in which he said he was at one time located.

"Because it gave promise of bringing me a good practice."

"From which section of the city did you draw most of your patients?"

"The West Side."

"How do you account for that?"

"Because many of the East Side dwellers belong to a section of the city which supplies free medical service at clinics."

I was beginning to be a bit impressed. All of his answers were of a nature which would stamp him as a bona fide physician. I asked him why he had abandoned the practice of medicine.

He appeared to hesitate a moment, then replied: "I was asked to do a favor for a friend, and the operation was one in violation of law. The matter was brought home to me, and I was convicted, and my license to practice medicine was revoked."

Then I asked the doctor about his early career.

With apparent frankness he confided this: "I got in trouble with the authorities during my thoughtless, younger days, before I had reached the years of discretion, and I was obliged to pay the penalty. Well, I paid it! Now it is a closed chapter in my life. I don't want to reopen it. I was taught a valuable lesson, and after I had learned it, I studied medicine and became a physician."

While his air of sincerity was impressive, I was not convinced that he was a doctor. I casually asked him several additional questions, with apparently nothing else in mind than a desire to acquire a little medical information.

"What would you do for a case of flatulence?"

The doctor shook his head.

"I would not undertake to treat that, Captain," he said. "I was a general practitioner. That disease requires the attention of a specialist."

"What would you do for an inflamed follicle?"

"No, Captain, I couldn't treat that, either. That's another ailment that calls for treatment by a specialist."

"What is a suture?"

"Only a specialist could answer that."

In terms more emphatic than elegant, I told Corthell what I thought of his veracity, explained the significance of my questions, and the meaning of the terms employed.

"You're a double-dyed liar, aren't you, Corthell?"

Corthell never blinked an eyelash.

"You've got me cold, Captain! I've sold people all over the country on this doctor business. For years they've believed me. You're the first one who ever trapped me at it."

I asked him where he got his idea of passing as a physician, and how he had acquired his knowledge of medical terminology. He replied that while he was in prison in Florida he had been an orderly in the prison hospital, and had there learned some stock professional terms.

Corthell was locked up, and held without bail. When eventually brought to trial, he supplied a perfect alibi: he was in a Western prison at the very time the Budd kidnaping had occurred.

The search for the Budd girl and her kidnaper is still on.

MISSING MEN

Little William Gaffney figured in one of the most important cases reported to the Missing Persons Bureau in 1927. Billy lived with his parents on Fifteenth Street in Brooklyn. He was four years of age, two feet, five inches in height, and weighed forty pounds. His eyes were blue, his hair dark brown. On the day he disappeared he was dressed in a gray blouse, dark blue knickers, and black shoes and stockings. Billy had a scar on the right side of his upper lip, the result of a fall, which had caused his teeth to cut through the lip.

The child was last seen playing in the street in front of his home at 5:30 P. M. on the day of his disappearance. At first the family thought he was visiting at the home of one of the neighbors, but after inquiries were made and he was not found, his father became frightened, went to the station house of the local precinct and reported the matter. The report was telephoned to the Bureau, and a detective was sent to the scene to make an investigation.

In conjunction with the local detective force, supplemented by members from the uniformed force, an immediate search of the neighborhood was commenced. Houses, roofs, dumb-waiters, areaways, yards, coal-bins and vacant lots were combed. Barges, canal boats, and other craft lying in the Gowanus Canal, near which the Gaffney family lived, were searched. The Marine Division of the Department was directed to send a boat for the purpose of dragging the canal on the theory that Billy might have fallen in and been drowned. The idea that the boy might have been kidnaped for ransom was not conceived of, since the family was very poor.

KIDNAPINGS

A general alarm was broadcast to other police departments. The widest publicity was given the disappearance through the press and, as usual, in cases where much newspaper space is devoted to a matter of this kind, communications began to pour in. All of these letter writers gave information regarding little boys supposed to answer the description of the Gaffney child. Many of the "doubles" had been seen simultaneously at widely separated points. Experience has taught us that information of that sort, although almost always well-intentioned, must be discounted. It was necessary, however, to run down each alleged clew in order to be sure that no chance was being overlooked.

A neighbor of the Gaffneys', a man of foreign birth, with whom the boy's father had had a quarrel, and who was known to be of a sullen, vindictive nature, was for a time suspected of responsibility for Billy's disappearance. It was believed that the deed was actuated by a desire for revenge. This man was shadowed night and day for a considerable period. His every movement immediately prior to the disappearance of the boy was traced until we were eventually satisfied that he had had no part in it.

As time passed with nothing of importance developing, we were forced to the conclusion that, except for the element of chance, the prospect of solving the Gaffney mystery was slight. From time to time, however, letters are still being received from far distant points, supplying what the writers believe to be authentic "tips." One of these letters came from North Dakota, and it seemed to give promise of something tangible, but when the information was run down, it was found to be worthless. Within a week of this writing, word was received through the Police of a New Jersey city that the Gaffney child, now nine years of age, was living with an Italian family on Staten Island. This "tip" had come through the gossip of a Staten Island woman who had visited at the home of Jersey relatives. The boy had aroused talk in the neighborhood because he was clearly not of Italian parentage. He was described as of a pronounced Irish type.

For a time it appeared that this clew was a good one but, upon investigation, it was found that the child was not "Billy" Gaffney, and his antecedents were clearly established. This in itself was a big job, for it was necessary to run down clew after clew in order to locate his mother, and get the facts from her. It brought us down a bypath which did not lead to Billy Gaffney and which, for a while, took us off the main road.

We are still following clews in the hunt for Billy. Perhaps he was kidnaped. Perhaps Gowanus Canal has not disclosed all its secrets.

Some mothers have a habit of parking baby carriages in front of stores while they go in and shop. Several kidnapings in New York have been directly traceable to this careless practice.

Reference to the records of the Missing Persons Bureau discloses the following, dated August 1, 1919:

> "Mrs. Elsie Wentz, of the Bronx, reported that at 5 P.M., July 29, 1919, her seven-weeks-old baby boy, Arthur Phillip Wentz, was stolen from his carriage in front of a department store on Third Avenue, by an unknown white woman, about nineteen years of age, blonde, dressed in white middy blouse, white skirt, no hat."

KIDNAPINGS

An investigation revealed that at about 4:30 P. M. on the day of the kidnaping, Mrs. Wentz had left the baby carriage containing the child about twenty feet West of Third Avenue in front of a dry goods store. She entered this store to make some purchases, and declared afterward that she had remained inside not more than five minutes. When she returned to the carriage she found it empty.

A woman who chanced to be standing in front of the store and near the carriage at the time the baby was removed from it described the young woman who had taken it. The witness said she had believed the kidnaper to be the mother or a relative of the child because she acted in a proprietary manner. She stated further that the girl had entered the store, carrying the baby, and her story was corroborated by another bystander, who had also witnessed the affair.

Numerous persons who might have had an opportunity of seeing the kidnaping were interviewed, including the carriage checker, the starter, and the doorman at the store, but none could give any helpful information. Full police machinery was set in motion in the hunt for the baby. There were telephone and general alarms, and patrolmen on post were instructed to make careful inquiries to ascertain whether any family or individual, with a young baby, had recently taken residence in the neighborhood. Motion picture houses were requested to coöperate, and a description of the baby was flashed on the screen, accompanied by an appeal to all those who saw the film to notify us if they came in possession of any facts that might have a bearing on the case.

After the lapse of a few months. it is almost impossible

to secure identification in cases involving a very young baby. Infants change rapidly, and even their own mothers would experience difficulty in recognizing them after the passing of months.

Lacking a definite description or identification of the person guilty of the kidnaping, it is almost impossible to secure anything in the way of a satisfactory result. If a baby should be returned to the sorrowing parents of a kidnaped infant, particularly after the passing of a considerable length of time, there would always be a doubt in the minds of the mother and father as to whether or not they actually had their own offspring. They would constantly be asking the unspoken question, "Is that child really mine?"

The Wentz baby is still missing.

We handled one kidnaping case which had a surprise ending and no more serious consequences than a wedding.

Late one cold winter night a few years ago, Giuseppi and Angela Corelli, two excitable Italians, rushed into a lower East Side precinct station house and reported that their daughter, Rosella, who had left home early in the evening to attend a neighborhood motion picture show, had not returned. They said they had gone to the motion picture theater, but were told that she had not been there that evening. The parents said Rosella was thirteen years of age, but appeared to be eighteen or nineteen. She had matured early after the fashion of girls belonging to her race.

When the Corellis were asked to describe Rosella, they said she had big brown eyes and dark hair, that she was plump, not very tall, and that she liked bright colors. She had worn a red coat over a black dress, a red beret, gold hoop earrings, a heavy, twisted gold chain, and gold brace-lets, old-fashioned jewelry which had once belonged to Mrs. Corelli. The disappearance of Rosella was imme-diately reported, by the precinct, to the Missing Persons Bureau, and the routine machinery set at work to trace the girl.

The Corellis called on me the following day, and I ques-tioned them about their daughter's friends. They mentioned a number of boy associates of her own age, and then rather hesitantly spoke of a man who was engaged in business in the neighborhood.

"His name is Tony Lazzari," said Mr. Corelli. "Tony is not a bad fellow, but he is old, much too old for our Rosella. He is twenty-eight. He likes Rosella very much, but she, too, thinks he is too old. She is polite to him, yes, but no more. Tony asked me one day if he could marry Rosella, but I told him, 'No, never! You are fifteen years older than my girl.' "

Upon further questioning, the Corellis said they had no idea why their daughter had left home, and that they could give us no clew—not realizing they had already done so. Our detective at once directed his activities toward finding Tony Lazzari, the "much too old" suitor for the hand of Rosella. He learned that Lazzari had been seen the previous evening in the neighborhood of the Corelli home, in a closed car, with several other companions. After the detective dis-covered Tony Lazzari's address in an uptown Italian section of the city, he called there, and found Tony's parents, a hard-working Italian couple, Tony, and the missing Rosella sitting in the kitchen eating minestrone soup and chatting with one another.

Rosella was not, however, as cheerful as the others, and when questioned by the detective said that, as she was walking toward the motion picture house the night before, a car had drawn up to the curb, and Tony Lazzari had jumped out and pulled her into the car. He had immediately taken her to his home, and here she was! As for the Lazzaris, they seemed to be fully in accord with Tony and sympathetic toward his desire to marry Rosella. The girl had been well treated while in the Lazzari home, and no improper advances had been made toward her by Tony.

When the Corellis were notified that their daughter had been found they appeared upon the scene and, oddly enough, immediately fell in with Tony's desire to marry their daughter. Of course Rosella must marry Tony! However, the Corellis were acquiescent for a different reason than the Lazzaris. They were merely exhibiting a certain phase of the Italian character. It is an accepted code among middleclass Italians that if a young girl is a party to anything savoring of impropriety marriage should follow. Feeling that their daughter's reputation was now damaged, since the girl had been involved, although against her will, in something which had already become a public matter, they decided that marriage was the answer.

"Will Tony marry Rosella?" was the first question they asked when they learned what had happened. That being exactly what Tony wanted, a hall was rented and a very gay Italian wedding took place, a wedding which, at least on the surface, appeared to be satisfactory to all concerned. Thus an occurrence which would ordinarily have resulted in Tony's being arrested and prosecuted for the serious crime of kidnaping ended, instead, in a marriage ceremony and an all-night fiesta, with cakes and wines served to a large gathering of voluble Italian friends of the bridal pair and their families.

XIII. THE UNKNOWN DEAD

THE Unknown Dead.

There is a tragic overtone to the phrase. One instinctively dreads a similar fate. Death is a lonely enough affair at best, and we like to think of ourselves, at the hour of passing, as surrounded by those who care for us and who will miss us when we are gone. But there are hundreds of unfortunates in the city of New York who face the Unknown without the comforting handclasp or presence of friends or relatives for the reason that they are themselves unknown. A tragic feature is that almost always there is some one somewhere waiting for a letter or message, which never comes, from the person whose death was so sudden he could not make known his name or address.

Of all the problems brought to the Missing Persons Bureau for solution, the one involving the discovery of the identity of these men and women is the most difficult of all. The dead are silent. They cannot tell us anything about themselves. It is our task to read and interpret those signs and symbols which they, unknowingly, have left for our interpretation. The teeth, the last portion of the body to be resolved into the dust, are often responsible for establishing identity. The laundry mark on shirt or collar often serves to prevent a grave from being marked "Unknown." A suspender or belt buckle, a shoe, a handkerchief, articles of jewelry, the name of a maker in a coat or hat, a tattoo mark, a scar, a fingerprint, may play a part in this sad business of establishing the identity of those who have died unknown.

These and many more clews which we have succeeded in interpreting have served to prevent between eighty-five and ninety-five per cent of those reported as unidentified from being placed in unmarked graves. More important still, these signs and symbols have made it possible for us to convey to their families a message of enlightenment as to the fate of those from whom they still hoped to hear. After I have described the Bureau of Unidentified Dead, a few examples of this phase of our work will be given.

This Bureau is maintained in connection with, and as part of, the Missing Persons Bureau, for the purpose of making identification of all persons dying within the city whose identity is not known at the time and place of death. The steps taken to identify the unknown dead are many and varied, depending largely upon circumstances. When a case of this kind is reported, a careful check-up is first made against all persons reported missing whose descriptions may tally with that of the unidentified body. Second, a careful examination is made of the personal belongings and effects for any possible names and addresses of relatives or friends. Third, inquiry is made among those who may have been in contact with the unknown person during his or her lifetime. Fourth, fingerprints of the dead person are taken and compared with fingerprints on file in the Bureau of Criminal Identification. Fifth, laundry marks on the collar and shirt are compared with the file of laundry marks maintained by the Missing Persons Bureau. Sixth, publicity through the daily papers is given, and there are still other steps we can take, if none of these bring results. We thus employ every agency which may serve to supply the needed identification.

An accurate physical description is taken of all unknown dead, with special stress placed upon teeth, clothing and articles found in the pockets. Fingerprints are taken; photographs made; and samples of clothing and personal effects which might serve as identifying media are preserved, in order to furnish means for possible future identification in case an inquiry is made at the Bureau later on. All cases of persons found dead and unidentified in New York City are reported to our Bureau; interment, if they remain unclaimed, is made in the City Cemetery. Now to describe a few cases of these unknown dead, and the manner in which we have established identity:

At 8 o'clock one morning a few years ago John Brady, a night watchman employed on a sewer construction job, was relieved by the regular day crew of workmen. He took his usual route to the B. M. T. station at Sheepshead Bay, and that was the last time he was ever seen alive.

John had been accustomed, during the lonely watches of the night, to visit a nearby purveyor of bootleg liquor, and by the time he was relieved each morning, he usually showed the effects of his "refreshment." His indulgence in fiery liquids did not, however, incapacitate him for his job, for he carried his liquor fairly well. But steady drinking, added to a night spent without sleep, tended to make him a bit uncertain on his feet. He used to weave his way toward the station, and although his course was zigzag, he always managed to arrive at his destination. But on the morning in question John failed to put in an appearance at his home at his usual time, and his family, after waiting his arrival for about an hour, began to worry about him. They telephoned the foreman of the construction work, only to be told that he had seen Brady a little before 8 o'clock, and that Brady had taken his usual course toward the Sheepshead Bay station. After awaiting news of him for several more hours, Brady's family reported the circumstances to the nearest police station, and in due course the information was transmitted to the Missing Persons Bureau.

The detective to whom this case was assigned made a searching inquiry, covering the ground thoroughly from the point where Brady was last observed, but he was unable to find any one who had seen the watchman after he left the place where the construction job was in progress. A description of the missing man was transmitted to all precinct units of the Department, and a check was kept on all records of Arrests, Aided Cases, Morgue records, and the like, for weeks following. Nothing developed to give us any line on Brady's whereabouts, or any clew to a possible reason for his disappearance. As I have said, motive is always extremely important in all our cases, and in this instance we, of course, made every effort to determine what it might be. Nothing supplied us with an answer.

Naturally, the fact that Brady was somewhat under the influence of liquor when last seen might lead one to believe that he had wandered from his usual route and become lost. However, there was nothing to indicate that he was any more exhilarated on that particular morning than on previous occasions. He had seemed to be sufficiently in control of his movements to be able to make his way homeward.

MISSING MEN

A copy of his description, in addition to being placed in the file of the Missing Persons Bureau, was also put in the records of the Unidentified Dead, and all these cases were closely scrutinized to avoid any chance of John Brady slipping through our fingers due to oversight. Eventually we decided that this case was one which would probably be included in those of unsolved mysteries, which number approximately two per cent of the total of disappearance cases. In time it passed from the minds of all except the detective working on it and our Morgue man, whose duty it is to check immediately on all cases coming to his attention in order to make sure that the subject is not among those already listed as missing.

A detective from the Bureau is assigned to each of the two largest Morgues in the city, King's County in Brooklyn, and Bellevue Morgue, better known as the City Mortuary, located on Twenty-Ninth Street near the East River. It is the sole duty of these men to watch each case sent to the Morgue, for the purpose of guarding against the possibility of an unaccounted for missing person being buried without identification.

About a year after Brady's disappearance, a report was received from the same precinct from which he had vanished that a human skeleton had been found by a group of boys in a swamp which at high tide was covered with water and overgrown with rushes. The boys notified the officer on post, and he accompanied them to the spot where they had made their discovery. He at once notified the Precinct detectives, so that every precaution might be taken to prevent any important clews as to the cause of death from being destroyed.

THE UNKNOWN DEAD

The clothing on the skeleton was in such a state of decay that it was impossible to determine anything as to the original texture or color. The shoes were of a nondescript variety, of cheap make, from which all marks had disappeared as the result of exposure to the elements. The only article which had survived exposure to the weather was the shirt collar. Inside of this the laundry mark or "indicator" was easily decipherable, and the collar was brought to the Missing Persons Bureau for comparison with our Laundry File. Within a few minutes the laundry indicator which corresponded to the one in the collar was found, and a detective was dispatched to the laundry which employed that type of marking, where the books disclosed the identity of all that was left of John Brady.

However, to make doubly certain of the identification, we examined the teeth found in the jaw of the skeleton, and noted that several of them showed dental work. Through information supplied by the family of Brady it was learned that a dentist having an office nearby had, on several occasions, treated his teeth. We brought to him the upper and lower jaws of the skeleton, and he, through comparison with his chart, identified the work as that done by himself on John Brady. In that way we were able to make certain that the skeleton was that of the night watchman.

A rather unpleasant procedure was necessary to effect the identification of the man in the following case:

Shortly after the close of the World War there was reported to us, through the Marine Division, the finding of the body of a soldier, apparently drowned, floating in the waters off Staten Island. A search of the clothing brought to light nothing permitting identification. The number tag worn by all of the enlisted or officer personnel of the Army was missing. The body had been in the water for such a length of time that the face had become bloated and distorted, making the features unrecognizable. There were no scars or tattoo marks, so frequently found on enlisted men, to help in identification, and a photograph, in this instance, would have been of no assistance.

Therefore, the detective working on the case was instructed by me to make an effort to secure fingerprints, which is no easy task in the case of a body which has been in the water as long as this, and soon the detective reported to me that it was practically impossible for him to carry out my orders. He said he had found it an impossible job, since when he made an effort to take a print of the dead fingers, the skin itself came off.

I suggested that he try wrapping the skin from the dead man's fingers around the tips of his own, and in this way possibly secure a classifiable set of prints. He was eventually able to secure an excellent set in this manner. A photostatic copy of this was forwarded to the War Department at Washington for comparison with the Fingerprint File of the enlisted personnel of the Army. Thus the identity of the dead soldier was learned, and the address of relatives located.

When I first thought of cases involving the unknown dead, I conceived them as rightfully belonging in a sort of Chapter of Horrors. And the case I am about to relate should certainly hold first place in it.

Several years ago an explosion, from some unknown cause, occurred in the hold of a freighter at one of the South Brooklyn piers while workers were cleaning it and preparing it for the stowage of cargo. A number of these workmen were killed instantly, and even those who succeeded in escaping were badly burned. As soon as the gas which caused the explosion was consumed the fire died out, but not until the dead had, in most cases, been charred beyond recognition. The task of the police was then to identify them which was a harrowing experience, to put it mildly.

When I arrived at the dock, the living had already been removed in ambulances to a nearby hospital, while the dead were being carried from the ship to the dock. The grim procession was one that invited the shivers of horror. Some of the bodies were burned almost to a crisp, others were only partially burned, but all were so blackened that it was difficult to believe that they belonged to members of the Caucasian race. Some of the bodies were literally roasted; others were burned on only one side, while the other was unscathed. The flesh fell from the bones of some as they were carried to the dock.

All of the clothing was in most instances burned off. The first task was to learn the identity of the injured men sent to the hospital, and that in itself was no easy matter, because some of them were still unconscious. But by careful and persistent checking through friends and relatives who hurried to the scene of the explosion as soon as they learned of the disaster, we were eventually able to determine the identity of all the injured. Then the real job was commenced: the identification of those who could give us no assistance.

In some instances portions of the clothing which remained, or a watch, or a pocket-knife, served as a means of identification, until nearly all the dead were known.

MISSING MEN

Perhaps as a welcome contrast to the kind of case just recounted, it will be well to include one of less unpleasant nature—though any of our work in connection with the unidentified dead is grim enough at best.

One day, several years ago, there was sent to the Bureau of Unidentified Dead, a report of the finding of the body of a guest at one of the uptown hotels of the city. The name entered upon the register was William F. Doane, and a small town in the northern part of New York state was given as the address. A telegraphic request to the Police of that city to notify relatives or friends of the dead man brought the response that no person of that name was known to live there.

After waiting a few days on the possible chance of inquiries being made for some one answering the description of the dead man, we gave the matter to the press. The news stories carried the name and an accurate description of the man and his apparel.

The day after the story appeared a man telephoned the Missing Persons Bureau and announced that he was a clergyman. He stated that he had read the newspaper account of the death of William F. Doane, and went on to say that several years before, while he was officiating in a church in a city in Pennsylvania, there was a member of his congregation with the same name as that which had appeared on the hotel register.

The minister said that the description of the dead man given in the newspapers tallied so closely with that of his one-time parishioner that he was confident it was the same man. The clergyman asked whether he might have an opportunity of viewing the body, thus making sure that he was right. An appointment was immediately made for him to meet the detective who had the case, and he was conducted to the Morgue where, after viewing the dead man, he identified the body as that of his former parishioner.

A telegram was sent to the Police of the Pennsylvania town and they wired us that there was a resident of that town by the name of William F. Doane, who had left on a business trip some days prior to the discovery of the body at the hotel. The description of the dead man tallied with that of the absent resident of the Pennsylvania town. The family was satisfied with the identification, and made arrangements for the transportation of the body from New York to Doane's home.

On the following day funeral services were held, with the usual accompaniment of weeping relatives and friends, floral offerings, and a laudatory sermon. While the minister was offering words of comfort to the sobbing wife and children of the departed, and reminding every one present of the exemplary life he had led, and the probability, therefore, that he was bound for a brighter life in a more glorious realm, a commotion was heard at the door.

A bluff but startled voice called out: "What the hell is going on here?"

And in walked Doane, suitcase in hand, to stare in amazement at his wife and children grouped about a bier, while they, the minister and every one else present, stared at him as though he were an apparition, for had he not a moment before been lying there cold and motionless in his coffin? This strange scene was described in detail to me later, when the whole affair, which might be termed a Comic Tragedy of Errors, was straightened out. Quite a novel climax to a funeral service!

But now, due to the well-intentioned but faulty effort at identification by the clergyman, and the strange circumstance of the similarity of name and description, we were just where we started as far as the William F. Doane found dead in the New York hotel was concerned. Back to New York came the body of the man, shipped here by the family to whose bosom *their* William F. Doane had been restored, as though by an act of God, and it was returned to its old resting place in the Morgue, to be buried eventually in the City Cemetery. It has never been identified.

Compared with the total number of unidentified dead brought to the attention of the Missing Persons Bureau, there is a comparatively small number of women. Most cases of women involve those who have, at the time of their death, reached the lowest level of society. We find, however, that some of them are women who came from fairly decent walks of life, but who, through dissipation and loose living, tasted the dregs before they reached their wretched end, either through acts of violence, drugs, drink, or fatal illness.

On February 28, 1931, the body of a well dressed woman, who appeared to be about thirty years of age, was found in Van Cortland Park. She had evidently been strangled, for a portion of a cord similar to a clothes-line was found tightly drawn about her neck. The body was removed to a City Morgue and examined, but nothing was found upon it which would serve to make an identification.

Certainly this woman did not appear to come in the class

of the ordinary drifter. She was handsomely gowned, and was described as five feet two inches in height, one hundred and thirty-five pounds, blue eyes, light brown hair with a reddish tint. As to her teeth, there was a removable bridge with three teeth in the upper left side and a gold crown on the last molar, upper left side. She wore a black velvet dress, trimmed with yellow lace at neck and cuffs, white kid gloves, black silk stockings.

Identification of this body was made through fingerprints. We took prints of the dead woman's hands, and when checked against fingerprints on file at the Bureau of Criminal Identification at Police Headquarters, they were found to correspond with those of a woman who had a previous criminal record. In fact, the body proved to be that of the notorious Vivian Gordon, whose real name was Benida Bischoff, queen of night life, habitué of Broadway clubs, cabarets and speakeasies, boon companion of criminals. Her alleged murderer was later arrested and brought to trial, but was acquitted. Incidentally, his acquittal by a jury was held by many to be one of the most scandalous miscarriages of justice which has occurred in recent criminal history.

Just a word about the Bureau of Criminal Identification, through which the Gordon woman's identity was established. All persons arrested on charge of commission of a felony are photographed, front and profile views, and are finger-printed. The fingerprinting is performed in the following manner. The under side of the end of each finger and thumb of both hands, to the first joint, is treated to a light coating of black printers' ink which, for this purpose, has been thinly and evenly spread on a piece of glass or other perfectly smooth, hard surface. Then each finger is lightly rolled on this surface. As each digit is inked, its inked impression is taken by lightly rolling it on a sheet of paper prepared for such record. If carefully and properly done, this results in a perfect reproduction of the tiny, almost microscopic, ridges present on the fingers. These fingerprints are then examined by men trained for the purpose and classified. The classification of the fingerprint is a highly specialized process, and space forbids a description of it.

After classification, the prints are compared with prints of similar classification to ascertain whether the subject has a previous criminal record. Having served their purpose in this respect, they are then filed away in folders with other prints belonging to the same general type. These folders are as easily located in the files in which they are kept as a book, the title of which is known, can be found in a book case.

Sometimes bodies are found floating in the water. On September 23, 1931, six or seven months after the finding of the Vivian Gordon body, a report was forwarded to the Missing Persons Bureau from a Bronx precinct that an unidentified colored woman had been found, evidently drowned, in the Harlem River. She appeared to be about twenty-five years of age. The body was badly decomposed, for it had evidently been in the water several days.

There was nothing upon her person by which she could be identified. The detective handling the case secured her fingerprints, and through comparison with the fingerprint records in the Department of Correction, her identity was revealed. She was Belle Gardner, alias "Pussy Cat," and she had many times been arrested for street walking and vagrancy. She had been riding in a taxicab with her lover when she suddenly opened the door of the cab, jumped out, and ran to the 145th Street Bridge, from which she plunged to her death.

XIV. EXTORTION ATTEMPTS

OCCASIONALLY as an accompaniment to a disappearance the crime of extortion or, more properly, attempted extortion, enters the situation. In cases where extensive newspaper space has been given a missing man or woman case, a certain type of racketeer seizes upon the opportunity to capitalize the distress of the vanished person's family. He cannily realizes that the family will do almost anything to have their missing member restored. Many people are under the impression that in numerous instances the missing person is restrained against his will; it never occurs to them that he might have left home voluntarily—which is true in the vast majority of cases.

Frantic at the thought that the one who has disappeared is being held captive for ransom or for some other reason, by a gang of criminals who are prepared to inflict upon him rare forms of torture if their demands are not met, those left behind are usually in a frame of mind to part with almost any sum of money in exchange for the freedom of the victim. It is better, they argue, to sustain a money loss than some day receive, through the mail, an ear or a finger of the one they love, or learn of his violent death.

Some of these attempts at extortion are unique. We at

the Bureau have never been impressed by any of them, since we long ago learned that the would-be extortionist, in virtually every instance, has had nothing whatever to give in return for the money he tries to secure. A variety of methods has been employed by this type of criminal. Perhaps the most recent is one in which carrier pigeons have been drafted to act as the medium for conveying the money from the victim's family to the extortionist.

This type of attempted "shakedown" figured in the Levy case, which was described in the chapter on murders. It had all the potentialities for success if we had not spoiled the plan. For the first few days of Levy's disappearance, no publicity was given the matter, but finally we believed that widespread news of the disappearance might help, and the story was handed to the press. A few days later Mrs. Levy received the telephone calls which have already been described. I instructed her not to accede to the demands of the would-be extortionist, who was attempting this spectacular form of sky blackmail, a type of crime fairly new in American police annals. I did, however, suggest that she pretend to fall in with the plan, and call for the five pigeons, to whose legs she had been instructed to attach ten one thousand dollar bills, before releasing them for flight to the home cote.

Several of my men trailed her to the cigar store in Queens where she had been informed that she would find the birds. Just as she had been advised, she found the five homing pigeons in a small crate at the store. Later one of my detectives questioned the proprietor of the place, who gave a description of the man who had left the birds, saying that he had sold them to Mrs. Levy and she would call for them.

The detective took charge of the pigeons, and we made plans to follow them by airplane upon their release. We decided to let them go early the next morning in order to avoid the chance of confusing them with other pigeons in the air. We adopted the plan of letting them go one at a time so that if any mishap occurred to some of the birds we would still have others in reserve, and in order to identify them we fastened a long, light streamer of orange ribbon to the leg of each.

Upon the release of the first pigeon, the plane started immediately in pursuit. It was a four-seater, and carried a pilot, an assistant pilot, an observer, and a homing-pigeon fancier, a man familiar with the habits of pigeons in flight.

Off went the first bird! Dangling behind him was the orange streamer, easily discernible as he winged his way onward. But then occurred the first difficulty. Pursuing pigeons by plane is not a simple matter; all the advantages are on the side of the birds. First, it was found that the plane was not sufficiently mobile to permit following the bird in its initial circlings, preparatory to setting a course for the home cote. We had no better luck with the remaining four birds. Each was lost in turn.

Luck was with us in one respect at least, however. Visibility is a very important factor in the pursuit of pigeons, and it so happened that the day of our chase was an ideal one. Before deciding on the time for the release of the birds, I had checked with the Weather Bureau and secured a report that visibility would be good on the following morning. But even this fortuitous circumstance did not offset the other discouraging factors. Carrier pigeons' habits differ from those of the racing pigeon, for the homing pigeon may alight en route.

One of the pigeons we were attempting to follow was found on the roof of a barn, clearly not its home, three hours after he had been released! However, so far as Levy was concerned it made little difference. His bullet-riddled body was found floating in Long Island Sound several days later, and in a condition which indicated it had been in the water for weeks, clearly proving that the would-be extortionist had written his first letter long after the man was already dead.

Attempted extortion through the use of homing pigeons first came to our attention several years ago when three pigeons were sent to a well-known physician, with orders to attach a one thousand dollar bill to a leg of each and release them, or else accept the alternative of being killed. The physician, not desiring to be mulcted out of a large sum of money, promptly brought the matter to our attention and we assigned a man to guard him. His instructions were to live with the doctor, to accompany him everywhere he went, and remain with him night and day.

After the birds, innocent aides of a would-be extortionist, were held for a few days, they were released from a point on Long Island where it was possible to follow them by plane. On the theory that three pigeons would be more easily followed than one, by reason of the fact that they would retain their identity better, they were released in a group. But, unfortunately they soon became mixed with a large flock of other pigeons, and were lost entirely. This was a lesson we profited by later when we trailed the pigeons in the Levy case, for although we did not succeed in tracing these birds to their cote, we did release them one by one, ribbon-marked as described, and would thus have been able to keep a single bird in view better than a group of them had we been equipped with the right type of plane. Sooner or later, however, the homing-pigeon extortionist will be caught by the use of mobile planes, similar to those employed in sky-writing.

So far as the case was concerned in which the physician figured there was an aftermath. When the disappointed extortionist received the pigeons minus the thousand dollar anklets, the doctor received a letter containing three pigeon feathers, which had been colored red, and the man who had attempted extortion wrote that they had been soaked in blood. He announced that he intended to "get even," and would take his own way of punishing the physician for not having responded to his demands. Extortionists are cowards, however, and no further attempt has been made to annoy the physician.

About a year ago still another case of attempted extortion by homing pigeons came to the attention of the Bureau. A boy disappeared from his home and, several weeks later the papers carried the story. Shortly afterward the father of the lad received a letter telling him to go to a certain candy store on the outskirts of the city, where he would find two pigeons in a box. The proprietor, according to the letter, had been instructed to deliver them to the father of the boy, whose name had been given to him. The boy's parent was further directed to attach a one thousand dollar bill to the leg of each bird. A one thousand dollar bill seems always to be the magic sum mentioned by extortionists. The father was warned that if he reported the matter to the police his missing son would be killed, but on the other hand if he obeyed orders and sent the ransom money, the boy would be sent home to him at once. Again we attempted to trace the birds to their source, but without success.

Two days later the body of the missing boy was found in the East River. His death was due to accidental drowning, and from the appearance of the body, it had happened weeks before the father had received the letter demanding money via homing pigeons. An additional confirmation of the fact that the would-be extortionist had had nothing whatever to do with the boy's disappearance came when the father received a second and more threatening demand for money, emanating from the same source, even after the boy's body had been found.

Means other than that of pigeons are employed by the type of criminal who seeks to capitalize grief over a missing person. Sometimes the relatives are told to place money in certain designated receptacles; to send it by messenger; to bring it to a deserted spot; or to keep rendezvous with the criminal in some such place as a cemetery. But the following attempt at "shake-down" was neither a pigeon scheme nor of the graveyard-tryst variety.

One day James Whittemore, a prominent business man, appeared at the Missing Persons Bureau in a highly nervous state, and asked us to help him locate his son, James, Jr., a young man twenty years old. Mr. Whittemore, although obviously a bit reluctant to do so, divulged a few domestic complications in order to familiarize us with the home life of the missing youth. He said that two years before his son, while still in college, had married a girl much against the wishes of his parents. This young woman was socially inferior, according to Whittemore, and the misalliance had greatly disturbed and disappointed the boy's father and mother.

Young Whittemore appeared to be very much in love with his bride, so much so that he was willing to relinquish his allowance, a sum of money which his mother had been giving him ever since he entered college. He seemed to think nothing of making the sacrifice, but promptly got a job, rather a humble one for a college man, for he became a shipping clerk. However, his salary was insufficient to support himself and his wife, and his father, not desiring to bring disgrace on the family because of the son's financial straits, volunteered to provide the young couple with an apartment.

"But I made it clearly understood that there was to be no social contact between the boy's wife and our family," said Whittemore. "Jimmy's mother and I did not want to have anything to do with our daughter-in-law. I must give my son credit for the fact that he is loyal to the girl he married, and apparently intends to stand by her. To tell you the truth, I admire him for doing that."

Whittemore, continuing his recital of his son's disappearance, said that his daughter-in-law had telephoned the evening before to tell him that James, Jr., had not returned from his place of employment. He was always punctual about his home coming, and the young wife was worried. She called the place where he worked, and was informed that her husband had not put in an appearance that day.

Mr. and Mrs. Whittemore immediately began telephoning friends, but could find no trace of the young man. It was then that Whittemore appealed to the Bureau. The usual routine of investigation followed: friends were interviewed, companionship analyzed. And then, five days after the boy vanished, and when his parents and his wife had reached a state of great agitation over the mystery of his absence, the father received a letter, printed in lead pencil, which read:

> "We have your son Jim in a secure place. We will let him go for five thousand dollars. We will send a messenger who knows nothing about this. He will give you a letter directing you where to leave the money. Don't fail!!! Otherwise you will never see your son again."

Underneath this message was a roughly executed drawing of a skull and cross-bones.

Naturally, Mr. Whittemore was very much upset over this communication, and came at once to me with it. It might be well to say here that the disappearance of James, Jr., had been dealt with as a confidential matter. There had been no newspaper publicity, and no way in which the general public could have learned of the boy's disappearance.

During our investigation of the mystery we learned that young Whittemore had been in the habit of gambling at a well-known whist club, and that he had given I. O. U.'s for rather large sums, credit having been given him on the strength of his father's business and social standing. We learned that his gambling creditors had made several efforts to induce him to settle but, of course, due to his straitened financial state, it was impossible for him to do so. Only the day before young Whittemore disappeared his creditor for the largest sum had threatened that, if he did not "make good" within twenty-four hours, he would go to his father.

We did a bit of deduction: no publicity had been given the

case, and this, coupled with the fact that the boy had found himself in urgent need of money, with the imminent danger of exposure should he fail to liquidate his indebtedness, led me to the conclusion that the demand for the five thousand dollars had its authorship in the young man himself. This theory was disclosed to Whittemore, Senior, who at first resented the implication that his son would be a party to such trickery and attempted fraud, but after I had analyzed the situation he began to feel that possibly I was right. We agreed that a gesture of compliance should be made regarding the money demand, hoping thus to produce the missing boy.

I assigned two detectives to the Whittemore home, with instructions to be present at the hour when the messenger was scheduled to appear. This messenger, it developed, was a precocious Italian boy who, when told he was engaged in a criminal act, confessed that he knew young Whittemore, who had paid him a small sum of money for the delivery of the message. The note instructed the boy's father to place the money in a securely wrapped and sealed package, and then give it to the messenger. Mr. Whittemore was warned not to permit the young Italian to know the contents.

The messenger confessed that young Whittemore had instructed him, upon receipt of the package, to bring it to a certain "L" station, and to drop it in a rubbish can at one end of the platform. The Italian, now thoroughly frightened, promised to do whatever was requested of him. He was given a package which had the appearance of being what it purported to be and, accompanied by the detectives, he set out for the designated "L" station.

The messenger had been told to go up the stairs to the platform, find the rubbish-can and drop the package into it.

EXTORTION ATTEMPTS

The detectives followed him up the stairs in the manner of any tired, homeward-bound workers. They watched him drop the "valuable" package in the can, hastily return to the stairs, and descend to the street. They noted that as soon as he reached the bottom of the stairs a young man awaiting there approached and spoke to him. According to his instructions the Italian youth nodded, apparently assuring him that all was well, whereupon the young man, none other than James Whittemore, Jr., hurriedly ascended the stairs, went directly to the rubbish can, and fished out the package. As he was in the act of ripping it open, the two detectives stepped up and seized him. After a short period of questioning the young man admitted that the whole thing was a put-up job.

He was taken to his father's home, where he broke down and confessed that his desperate need of money had made him try this means of securing it.

"I couldn't help it, Dad," he cried. "I was up against it for funds. Can you ever overlook this rotten trick of mine?"

His father forgave him, delighted that no harm had befallen him, and the suspense endured by the family was at an end.

XV. CONCLUSION

I AM frequently asked: "How do you endure the strain of work such as yours at the Missing Persons Bureau? How do you react to this constant necessity of listening to the troubles of others?"

Perhaps readers of the foregoing chapters will feel like putting the same questions to me, since in these pages I have tried to indicate in some measure the many ramifications of my unique job. It is true that my work is a mixture of strain, suspense, and anxiety. But the strain, suspense and anxiety are suffered mainly by those attached, either through blood ties or affection, to the man, woman or child who is, for the time being, among the missing. If my efforts in behalf of the person who has disappeared and those he left behind are to be effective, it is incumbent upon me to retain an objective viewpoint and a detached attitude. I suppose that the years have inured me somewhat to human suffering, though I do not believe that I am any the less sensible to the griefs and heartaches which it is my daily lot to witness. Quite the reverse: my job has taught me much of the good in human nature as well as the bad, and there is no deeper satisfaction I know of than to bring a person who has lost his moorings back to his proper place in society.

CONCLUSION

While I must, in a measure, identify myself with the missing person and his problems, I must not let that identification become so marked that it plunges me into a morass of intense personal concern, thus defeating my purpose, which is to locate the one who has disappeared and give him back to society. The vicarious rôle must be played with discretion.

Missing persons cases usually come into being in the first instance because some person—or group of persons—has lost perspective. They are too close to their individual difficulties to appraise them properly, and as a result they magnify them, color them, and imagine them as insolvable. If a man like Morris Belker, for example, whose case was described in the chapter entitled "Why Men Leave Home," we.e surfeited with his wife's demonstrativeness, it would have been a comparatively simple matter for him to straighten out the difficulty, granted, of course, that he had the courage· to face the situation in the first place.

He would then go to his wife and say: "Mary, I'm not up to this continual love-making. We're grown up. We've been married twenty-eight years. Let us behave like adults, not like children afflicted with calf-love. If you will accept the fact that our honeymoon is over, and settle down to a more placid way of married life, I will be satisfied to remain at home. Otherwise I will be forced to establish a separate home for myself, making every provision, of course, for your comfort. I am sorry, my dear, to be obliged to tell you this. But we must face facts."

Had Belker pursued this straightforward course, he would probably have settled his problem after a few uncomfortable hours—and possibly some recriminations from a tearful Mary. But, too near his own tribulations to see them in correct proportion, Belker staged a mysterious disappearance. However, it is perhaps asking too much of humanity to be level-headed where its own emotions are involved.

"Do you not become hardened to the woes of others after being obliged to listen to them year after year?"

This is another question which is put to me often, and to which I reply: I have trained myself so that, when I leave my office, I close the door of the "shop" firmly behind me, thus permitting my mind—and my heart too—to have a brief overnight vacation, a respite which will enable them to regain, through natural resiliency, their normal tone and responsiveness. I never carry my day's tasks home with me. I quickly arrived at the conclusion that if I were to maintain my mental equilibrium, it would be necessary for me to free my mind of all details of my labors as soon as I left my office. After a day given over to listening to the troubles of others, attempting to relieve their anxieties, offering words of reassurance to bolster them up during their period of worry and suspense, it is absolutely necessary for me to erase all thought of the specific cases which have been brought to my attention.

I learned also, early in my work at the Bureau, that in order to be of assistance to another in the "ironing out" of difficulties, one must be able to remove oneself to a sufficient distance from the picture to be able to see all the lights and shadows. One must, in short, get the right perspective. This, I contend, is a rule also applicable to most of the other problems of life. Few people are able to map out an effective plan for the conduct of their own lives or to evolve or cultivate a workable philosophy. For this reason they find it necessary to appeal to others to help unravel the tangled threads which weave themselves in and out of their lives. It so happens that I am one of those others to whom many turn in time of trouble. My function is that of analyst—psychoanalyst, if you will—or a sort of father confessor. The rôle calls for a variety of qualifications: above all an objective viewpoint. A knowledge of practical psychology, sympathetic understanding, and intuition are also necessary—together with a chameleon-like ability to project oneself under another's skin, as it were, in order to think for a time as the central figure in a missing person's case would think, to visualize how he might act and react under certain circumstances.

I stand at a distance and am thus able to look at a situation calmly and clearly. I am sufficiently disinterested to achieve the objective viewpoint—the detached perspective. This also applies to a lawyer in relation to his clients, or a physician to his patients. We are all specialists in our different ways; we must evaluate things as they *are*—not as they seem to be. A doctor knows whether a man's lungs are sound. I generally know whether a man's reasoning is faulty or not. A physician has much to do with unsound organs; I have a great deal to do with unsound logic.

This brings to mind another question which is often put to me: "How is it possible for you to retain a cheerful attitude toward life when most of your waking hours are devoted to listening to the troubles of others, to observing the abnormal reactions of many to the normal things of everyday life?"

And I reply: "Just because a doctor deals only with sick

287

people is no reason for him to believe the whole world ailing."

While my work is at times trying, it nevertheless appeals to me strongly for several reasons. I like to solve a mystery. This tendency is shared, I think, by most people. We all like to let our minds race ahead in order to see if we can work out a solution of that which is, seemingly, of an incomprehensible nature. As proof of this, observe the popularity of the mystery detective novel and short story, the crossword puzzle, the anagram. Perhaps my love of and faculty for solving mysteries has been accentuated as the result of almost a lifetime devoted to that occupation. I have been a detective, or supervisor and director of the activities of detectives, for more than half of the thirty-five years I have been a member of the New York Police Department.

Then, too, practical psychology holds a strong interest for me. Therefore the ease with which an apparently insolvable problem may be worked out by one sufficiently detached and with the necessary experience is fascinating to me. Most of the cases presented to me for solution contain the element of abnormal reaction, and it is surprising to note the extent to which a quite ordinary occurrence may be colored, distorted, and magnified out of all proportion to its real significance. The solution is often almost too easy—though it often looks like black magic to the uninitiated!

One of the satisfactions attending my work is the opportunity afforded me of stabilizing some of the persons brought to my attention. I try to give them a more wholesome and intelligent outlook on life. This mental prophylactic treatment I employ not only with many of the men, women and children I succeed in locating, but also with members of the

CONCLUSION

families involved, for often I find that those left behind are, in a measure, partly responsible for the original disappearance. This treatment frequently serves a double purpose: first, it assists those involved, and, second, it prevents a possible recurrence of the act that brought the matter to the attention of the Bureau in the first instance.

While I realize that frequently my efforts at stabilization will be fruitless, I am convinced none the less that in most instances the fact that I have been in a position to suggest and advise and sketch a proper outlook to replace a faulty one has had salutary effect. I know that many people who might have continued to go through life maladjusted have been able to pull themselves together and take a proper view of the future—largely because of some straight talking on my part.

While intuitiveness is supposed to be a feminine quality, I believe that it is possessed in some degree by most people of either sex who have an alert mind and a sympathetic nature. Certainly the ability I have acquired to penetrate deeper than the spoken word helps me greatly in my work. I have learned also to read character from faces. Most intelligent people can do this to some extent, but my long years of experience have sharpened my faculties in this respect. I firmly believe that in most cases facial expression offers a key to the predominating mental traits of any individual. More often than not the photographed likeness of a missing person will give me a better insight into his character than any amount of assistance by intimate friends and relatives. I have learned that the views of those who come to the Bureau for assistance, as far as such views pertain to the one who has disappeared, are seldom to be relied upon. The people who express them are too emotionally involved to be of much assistance.

My description of the outstanding traits of character of a missing person, particularly if a photograph has been made available, often surprises those who come to me for help. They exclaim: "Why, you have never seen this man! You do not know him. How have you gained this knowledge of him?" Hard common sense, plus knowledge gained through experience, supplies us with the perception which some people are prone to look upon as uncanny. There is nothing magical about it. A policeman in his work is obliged to resort constantly to the application of commonsense principles. He must above all be a realist.

My experience in dealing with the seamy side of life has in no sense destroyed my original faith in the general worthwhile qualities of men and women.

This declaration may sound overoptimistic, but it is, nevertheless, sincere. I never lose sight of the fact that, although most of my own work has centered about the maladjusted, the criminal, the wretched and the forlorn, these people make up but a small part of the human race. It is similar to the matter of happy marriage. People hear so much about unhappy unions they are inclined to think the institution of marriage is very much frayed at the edges. Publicity is given to the exceptional, not to the ordinary circumstances of life.

My work has never led me to believe that mankind is on the down-grade so far as common decency is concerned. After all, human nature is very much the same now as it always was. Potential criminality is no more prevalent today than it was five thousand or more years ago. If it appears to be

CONCLUSION

so it is simply because the opportunity and the means provided for fostering it have been many times multiplied. Crime today is better organized than it was in the past. It has become, if you will, motorized. But then, to offset this, we have improved modern methods to combat the criminal, and to frustrate at least some of his malevolent intentions. Modern police methods are vastly improved; they, too, have kept pace with the changing times.

As for Missing Persons cases it is true that more people disappear today than ever before, but this is because of the greater ease with which they can drop out of sight. Airplanes, automobiles, fast ships can carry them far from their usual haunts, much farther away—and much faster—than in those days when the speediest method of movement was by leg power of the individual himself or of his horse. But facilities for tracing these missing persons have kept pace in corresponding degree. We have intercity and interstate police coördination; the telegraph, the teletype, the telephone, the airplane, the radio, mechanical means of transportation, improved ways of transmitting messages from one police department to another—all these help in our searches for the missing. Coöperation between the Police departments of the world is a vast step forward in all branches of our work.

People tell me that I have retained to a surprising degree my human qualities. Perhaps this is because by nature I am not excessively suspicious or sceptical regarding mankind. I have managed somehow to keep my fundamental faith in the essential goodness of human beings. Many detectives defeat their purpose by being too suspicious of all human motives. Much of their good work is negated by the fact that they are prone to disbelieve almost everything that is told them. A certain amount of scepticism is necessary, but it can be overdone. A good plan to follow is to keep the mind free from conclusions until one is warranted by all the facts available.

My philosophy of life has always been a simple one. I live from day to day and cross no bridges in advance. Cynicism has no place in my make-up. I strive to be not too mistrustful of people, accepting people at face value until something develops which causes me to change my opinion. Then I deal with the situation accordingly.

If it should appear to readers of this book that everything accomplished by the Bureau has been due to my efforts, this impression was far from my intention. We in the Bureau are above all an organization. We do not dramatize ourselves as super-sleuths of romantic fiction. We are practical men who must subordinate ourselves as individuals to the efficient functioning of the department as a whole. If by reason of my position I have come in for more than my share of credit, this is ever the case in situations of this kind. The general receives the praise while his staff officers, who worked up the successful plans, are too often not even known by name. Without an efficient staff behind me and without the loyal coöperation of the entire Police Department of New York City I could have accomplished little. As a matter of fact, my work is largely that of supervision and direction.

The success of the Missing Persons Bureau—and we are an extremely successful unit, I say with pride—has been mainly due to the intelligence, diligence and loyalty of the men and women who make up its personnel, all of whom are

CONCLUSION

specialists in their work. Our duties call for a profound knowledge of human nature and a sympathetic attitude toward all who come to us in their anxiety and distress. Efficient teamwork is essential. We have it in the Bureau.

www.ingramcontent.com/pod-product-compliance
Lightning Source LLC
Chambersburg PA
CBHW030939260626
47169CB00002B/540